ALL THAT'S LEFT

KA Allen

Dedicated to my ever patient Lynne, who encouraged me throughout the writing of this book.

Also the indomitable people of Mission Beach and the Cassowary Coast, who have shown me the better side of human nature in the face of absolute disaster.

PROLOGUE

Hi, I'm Jessica Bell. Our group calls me 'Doc,' which annoyed me at first, but I guess I'm used to it now. This is my account of what happened after the aliens invaded. I don't know if anyone will ever read it, but at least it was written.

They landed in the deserts in three ships. One went to the Sahara Desert. One went to the Atacama Desert, and the last to the Simpson Desert here in Australia.

It was days before the right people got to where they landed. To start with, it was just the residents. It must have been hilarious when a bunch of locals from '*the Alice*' went out to meet some aliens.

All the world's major powers came to meet them, all jockeying to be the favoured country. They brought with them the best linguists on the planet and managed to develop a dialogue fairly quickly. The aliens said they wanted to meet us to exchange knowledge, and one of the first things we wanted to know was how they travelled faster than light. But our visitors seemed to be reluctant to tell us. They just kept saying, (translated) "You don't understand the question you ask". That cryptic answer went viral and became the catch phrase for everyone across the globe.

As you'd expect the world went alien crazy and there were images and videos of them everywhere you looked. To be honest I got sick of hearing about the aliens pretty quickly, it was all anyone could talk about! Although, I must admit there was that one viral video of an alien, kind of throwing up during a meeting with the worlds leaders that was well worth watching. The smell of their vomit made everyone in the room throw up, world leaders, reporters, and photographers. It was hilarious!

It turned out, that's how the aliens defecate (poo). Apparently, they don't get to choose when that happens, like a cat coughing up a fur-ball. When it's time, it's coming up whether it's convenient or not!

After about five months of badgering from the world's leaders, the aliens finally released the formulas for how they travel faster than light. All the military powers put their best people on the task and they failed to decipher it. They went to the worlds greatest minds in the top universities and space agencies, which also failed to crack the formula. It was released to the population to see if there was an, as yet, undiscovered genius that could solve it. There wasn't. The consensus from the experts was that the formula wasn't solvable. It was utter nonsense. I had a look, as everyone across the globe did, and to me it was gibberish. I'm far from an expert but even to me it didn't make any sense. It was almost like someone had replaced every third word in a sentence, with a random word.

They flatly refused to subject themselves to a DNA test or discuss their weapons in any way. Our scientists did test their poo for DNA but were unable to identify anything familiar and there were some very embarrassing failures by various Special Forces soldiers, trying to find out more about their weapons systems. But they learned nothing. These creatures were being very secretive and within six months of their arrival, suspicions of their motives started to circulate. It seemed the exchange of information was all one way; they plugged into the Internet and downloaded absolutely everything mankind had to offer. Yes, that included ten million cat videos. They knew everything about us… but we still knew nothing about the aliens.

A popular joke meme about an alien invasion started a social media group page, and before long, there was a Cairns splinter group that met for drinks a few times.

In truth it was really just social, but we half-heartedly planned for an invasion and set up a meeting point locally… you know… just in case. It was just a bit of fun over a few drinks and nobody took it seriously.

Around ten months from the alien arrival, relations started to become tense. Their secrecy was starting to raise a lot of suspicion and they fell out of favour with much of the world. The Russians cut off all communication with them and made it clear to the world that they had ballistic missiles permanently targeting two of the alien ships. The media talk was that the Russians were being paranoid and just trying to invent an enemy; but hearing about it made me a little nervous. I was certain we weren't getting the full story…

Jessica

There are two great days in a person's life, the day they are born, and the day they discover why.' - William Barclay

It was August 3rd, 2025. A date remembered by all those who survived. The meme referred to a line from a popular movie about an alien invasion.

They're counting down!

I guess it resonated with many of us who harboured some suspicion of our new guests. They were arrogant and elusive and with no real facial expressions, or none that humans could read anyway.

Like most people, I found them difficult to trust.

When the post popped up on social media that there was going to be another get-together to celebrate one year to the day of the alien arrival, I decided to go.

I was from Charters Towers studying university in Cairns, and while I had plenty of friends at uni, I really resonated with the 'alien invasion' mob. They were just good fun. They didn't take anything too seriously, and I didn't have to discuss my studies with them. Don't get me wrong, I liked pharmacy, but there has to be more to talk about than your studies.

We met at a grubby backpacker bar in town and had a few drinks. I'd had a few glasses of wine with some girls at uni earlier so I arrived late. Spotting Jared, who I'd met at the last drinks night, I ordered a beer and planned to go talk to him. While I waited for my drink I took in the scene; the place smelled of stale beer and an extra funky smell I probably didn't want to know the origin of. Everything I touched felt sticky so I tried to keep my hands to myself. I guess it's your typical backpacker bar, which was packed with people trying to chat each other up over some awful loud music. Yeah... I know, 'If it's too loud, you're too old.' But these places seem to be making up for a lack of cleaning with the volume of the music.

So with a beer in hand, I headed over to where Jared was. I'd chatted with Jared before and liked him. He was easy-going and smart. He was also tall and fit, obviously well toned with a great smile, which may have swayed my opinion of him. Don't get me wrong, I wasn't interested, but he would turn heads at uni. He was chatting with a guy called David and a couple of others so I propped myself up on a barstool where I could look them in the eye.

David, with a beer in hand was telling everyone about some of the funny things that happen when working on boats, like the passenger who wanted to get an Uber back from the reef because the boat was too bumpy, and the woman who was very upset that she would have to get wet if she wanted to go snorkelling. "Seriously! She wanted to sue us because she couldn't get her thousand-dollar bathing suit wet, but demanded to see the coral. I suggested she take the bathers off..." He shrugged innocently. "Well, she went right off! I meant put a wet suit on instead of the bathers... But she didn't get that." He shook his head ruefully and then laughed.

David was a pretty funny guy; we were all laughing hard when the music ended abruptly and everyone stopped talking. The big-screen that dominated one wall showing music videos, suddenly changed to a news channel. We all turned our attention to the screen and that's when we saw the footage of the bombings. The text scrolling at the bottom of the screen said, **"The aliens have begun bombing all major cities across the world. Citizens are encouraged to find shelter or evacuate immediately."**

"Is this for real?" I heard someone ask.

"Looks like it," Jared said.

Like most people, I didn't believe it, not deep down. When they blasted Russia off the map, it looked like footage from a sci-fi movie, and then the picture became pixelated momentarily before it went completely blank. When someone from the bar rang a relative in Russia and got nothing, we all started to take notice.

"They aren't answering, there's nothing... Not even ringing," the upset girl said in a strong accent. Another rang home to a neighbouring country and was told it was real, and that they'd seen the dust cloud that was already drifting across Europe. It was then, that the reality sunk in for most of us.

People became frantic, all trying to ring home across the globe. It was only a moment later that everyone's phone signal went dead and the lights went out, plunging us all into darkness.

Jared yelled at the top of his voice, "LOOKS LIKE IT'S REAL, PEOPLE... I'LL SEE YOU AT THE MEETING PLACE...

BRING AS MANY SUPPLIES AS YOU CAN CARRY."

In the dark I didn't see him leave, but I left immediately, fighting my way through the now panic-stricken crowd to get out of the bar and head back to my accommodation. The streets were full of people, a few grabbing at others passing by, asking to confirm if it was real. I saw people throwing things at shop windows trying to break in. It seemed every police, ambulance and fire truck in Cairns had its siren on, and the noise was bewildering. Traffic was bumper to bumper with people trying to flee, but to where I have no idea. It was so surreal!

By the time I opened the door to my unit I was getting a little upset. I grabbed my backpack and started stuffing clothes into it and then changed my mind. I pulled them all out and went to the little kitchenette in my room. I emptied all the food I had into the backpack. Instant noodles, microwave meals, packets of chips, lollies. It was all just snack food really, but it was all I had. I spotted the saucepan I'd carried around forever, I thought it might be useful so stuffed full of noodles it was thrown in. I grabbed my toiletries and any medications I had in there as well. My sleeping bag with a small tent was strapped to the top and I was ready. For what, I didn't know.

I really was running on adrenaline and it was at that point I must have sobered up and realised what I was doing... *My God, what if this is all real?* I had another little adrenaline rush and took a deep breath to calm myself. Panicking wasn't going to help.

Heading off to the meeting point on the outskirts of the suburb, the walk gave me time to calm down. The quieter backstreets, away from the hysteria helped me gain some perspective. In fact, I'd reasoned myself around to half expecting nobody to be there, or maybe a few TV cameras and a presenter saying, "Jessica, you've been pranked!" But hearing the sirens still wailing in the distance, kept one of my feet in reality.

When I reached the meet point, I was a little surprised to find a large group there already. I thought I'd packed fast, but most were equipped with head torches and full backpacks. *They must have had their gear already packed!*

Jared was talking with a small group of people when he saw my arrival and he made his way over to me. "Hey, glad you could come along," he said with a warm smile.

"I'm not sure why I'm here… should we be doing this? I mean… Is this all real?"

"You know as much as I do, Jessica. But it's not looking good. Hey… Look, at worst we'll spend a night in the bush while we work out what's happening. At best… well, who knows what the hell is happening, but I know I don't want to be in Cairns."

"Well, I can't argue with that. Where are we going?"

"This is the start of a walking track that heads up the mountains. Eventually, it gets to Kuranda."

"Kuranda! I'm not walking all the way up there."

He held his hand up to stop me.

"I'm thinking we just head up over the ridge, camp until morning, and we can look down over the city and see what's happening. The track is easy and shouldn't be a problem in the dark. We're all going and I'd like you to come."

At that point, one of the alien aircraft screamed over the city. The high-pitched whistle was heard long before the deeper hum that followed as it passed a few kilometers away. I could see the sky where it *should* be, but all I saw was black. It had no lights on it like any of our airplanes and even with the moonlight I couldn't see the aircraft.

"I'm coming," I said. *I have nothing to lose, and this is getting a bit scary,* I thought.

Jared seemed pleased. "Great, good to have you with us, we're going to give it another half hour for anyone else to arrive." As he finished speaking, the aircraft returned, it slowed and then fired. Even at a distance, the sound was phenomenal. There was a large BOOM and everyone covered their ears instinctively.

"Nup. We'll be leaving now," he said and turned to the others. "Right everyone. Let's move. I run this part of the track once a week so I know it well, I'll lead."

There was a chorus of agreement and everyone filed in behind Jared as he headed up the track.

It was fairly easy walking along a well-maintained track. The talk amongst the walkers was varied. Many kept trying to ring their families, but all the mobile networks were down. Some were excited, some were stoic, but I could tell many were just plain scared, like me.

The night air was cool against my skin cool, but I soon warmed up from the mostly up-hill hike. The only torch I had was my mobile phone. It occurred to me about fifteen minutes into the walk that I had nothing with me to charge the phone, so I turned it off and found there was enough light from the half-moon and other people's torches for me to find my way. At least until we entered the forest, it was so black in there, and barely any moonlight made its way to the ground, so I turned the torch back on.

I don't know exactly what time we started, maybe midnight, but it was nearly dawn by the time we came to a small clearing where Jared stopped and said, "This is far enough folks. We can camp here and have a look in a couple of hours to see what's happened."

Everyone bombarded him with questions, which he fielded with ease. He knew nothing more than they did, but somehow he made them feel better and they set about making camp.

I didn't bother with my tent, I was hot and a bit sweaty, in spite of the cool dry season air. So I just stretched out on my sleeping bag and lay there with absolutely no hope of sleep. I doubt anyone else would have slept either.

When the sky lightened enough to see we were in a bowl between ridges, Jared set off to climb the eastern ridge. He was followed by almost everyone. It was a short climb and as we broke through the low scrub at the top, Cairns came into view. We could see the airport and the great plume of smoke rising from it. It wasn't a dream, it really happened. Almost in unison, everyone checked their phones for a signal, but there was none.

A few took photos, many burst into tears, which made me feel like crying with them. I choked back my tears, as I knew they weren't going to help.

A discussion began about returning to Cairns. Jared was amongst those who said that we should wait. "Look it's going to be absolute bedlam down there, I'm pretty happy up here and I think there's little to be lost by staying out of Cairns. If you feel you need to go back, then we'll wait for you here."

I didn't know what to think. I didn't have any family there, all mine were on our cattle station outside Charters Towers and the thought of them pushed me over the edge into tears. The girl beside me saw me get upset and put her arm around my shoulders. I didn't know her name but her kindness helped immensely. Actually I didn't know most of these people, and the ones I did know were online people I'd had a couple of drinks with a few times. There were hundreds of people in the online group, some names you get used to seeing, but most you've never heard of. We were virtual strangers, thrown together by circumstance.

After some discussion, a few people decided they were going to go back to Cairns, while the rest stayed put. I chose the latter as I could only imagine the chaos that Cairns would be in. At least up high on this ridge, I could feel a little distance from it.

One of the guys pulled out a small drone and unfolded the arms ready to fly it. "Well, I'll save you guys a walk." he said proudly. We were all pretty interested in what he was going to be able to see with it.

He stood there for a few moments pushing buttons with a furrow in his brow, looking intently at the screen. "I can't get a GPS lock."

"Can it fly without GPS?" asked one of the girls.

"Yeah, but I might lose it... Guess it doesn't matter now I 'spose. I'll give it a crack."

He placed it on the ground in the middle of the clearing and we all stood back to watch. When he turned it on, his face was full of concentration, the propellers all started spinning but when it lifted into the air it was erratic. It wobbled and spun around all over the place. "It's not responding, it says it's got a signal problem, but I dunno how, it's got a range of ten kay"

The drone made a few more erratic swings before suddenly taking off vertically like a rocket for maybe fifty meters and then headed for Cairns before beginning to tumble through the air, all the way to the ground where we saw it hit a rocky outcrop. It was destroyed. "Bugger it!" said the owner.

"Maybe the signal was being jammed?" someone said behind me.

"Maybe… Doesn't matter now though, it's gone," said the guy, throwing the remote controller in his backpack before sitting down hard on it.

There were twenty of us left when the group of about a dozen headed back down the hill. When they left, Jared addressed us all informally. "Guys, it's gonna get hot later, I'd suggest we all grab some food and sleep if you can."

I ate some rice crackers and had some water. I wasn't hungry but thought I should try to eat something. Stretched out on my sleeping bag again, I slept fitfully for about an hour.

I woke to the sound of an approaching alien aircraft. We heard several large BOOMS as it approached us from the south. Everyone stood and squinted against the morning sunlight trying to see the black spaceship. It looked a bit like a stealth bomber; it was all angular and pointed at the front. It was moving so fast it was hard to get a good look at it and it didn't seem to reflect light, like it was there but not really. I saw it bank and head for the Barron Gorge, which was quite close to us. It slowed over the gorge momentarily and Jared yelled, "GET DOWN" just before it fired. The shock wave was tremendous. Anyone still standing would have been blown flat on the ground. My ears were ringing with the impact. When we regained our senses, a few raced back up the eastern ridge to see what happened. As my ears recovered, I could still hear a low rumble, and it turned out, the rumble wasn't hearing damage. They had hit the dam wall and *billions* of litres of water were now roaring down the river. There was also water coming from the south to meet it and we watched in horror as it all swept towards the coast, taking houses with it.

"That's the water from the Copperlode Dam meeting the Barron Gorge water down there. They're going for the infrastructure," said a voice behind me. It was James, our online group's resident conspiracy theorist. He was a thin, unhealthy looking guy with dark hair and a complexion that hadn't seen the sun in a while. We met at the first drinks night and I quickly worked out not to get into a conversation with him. A nice enough guy, but he has some pretty different ideas.

"It's their plan. Take out the infrastructure to bring the population under control. They'll be doing it in an order of priority. First, they'd disrupt communications, which explains what happened to the phones and the drone, as they'd be jamming all the frequencies. Then they'd bomb the airports to gain air superiority, and then power generation. Fairly textbook really," he said with a shrug.

"So what's next then?" asked a cynical voice.

"Depends on what they want to do... beat us into submission or wipe us out. Ports and rail are next if they want us to submit, roads are if they want to contain us for extermination."

Jared interjected with an exasperated edge to his voice. "*Jesus*, James, I don't think anyone needs to be *more* scared. We don't know what they are planning."

But not everyone was done with the subject.

"Yeah?" said one of the other guys. "And why not do it all at once instead of bits and pieces?"

James rolled his eyes. "Because it's a big planet. Can you imagine how many cities there are to bomb? How many aircraft do you think they have? They will be prioritising the major cities, everywhere else will be covered based on a different set of priorities, until the job is done on the capitals and more aircraft are freed up."

Nobody spoke for some time. What he said made disturbing sense.

Jared was the first to speak, which he did so quietly to James. "Well, until we know more, let's not scare everyone *unnecessarily...* Look around, mate."

James and the others looked at the rest of the group. There were more than a dozen terrified faces, many wet with tears, and most were stricken with grief. They were all looking at James and Jared.

"Fair point... sorry," he said, before saying loudly to the group. "Sorry folks. Don't mind me. I've just read too many sci-fi books."

Jared turned to address the group. "How about we have a change of subject, I know a lot of you from the alien invasion group, but there are some faces I don't recognise. How about we go around the group and introduce ourselves?" There was a murmur of agreement.

"I'll go first," he said. "My name is Jared Faulkner. I'm a boilermaker and I spent a few years in the Army Reserves until a trigger finger injury got me kicked out." He held up his right hand, which was missing part of his index finger. "I like bushwalking, cold beer and long walks on the beach." He grinned.

A few people chuckled.

"Ok, clockwise from the top. He pointed to me, as I was sitting beside him. I really didn't feel like doing this, but the group's mood had lightened already, so I could see his reasoning.

"Ok, I'm Jessica Bell. I'm a third-year pharmacy student at uni in Cairns. I also like cold beers and walking, and I'm not missing any body parts." I smiled at Jared, and he laughed.

I looked to my left; it was the girl who put her arm around me earlier. Her name was Julie and she worked in childcare. I smiled at her. It made sense that someone in childcare would see when a hug is needed. She looked like a presenter from Playschool, with her round welcoming face, soft voice, and warm smile. She was just someone everyone instantly liked.

Next came Paula the barmaid, and then Louise, who was an assistant shot-firer in the mines out west so she worked with explosives. Both were tall, fit looking girls. Louise had short blonde hair, with an almost boyish cut. Paula was the complete opposite; she wore a long thick mane of dark brown hair that went halfway down her back. I was jealous. I always wanted hair like that but instead got thin mousy blonde hair that always struggled to get past my shoulders.

There was much laughter and joking as each of us shared something of ourselves. Faces lightened, and tears dried up. It was a genius move by Jared.

As we neared the last in the group, I could see we actually had a pretty useful mix of skills. There was an auto electrician, a second-year apprentice plumber, a butcher, a divemaster from a scuba diving boat, and a pig hunter. Plus a whole range of other skills and it occurred to me that Jared wasn't just boosting morale. He was finding out what resources he had in his team. It seemed Jared wasn't just a pretty face; he had brains to go with it.

Most of us were in our early twenties; a few may have been in their late teens. Jared I think would have been one of the oldest, maybe late twenties?

When it came time for a girl sitting by herself at the back of the group to introduce herself, she seemed reluctant. She looked younger than the rest of us but that may have been her size, as she was quite petite. She wore new looking cargo pants and a long-sleeved shirt with pockets all over it.

Jared spoke to her. "Hey, you're a new face. Come on, tell us about yourself."

She looked quite worried, fiddling nervously with her backpack straps. "Um... I'm sorry... I hope you don't mind, but... I'm not actually part of this group. I just saw you all gathering at the bottom of the hill and I kinda just tagged along. I'm sorry," she said in a tiny, almost child-like voice.

"Ha, don't worry about that," said Jared. "We're all just tagging along." He smiled at her and the group echoed his sentiments.

She seemed to relax a little and told us her name was Amy Kitchener, and that she was a first year botany student at uni.

Jared asked, "Tell me. You have a backpack that looks well prepared." He looked down at her feet. "New hiking boots and you were heading bush as well. How did you know we were heading up here?"

"I didn't, my dad told me to."

"Your dad? Why did he send you up here?" Jared asked.

"I guess I can say now... now all this has happened." She took a deep breath. "My uncle works in an observatory in South America.

He rang my dad last week and said we should all get out of the city. He said there were more ships arriving, and they were all parked behind the moon, dozens of them. They'd taken out the lunar satellites so we couldn't see them, but the radio telescope he works on was seeing spikes each time one arrived. He said that they must be planning something and that we should go bush."

"Jesus Christ. So they knew and said nothing!" said a man I now knew was Peter the accountant.

Jared responded quickly, "What could they do, mate? To say something to the people would have caused worldwide panic, looting, and chaos. They've probably been negotiating all week trying to avoid what happened."

Nobody spoke until Jared turned to Amy again. "Amy, please … go on."

She took another deep breath. "So, anyway, my dad lives in Brisbane but grew up here. He rang me and told me to get some gear." She nodded to the backpack. "And head up this track and stay here for at least a week, or until something happens. I should have been here days ago, but I had an assignment due… and it all seemed a bit silly."

A few people chuckled.

"We all thought so too," Jared said with an easy smile. "Anyway, welcome to the group Amy." He turned to the rest of the group. "I guess we can call it that now. I think we are far stronger together than we are apart. Nobody is under any obligation to stay, but if you do, you are expected to contribute in whatever way you can. I think we stay close to here and wait to see what the-."

"Who made you leader?" interrupted the voice of Craig, the overweight Duty Manager of a bottle shop, with one of those short cut beards some guys wear to hide their extra chins.

Jared paused and turned to face him. "Nobody made me the leader, and I'm not claiming the job. I'm offering suggestions because nobody else is. Got some suggestions on what to do next? You want the job?"

"No... I just don't like that you're telling us what to do, when none of us is the official leader. There are some of us who have leadership training and might be better suited to the job."

Jared stayed quiet for a moment and then smiled. "Ok, if the Army Reserves taught me anything, it's the importance of leadership structure. I'd thought it was a bit soon to elect leaders, since we have no idea what's going on, but since you've raised it. What does everyone think?" Jared looked around the group.

"I think we should put it to a vote," said Craig. "Hands up who wants to be a leader?" He raised his own hand. I noticed two others raised their hands, but Jared wasn't one of them.

This is silly. Just boys wanting to be leader of the club, I thought. *But why isn't Jared putting his hand up?* I looked at the other contenders. None of them struck me as someone I'd follow down the street, let alone into the bush. And Craig? *Manages a bottle shop and thinks that automatically makes him a leader here?*

Craig spoke again. "Right, let's put it to a vote, we can start with me. Who votes for-"

I had to interrupt. I didn't know any of these guys but it was clear to me that Jared was our best hope. I just had to say something. "I nominate Jared for leader."

Craig gave me a glaring look. "I wasn't calling for *nominations*. We nominated ourselves."

"I nominate Craig," said Reece, a greasy haired guy that worked in a service station.

"I nominate Jared too," said Julie the child carer.

"Yeah me too," said David the divemaster.

I could see Craig gritting his teeth, eyeballing David and I, he said sharply, almost hissing, "That's not how this works. You can't have three nominations. And we aren't doing nominations. Jared didn't put his hand up, so he's not in the running. Now who votes for me as leader?" he looked around the group.

"This is crap," David said loudly, shaking his head. "I've worked on boats long enough to recognise a good skipper when I see one. You can all vote for whoever you like. I'll be going with Jared."

There was a murmur of agreement from the group.

David stood up. "Who votes for Jared?"

I counted the thirteen hands that shot up.

"*Jared* isn't in the bloody running! He can't be voted leader," objected Craig, standing up and facing David.

"Give it a rest Craig." David squared his broad shoulders towards him.

Another guy, Kieran, also stood up and faced Craig. I thought his name was Kieran, anyway he was a pig hunter and a pretty solid guy with a big chest and a short neck.

"Jared is the leader and that's the end of it." Kieran turned to shoot Jared a grin and added, "Whether he likes it or not."

There were a few chuckles from the group, and Jared stood up.

"Well, thanks for the vote of confidence, guys. I'll do my best for you all. I should say now that this isn't a dictatorship. I accept ideas and constructive criticism for anyone in this group. Now one of the reasons I didn't think deciding on a leader was something to do yet, was that we have a large part of this group currently down there." He pointed towards Cairns.

"They may have other ideas and have maybe decided on a leader of their own. We'll cross that bridge when we come to it. Now, I think we should move into the forest a bit. It's going to get bloody hot out here soon and we're a bit exposed to aircraft."

"How long will we stay here?" asked Julie.

"I don't know yet," Jared said. "A return time for the others wasn't discussed, but I don't want to hang around here for too long. I think we should move away from Cairns as soon as we can. It's a big target."

"Maybe you should have set a time for the other group to be back." Craig, obviously still fuming over being out voted for leader, just sat there, glaring at everyone and huffing now and then.

"I didn't hear you say anything about it at the time," said David, in Jared's defence.

"Hang on guys." Jared held up a hand. "Them taking off was their choice. Now we don't have to stay here and wait for them, but I'd like to. They may have access to some news that we don't have. What does everyone think?"

There were a few comments in agreement that we should wait.

We picked up our gear and followed Jared back down the path about one hundred meters to a creek, which we then followed up stream about thirty meters to an area with large trees whose canopies almost completely blocked out the sun. The understory was clear of trees and relatively flat.

"Let's set up a bit of a camp here for the day. We can see the path from here, so we'll see the others come back."

Everyone spread out and threw down their backpacks. I'd by chance thrown mine down near Jared's, between some large boulders.

A group of three went and sat on a big, mostly decomposed log at the edge of the creek. One of them was Craig, and the others were Reece and Jamie who supported him for the leadership. I really didn't like either of them. Jamie was a pudgy sleaze and Reece looked like he needed a bath.

They immediately began a quiet discussion amongst themselves in hushed tones.

Kieran spotted them and said loudly. "Oi, you blokes." They looked up. "I wouldn't sit on that log if I were you. You'll get scrub itch."

"We'll get *what*?" asked Reece.

"Scrub itch. Little sores from the mites that live in dead wood. You wanna sit on sumthin', find a big rock."

"That sounds like crap to me. I've lived up here for five years and never heard of that," Craig said.

"Suit yourselves." Kieran shrugged.

Reece sat on his backpack, but the other two stayed put.

I saw Jared smile slightly and wondered if he knew something but chose not to share.

Once we were all settled, Jared stood up and spoke again. "Everyone, I've been doing some more thinking. The country from here gets steeper to the north. From here south might be an easier route to get us some distance from Cairns. There are houses further up the hills as well, where we might be able to get more fresh water."

"What's wrong with *that* water?" Craig pointed at the rainforest creek, with its burbling clear water. "It's as pure as it comes!"

"Not quite mate." Jared shook his head. "There's potential bugs in that water. As the weather warms up and there's less rain during the dry season, it'll get more and more risky to drink it."

"Buuullcrap." Craig rolled his eyes and shook his head.

"I have to agree with Jared," I said. "We did a unit on tropical waterborne infections last semester. Unless we can boil it for at least one minute, two to be safe, none of us should drink the creek water."

Craig just shook his head.

"You heard the Doc, people, don't drink the water unless it's been boiled, and if you need a drink, ask around to see if someone can spare some. Remember we're all in this together."

Being called *Doc* irritated me. My last boyfriend did that all the time just to annoy me... It worked.

When he sat down, I spoke quietly to Jared, "I'm not a doctor, Jared. Far from it, I'm not even finished with my pharmacy degree."

"You're the closest thing we have to a doctor, Jess."

Another thing that annoyed me was being called *Jess!* It's what our neighbours call their cattle dog! But I chose not to say anything, for fear of being considered hard work.

It was important to be accepted in this group. If things really were as bad as we thought... They were all I had. Thinking about that started to upset me again. I swallowed the sob in my throat and thought about getting something to eat instead.

Jared pulled out a map and was studying it over his knees.

"That'll be handy. I didn't think to bring one," I said as I rummaged in my pack for some food.

"Yeah, I'm just trying to find the easiest route south. Some of that bush is pretty steep."

"You can tell that from the map?"

"Yeah, it's a topo' map... sorry, topographical. Here I'll show you." He stood up and slid his backpack up alongside me and sat down again. He spread the map across our knees and pointed with his left index finger to the millions of lines on the map.

"See these lines? They indicate heights above sea level. The closer they are, the steeper the gradient. See that valley there?" He pointed at an area that was almost black with lines. "That's as steep as hell and we'd never walk it. Not with this lot." He thrust his chin at the group.

"It's better if we look for areas where the gradient lines are further apart. Like here." He pointed to an area where the lines were about two centimetres apart. "*That,* we can walk... across the slope that is, without too much trouble."

"Where did you learn this?" I asked.

"Army Reserves... it wasn't all guns and parades." He gave me a wry smile. "Anyway. I think we'd better get some rest," he said, folding the map. "If we're stuck here waiting for the others, we might as well catch up on sleep." He slid down his backpack till he was sitting on the ground and leaned back against it with his head against the boulder. He pulled the brim of his baseball cap over his eyes and exhaled loudly.

I did the same and wished I had a cap to cover my eyes.

"Thanks for taking the job, Jared. I feel better knowing you know what you're doing."

"Don't sweat it. I'm out of my comfort zone too. I've just spent more time there than most." He lifted his cap enough to give me a wink. "And thanks for coming along. I feel better knowing you'll be there to keep us in one piece."

I was about to object, but he sighed and settled himself down to sleep.

Let it slide, Jessica, I thought to myself.

No Going Back

'How do you move on? You move on when your heart knows there is no turning back.' -JRR Tolkien

About an hour later, those who were sleeping were woken by the sound of an alien aircraft approaching. Jared was instantly awake and listening. It was coming in fast from the south. BOOM there was a loud explosion of sound and as it echoed away, we could hear the aircraft still coming.

"EVERYBODY COVER YOUR EARS!" yelled Jared. "Lay flat on the ground!"

We all did as we were told. I ducked in between two boulders and just as the last person hit the ground there was an almighty BOOM...!

The shock wave sucked the wind out of my lungs and knocked me half unconscious. Branches and leaves started falling from the treetops above, some of them quite large. I could hear one of the other girls bawling, almost screaming, and trying to get her breath. I couldn't tell who.

Even with covering my ears, they hurt with the impact of the sound. I could barely hear anything above the ringing. Branches were still falling from the trees above us. I felt myself being part lifted, part dragged, and then propped up against a boulder. Then there was Jared's face in mine, mouthing the word. "OK?"

I didn't know if I was ok or not, but whoever was bawling had to be worse than me! At least the bawling had turned into a whimper now, so whoever it was had calmed down a bit.

I looked around, fighting the daze and fogginess in my head to try to work out what was happening. I couldn't think straight, and my ears were ringing so badly, I couldn't hear anything. But I could hear that poor girl's crying. I couldn't understand it.

Jared was running from person to person, checking on them. But now the branches had mostly stopped falling, but the shredded leaves were still falling like confetti. Once Jared had checked on a few of them, he came back to me. He took my face in his hands; he smiled and yelled, "IT'S OK." He pulled me into his chest, and I immediately felt safer. It felt like being a little girl getting a hug from mum or dad after an accident.

The bawling and whimpering slowly stopped and through the fog of my concussed mind, I realised the sounds were *mine*... I burst into tears, sobbing uncontrollably.

Jared held me for the longest time. I could sense him looking around and I *felt* more than heard him yelling through the vibrations in his chest. He was yelling orders, and as my sobbing subsided and the fog in my head cleared, I became more aware of the situation.

People might be hurt! I dragged myself away from his chest and looked up. He looked down and smiled. "Back with us?" he asked.

"I think so." I tried to focus. "Is anyone hurt?"

"Nothing serious. I have a couple of the guys going back to the ridge for a look."

"I feel so silly, I'm sorry I-"

"Never mind that. We all deal with stuff differently. I go to water at the sight of a needle." He winked.

He pulled away and looked into my eyes, one and then the other. He then grabbed a torch and did the same. "How many fingers am I holding up?" he asked, holding up two fingers on his right hand.

I concentrated hard and finally saw two. "Two fingers."

"Close... it's one and three quarters," he laughed. "But you were a bit slow on answering that Jess, I'd say you're a bit concussed."

"What about you?" I grabbed the torch from his hand.

"Not enough brains in there to damage, Jess," he said with a grin.

I'd never done a concussion test for real before, but when I did the test on him, as best I could tell, he was fine.

"I gotta go, when you feel up to it, there are some minor injuries to look at Doc." He winked and got up. He raced off towards the path.

There it was again... *Doc. I'm no Doc*, I thought. *But I have to see if I can help.*

I got up. A little shakily at first, but I steadied myself against the rock. When I looked around, the scene was chaotic. Everything was covered in a blanket of shredded leaves and there were people just sitting, looking dazed. One of the girls had a trickle of watery blood coming from her left ear. I didn't have to be a doctor to know that it was a burst eardrum. God knows mine felt like someone had bashed them with a hammer.

I spotted one of the guys lying down and two others leaning over him. His name was Tony, that much I remembered. I made my way, unsteadily at first, to where they were. "Is he ok?" I asked.

"Yeah, it's a cut on his leg. I was just looking for something to strap it up," said the man closest to me.

"Let me have a look." I knelt beside him.

The wound wasn't big, only about forty millimetres long, but it was deep and I could see pieces of wood poking out of it from deep within the muscle. I'd seen worse injuries in cattle growing up. I'd once pulled a star picket out of a horse's chest when assisting the vet, so at least I wasn't squeamish.

"We need to clean it first. The wood will cause infections, does anyone have any tweezers?"

"I do," a voice said from behind me. It was Julie. She rummaged in her backpack and produced a small grooming kit. She pulled out a set of tweezers and handed them to me.

"Thanks," I said, looking at them. "They aren't going to be sterile. I don't suppose anyone has rubbing alcohol? Or maybe a lighter?"

"I have a lighter." Tony dug into his pocket and produced a disposable lighter.

He handed it to me and I set about burning the end of the tweezers with the flame. I handed him back the lighter and started to remove the wood splinters from the wound. Some of them were deep and the poor man couldn't help but swear when I dug too deep and hit a nerve.

"I'm sorry," I apologised each time.

Tony winced, gritted his teeth and grunted. "All good."

By the time the wound was clean, Jared had returned. He looked over my shoulder to watch what I was doing before commenting. "Nice work, Doc. Sorry I should have mentioned I have a basic first aid kit in my backpack. It has a set of proper tweezers, a scalpel, and a few other things. I'll show you where it is for next time."

"Ok, good. You wouldn't happen to have some sterile gauze and bandages in there as well?"

"I've got some battle dressings in there, but we'd best save them for more serious injuries. Might have to tear up a shirt for that one."

I looked up at Tony. "Got a shirt you're not fond of?"

"Ha. I'm wearing the only one I brought with me," he laughed.

"I have some bandages," Amy said.

She brought over her backpack and opened it, revealing a large pocket full of first aid supplies.

"Oh you're well prepared." She didn't respond. I looked at her and saw the clear fluid and a little blood dripping from her ear.

"Amy, can you hear me?" I said, a little louder.

She turned suddenly and spoke a little too loudly. "Sorry. I don't seem to be able to hear on that side right now. It hurts like hell too."

I took the offered bandage and wrapped the man's leg. It wasn't pretty, but it would do and should keep the wound clean.

I turned to Amy and thanked her, then grabbing Jared's torch I checked for concussion. There was none. *Why can Jared see it and I can't? She must be concussed, Christ it burst her eardrum,* I thought.

Jared was standing behind me. So I asked, "Can you check please? Just to make sure."

"Yep no worries." He took the torch to check her eyes, and asked her to count his fingers.

"Nup, she's fine." He stood up. "Right folks, while doc's checking you all out, I'll fill you in on what's happened. That alien ship has bombed the road into Cairns and the Kuranda range road which heads west. The blast we got was the one that took out the Western Arterial road. I can only assume that means Cairns is cut off by road, from all directions." He glanced at James, who gave a nod.

"The blast that wrecked the Western Arterial road, also took out the bottom half of this track. We won't be going back that way, that's for sure, and the others won't be coming up this way... Look, it's about noon so we have plenty of daylight left. Now I'm sure nobody feels like walking right now, but I think we'd best make some tracks and get the hell away from Cairns. All agreed?"

Nobody disagreed.

"Alright... Once Doc has given you the once over, help the wounded, assemble down to the track with your gear and we'll get under way." He grabbed his backpack and hoisted it onto his back. "I'll go get the guys on the ridge and see you down there." He turned and headed back towards the track.

The others reached for their packs and started after Jared when Kieran stepped in front of them. "You heard the man. If you need it, Doc will check you over. If not, help the wounded. Might be nothing wrong with you, but there's plenty that need a hand."

Most turned around, looking embarrassed, and searched for someone to help. Craig stood his ground and eyeballed Kieran.

"What's this make you? His lackey?"

Kieran laughed in his face and said, "Part of a team, mate. It makes me part of a team. You're either in it, or out of it. Which one you choose; I couldn't really give a rat's arse. But I can tell you now, if you're in it, you'll do your bit, like *everyone* else."

While Craig was big, most of him was fat. Kieran stood almost a head shorter than Craig. But he was solid and way fitter. Craig squared up to Kieran momentarily and then thought better of it. He turned and grabbed one of the wounded people's backpacks from one of the other men and marched off down the track.

Kieran smiled, "Right, does anyone else need the Doc?"

I looked around and saw the pretty blonde girl standing with her backpack; she was unsteady on her feet. I couldn't remember her name, but Kieran saw where I was looking. He grabbed the shoulder of one of the able-bodied men and said. "Mate, I think that girl might need a hand. Help her out, hey."

"Yep, will do. Hey Louise, hang on, I'll give you a hand with that."

That's her name. Louise. Remembering names is going to take a while, I thought, before remembering about inner ear problems.

Hey, anyone with blood coming from their ears is maybe going to have balance problems. Can someone walk with them in case they get dizzy?"

"You heard the Doc folks. Help out the brain damaged ones." Kieran ordered with a smile.

Before I knew it, Kieran was beside me, carrying my backpack. "Oh no, I can carry it," I insisted.

"Nah, you'll be right," said Kieran. "I think you might be one of the damaged ones." He winked.

The others had already started off towards the track when Kieran and I fell into step behind them.

"I really am ok, Kieran. I feel pretty stupid about it all now."

"Doc..." Kieran began quietly. "I near crapped my pants. I thought it was *me* makin' that noise... I've never felt anything like that, so I reckon you've got nuthin' to feel stupid about, hey."

"Well, thanks, Kieran," I said, but I still felt guilty that he was carrying my backpack.

I liked Kieran from the start, as he seemed to have a good heart. I recognised him as *'boy from the bush'* straight away; so I guess having grown up around guys like him, I knew where I stood. He's one of those guys with a real sense of fair play. He'd be a terrible larrikin I'm sure, but he would always fall short of hurting anyone. I felt he was someone I could trust and I was pleased he was part of the group.

FIRST MARCH

'Perseverance, secret of all triumphs.' -Victor Hugo

We marched all afternoon through the forest. In spite of the pulsing pain behind my eyes, my head became clearer, but my body felt like I'd done twelve rounds with the world champion boxer. I felt certain the others must have been feeling the same way, so there was no point in complaining.

Jared led us, and from what I could see was doing a pretty good job of avoiding the steep and thick scrub parts of the trip. He had a machete, but he hardly used it. I have no idea how far we'd walked, but we certainly seemed to be covering some ground. I remember being amazed at how different the forest could be from one ridge to the next. I'd been in Cairns for three years and always just looked at it as the rainforest. I had no idea there was so much diversity compared to home. Out there it's all the same except for a few small pockets of green along the creeks, but here it's all so different.

At one point we could see out from the forest, all the way to the centre of Cairns in the distance. We could hear lots of squealing tyres and revving engines. The consensus was the petrol heads were enjoying some freedom while the police were busy. But I suspected it was just our society slipping into anarchy in the wake of a disaster. The occasional rifle shots we could hear didn't bode well.

The terrain was mostly open under-story forest. The canopy of the large trees block out the sunlight so nothing but small saplings grow under them until a tree falls and the light hits the ground. When it does, the forest springs into life in a race to reach the sun before the canopy is closed by another tree.

It makes for much easier walking than the few patches of re-growth forest we crossed. Places where the trees have been cut or fallen down and the seed bank in the soil has exploded a plethora of plant life into the void. Those stretches were just hard work.

We crossed a few creeks and as it was towards the end of the 'dry season' most of the creeks had very little flow, but you could see evidence of much bigger flows by the debris pushed high up the banks. Traveling through this area during the summer or 'wet season' would be a whole lot more challenging.

One of the larger creeks we crossed still ran waist deep and fast. It was strewn with boulders, and impossible to cross with a full backpack. Jared organised the boys to form a human chain and got all the gear and the people across safely. But everyone was now wet from the waist down; it made walking so much more uncomfortable having your feet squelching in your boots.

As it grew late in the day, I noticed we were climbing higher. I'd much rather climb *up* when we were just starting, as climbing when you're tired is so much harder.

Just as it was beginning to get quite dim in the forest, we crossed a small ridge and descended into another valley with an open under-story. Jared stopped in the middle of the widest part and spoke.

"Everyone had enough? Wanna camp here for the night?"

There were groans, and everyone just collapsed onto the ground.

"I take that as a yes," he laughed. "Folks, that was a hard march and you pulled it off. Well done everyone. Now I'm going to chase up some firewood. Anyone feel up to helping?"

Nobody spoke for a moment before Kieran dragged himself up off the ground and said. "Yep. I'll help."

"Good onya, mate. I think the ridge is the most likely place to find some dry stuff."

The two headed back up to the ridge they'd just crossed while the rest of us sat there panting on the ground, in our still very wet clothes and boots. After a couple of minutes, I couldn't stand it anymore and decided to take my boots off and begin setting up my tent. I really didn't feel like doing it, but I could feel my legs stiffening already and knew I wasn't going to feel any more inclined to do it later. As I stripped my socks off in the dim light, I saw my foot was discoloured with short black lines all over my feet. I grabbed my phone from my backpack and using the light from the screen while it turned on, I saw the lines were *leeches*. I gave an uncontrolled shiver. Much of the squelching in my boot had been my own blood from the leech bites after they'd drunk their fill and released themselves from the flesh. The anticoagulant produced during the feeding process kept the blood flowing from the wound and into my socks. I shivered again.

It was gross, but I knew the worst thing to do was yank them off. They leave their jaws in your skin causing infection. I remembered getting leeches when I was younger, playing in creeks after heavy rain and my mother lecturing us about not pulling them off.

"Does anyone have a lighter I could borrow for a minute?" I asked.

"Yep, I've got one," said Tony and I got up and walked over to him.

"Thanks," I said as I took it from him. "How's the leg?"

"Yeah it's fine, thanks. It's a bit sore but it'll be right. Just walking makes it bleed a bit."

"Yeah, I don't know how to get around that, anyway this will only take a minute." I said and walked to the edge of the camp and set about burning the leeches to make them drop off. Most of them were big and full of blood, so it didn't take much encouragement for them to drop off.

"What are you doing?" A voice asked from behind me.

"Getting some leeches off," I said, closely inspecting my foot for any more. "You'd probably want to do the same. In fact you should all check for leeches," I said a little louder. "Take your shoes and socks off. Grab a torch and have a look. Check in between your toes."

"Leeches! Bugger that." I heard a guy say.

One of the girls sounded a bit distressed. "Get it off, get it off!" I suspected she'd removed her sock and found one.

"Relax. They won't hurt you. I'll come get it off for you," I said, getting up and making my way over to her. It turned out to be Julia. "Argh, I hate leaches, Jess," she said looking away from where I was removing the leech from her ankle.

"Yeah I'm not a big fan either, but there are worse things I guess."

"I guess so... But... Will we come across them?" She lowered her voice to a whisper. "I'm a bit scared, I've never done anything like this before."

I looked up at her; she had tears in her eyes. The enormity of our situation was maybe getting a bit much for her and I knew exactly how she felt. It had happened often enough for me today.

"I don't know what's going to happen, but I think we're safe in this group, as safe as we could be anywhere right now. We'll be ok." I smiled at her.

"Thanks," she said smiling back at me.

There were many comments from around the camp now. "Yuck" was a common one. "Gross" was another and I couldn't blame them.

I spent the next ten minutes going from person to person removing leeches. One of the guys handed me a torch to use instead of my phone, which I was grateful for. I really wasn't very prepared for this trip, but I guess it was impossible to know how it would turn out.

One of the guys had walked a short way out of the camp to urinate and I heard, "Bugger thaaat!"

All I could see from behind was his silhouette from the torch he was shining on his crotch.

"I've got one on my *nads*...! Jeeezus," he cried.

"I'm not getting it off," I yelled in his direction and suppressed a laugh.

"Oh c'mon Doc. The man's in need of *help*!" David the divemaster said with a laugh.

"Gotta draw a line somewhere... I'm sure he's capable of taking it off himself."

I suspected David might have been one of the good guys. He seemed genuine and always up for a laugh. I guess you'd describe him as lean but toned. He looked pretty fit, and he had a big smile that lit up his dark tanned face.

Jared and Kieran returned to camp with armloads of firewood. They were amused to hear of the leeches and agreed to check their feet.

With a fire lit and my tent up, I was content to sit by the fire and hold my boots and socks up to dry. The steam rose from them and there were plenty of others doing the same thing. Some of them possibly benefited from the washing in the creek, as they didn't smell too good already.

My pants were still wet, but I didn't bring anything else to wear, so I had to hope they dried in the tent overnight. Some of the guys, less concerned about modesty just sat in their underwear drying their pants. I envied them.

"Right, guys. I guess we'd better start thinking about food and working out what we have," said Jared. "Some of us got away better prepared than others and while I understand that some of you may feel that it's not your fault others weren't prepared, I think we'd be better to pool our resources. We don't know how long we'll be out here."

"I agree with Jared," David said. "We have to treat it as being in a survival situation like on the boats. We pool our resources and ration the food. It's how you survive."

"Well I'm not," said Peter, the accountant. Where David was lean and toned, Peter was skinny and a bit weedy. I guess an office job doesn't do much for the figure.

"I was organised enough to bring enough to feed myself for a week. I don't see why I should have to give it away to someone who wasn't prepared."

"I can tell you why," began Jared. "It's because we're *it*... It's just *us* now and we all have to look out for each other, at least until things settle down and we don't know when that will be. We should stick together; help each and every one of us get through it. Being selfish is not how we are going to do it."

"You can have mine," said Amy. She dragged her backpack over to the fire and upended it on the ground. She had dozens of dehydrated hikers' meals, packets of carbohydrate sweets, sachets of electrolyte powders to add to water and water purification tablets. Enough to keep a small girl like her going for a month or more.

"And mine," David the divemaster said. He'd walked over to his backpack and grabbed a dry bag, which he then upended beside Amy's food.

It was full of Army ration packs and bags of sugar lollies.

"Where did you get *those*?" Jared asked.

"I've got a mate who worked in an army surplus store. I got them from him last year just before it closed. I love 'em, but I've pinched the chocolates out of them ages ago. Can't leave 'em alone!" He grinned.

There was a murmur of chuckles from the group.

"Ok, folks, it's a bloody good start, thank you. Seeing how much some of you are carrying makes me wonder if there aren't some with lighter packs that can share the load."

"I'll second that. I carried Amy's pack today and no offence to you Amy, but someone your size isn't going to get far carrying that lot," said Kyle.

I can't remember what he said he did for a living, but while he was fit looking, he wasn't a big guy and two packs must have been hard work to carry today.

Jared nodded. "Yeah, that's a big load on a small frame... Look I think instead of trying to divvy up all the food how about we just go by weight of the backpack compared to the person and try to even things out. Each mealtime we each eat something from our backpacks, regardless of who it was from. Agreed?"

There was a murmur of agreement from around the fire.

"Good, well how about we get some food on the go, I'm starving. If anyone is short of anything, give a shout. I've only got one pannikin, but anyone is welcome to use it after I've heated up a feed."

This was my moment to admit I'd brought next to nothing. I'd been wondering what to do about that all day. "Great," I said. "All I did was empty my kitchenette at uni. I'm one of the seriously unprepared, I'm afraid."

"Ha, Jess, you brought along something far more important... *skills,*" Laughed Jared. "Have dinner with me and we can talk about what we need."

"Ha, ok thanks."

The fire was a spread out affair, which gave room for a few to cook or heat their meals at once. Jared had a tin of stew, and I had some noodles, which we threw in together. I was so hungry I would have been happy with dry noodles, so the noodle stew was almost gourmet. Jared heated it in my saucepan, the same one I felt silly having brought along all day, but now I was glad I had it.

"So, Doc," he began once we were sitting down to eat. "We need to work out what supplies you're going to need."

"I'm not a doctor."

"Jesus, are we going to start this again?" he laughed. "You're all we've got. Now I'm sure we have a few bits and pieces between us all, but that's not going to go far. Especially if they keep bombing near us."

"Yeah, that was something else. What sort of bombs were they?"

"No idea, I was only in the reserves. We trained a lot, but I've never been in battle where they dropped bombs, so I've only heard ours. They certainly didn't sound like anything I've heard before."

"Well, as I've said, I'm studying Pharmacy, so I have some idea of the drugs we could use. I have some basic skills in first aid and although I've never stitched anyone up, I have seen it done."

"Now we're talking. So we ideally need to get to a chemist shop, yeah?"

"Ideally yes. They'll have all the first aid and wound care as well as the drugs. But Jared, I'm not qualified, and I certainly can't *prescribe* drugs. You'd need a doctor to do that."

"Jess... I think the way things are going, the rules don't apply anymore."

"You... Think things will stay like this?"

He paused for a moment and shrugged before saying, "I don't know anymore than you do, Jess. But it's not looking good, is it?"

I was unable to speak. Like Julia just before, it was dawning on me once again that this wasn't a bad dream. I wasn't going to wake up tomorrow and head back to uni. Nothing was ever going to be the same again. I felt a sob rise in my throat, and tears welled in my eyes. I tried to be strong, but I couldn't hold it in. The reality had just hit me like a brick.

Jared slid beside me and put his arm around me and let me sob quietly. After a couple of moments, I got a hold of myself and wiped away the tears. I had to be brave and crying into this guy's shoulder every time things got hard was not a good look.

"I'm sorry," I said. "I'm being soft."

"Nah, not soft… human. I've seen most of this lot wiping away tears at some point, don't you worry."

I thought about that for a moment before asking. "What about you?"

"Can't say this all doesn't bother me, Jess. Just internalise it. Like my ex-girlfriend used to say." He put on a female voice and said, "You bastard, it's like talking to a brick wall, why don't you show any feelings when it gets hard."

I laughed. "You do that very well."

"Thanks, I heard it often enough to memorise it. Truth is, I just really hate confrontation with people I care about." He shrugged.

"How did that go in the army? Isn't war kinda the ultimate confrontation?" I laughed.

"Ha, yeah I guess it is, but I didn't mind taking on the enemy. I spent a bit of time on peacekeeping missions, so I did see a bit of action, mostly just guerrilla skirmishes. I don't mind that stuff, its just people close to me that I hate arguing with… So anyway, I suppose we have to get you to a chemist as soon as we can," he finished, changing the subject.

I nodded and let the subject go. "Yes, and I could really use some books on treating people. I've really only learned about drugs and their effects on the human body. I don't know how to diagnose things or treat wounds. Not serious ones."

"Right, where would we find books like that?" he asked.

"I'm sure there are plenty of them in the university library. But that's a fair way from here and it's to the north."

He looked deep in thought. "Yeah, that's not ideal, but from memory the forest comes right down to the back of it... Unfortunately it's on the other side of both the Kuranda range road and the Barron River. Both of them have been blown to buggery. It'd take days to march this lot there anyway. Can't follow roads really, coz they'll be chaos and they may come back and blow more of them up anyway."

"If it's too hard, we might find those books in a doctor's surgery," I interrupted.

"Yeah, it looks like it'd be tricky to pull off. But maybe there's another way to get the stuff. Would it be possible for you to give me a list of the things you'll need?"

"Um yeah, for the drugs, I could do that. But I don't really know which books without seeing them. It'd be hard to describe the sort of thing I need."

"Yeah, I was afraid of that. I wouldn't have a clue what you'd-." He stopped speaking.

"Incoming!" He stood up and spoke loudly to the group, "Everyone on the ground, men cover the girl's heads, so they don't blow more eardrums and cover your own ears."

I could hear it now, the sound of an alien aircraft close by. Everyone dived to the ground.

He sat back down and grabbed me, pushing me backwards as he lay on top of me, covering my head with his body.

BOOM...BOOM...BOOM. There were three explosions. They were close, but the shock wave didn't hit me this time. I could feel something dropping onto my legs, and Jared slowly took his weight off me. He was on all fours over me while twigs, branches, and the confetti of leaves rained down all around us and onto his back. "They're gone... Ok?" he asked.

"Yes, fine, I didn't feel a thing... Thanks."

"I'm not sure I did much. I think the ridge protected us," he said, getting up.

"Where did the idea to cover the girls' heads come from?"

"Yeah, I was thinking about it on the walk up here. It was only the girls who got blown eardrums after this morning's bomb. I dunno much about it, but I thought that it was possible they had weaker eardrums." He shrugged.

"I've never heard of that." My feminist side felt slightly triggered by the word, *weaker*.

"Nah me either, but look, I figured it had to be worth a shot if it might save your ears." Jared shrugged.

"GET OFF ME!" Came a muffled shout from the other side of the fire.

Kieran got up quickly and held a hand out to Louise, who was climbing to her feet. She swatted his hand away.

"WHAT, the hell was that all about?" She glared, looking from Kieran to Jared.

"It was to protect your ears," I said before Jared could respond.

"What? How is this big boof-head climbing all over me going to protect my ears?" She pointed at Kieran, who just shrugged with a big smile.

I explained the theory to her and the other girls who were all listening in.

When I was done, I said, "Look, I don't know if there's any truth to it, but at this point we don't have anything else to go on and burst eardrums are pretty serious. I for one am thankful the guys are willing to look out for us."

"Well I for one, am happy on my own thanks." Louise stomped off towards her tent.

"Thanks for that," said Jared quietly.

"I thought it would sound better coming from a girl. Plus I think your motives are sound and in the absence of any other information... Well, we don't have any other theories." I smiled at him. "But if you're not careful you'll be labelled as sexist."

"Nah... I'm not like that."

"I know, but Louise might take some convincing," I chuckled.

"Yeah, well I'm awful glad it came from a girl." He turned and looked wide-eyed towards Louise's tent. "Anyway we haven't finished our discussion, but I think we can do that in the morning." He reached down and grabbed his pack and began removing the tent from the top of it. "I'm not going to go investigate what they hit this time. Knowing won't change anything tonight."

"Yeah, I'm pretty tired too. I'll head off to bed. Thanks for dinner. Good night," I said and headed for my tent.

"A pleasure... Night," he replied.

So I went to bed thinking about our new leader who hates confrontation. There seemed to be more to him than I'd first thought. I guessed everyone has a story.

SHOPPING

'Success is getting what you want. Happiness is wanting what you get.' -Carl Carnegie

There were no more bombing runs that night. We all awoke just as it started to get light. Well, Jared was up, clanking around in the dark making coffee while the sky began to lighten. That woke everyone else up. The smell of coffee had tent zippers opening all over camp and people were soon up and moving about. I lay there for a moment listening to an amazing array of birds, all calling in the sunrise. It was a great way to start the day.

I rolled out of my sleeping bag and pulled on my pants; they were cold and damp. Wearing wet clothes is one thing, putting them on wet in the morning is a whole other world of *yuck*. But I had nothing else, so I zipped them up and went outside the tent.

As I looked around, I saw a few others wearing screwed up facial expressions and a strange bow-legged walk, which told me they too, had just pulled on damp pants. At least I wasn't alone.

"Mornin' Doc, Chasing coffee?" asked Jared. He was crouched beside the fire with three of the guys, deep in discussion in low voices.

"Oh, I'd kill for one... But I gotta go first." I thumbed behind me.

"All good. Seems to be girls behind you and boys over there." He pointed at the far side of the fire.

"Thanks," I said, heading into the bush. When I got back, Jared handed me his pannikin. It had coffee in it, which was black, but I wasn't arguing, as it smelled so good! When I sat down by the fire, I welcomed the warmth it gave. Even in the tropics, it gets cool in the dry season.

"Thanks," I said and took a sip. "Hmmm that's good... How'd you sleep?"

"Not too bad. And you?"

"Like a log. I haven't hiked like that in a long time, plus yesterday was a big day in general."

"Yep, it sure was." He nodded slowly.

"So what's the plan for today?" I asked.

"Well, we've just been talking about that. Couple of us went up the hill earlier and had a look. Those bombs last night hit the city. We're thinking that if we don't do a bit of shopping soon, there might not be much left to get."

He picked up the map from beside him.

"Looking at this map, I'd say we're behind Redlynch. Most of it seems intact after the bombs last night. Now there's a chemist, a supermarket as well as a doctor's surgery. That would pretty much cover what we need for now I think."

"When do we leave?" I asked.

"Well, that's just the thing. I was thinking of taking some of the fittest people and doing a run in there. Hit-and-run so to speak."

"Oh... yeah, well I can stay here. I can make a list if you like." I admittedly felt a little disappointed.

"Well... Actually, I'd kinda like you to come if you feel you can. We're going to go pretty hard. I don't want to spend any more time down there than we have to. But I really wanted you there because you know what you're grabbing. We're all regular runners and are pretty fit, so we'll do all the carrying to make it easier for you to keep up. All you have to do is carry yourself. Up for it?"

I answered without thinking about it. "Yep, I'm not very fast though."

"I doubt we'll be fast carrying backpacks, especially once they're loaded, but if you can keep up, it's all we can ask." Jared turned to Kieran. "Mate, can you round up the biggest backpacks we have amongst us? I'll ask their owners if we can borrow them. I'll have a word to everyone now."

Jared stood up and called everyone in. He described the plan and asked those with the biggest backpacks to empty them and hand them to Kieran.

"I'll be coming," said Craig.

Jared sighed. "Mate, I've got the team organised, the fittest and the fastest. This is a hit-and-run job."

"I'm coming, I'm fit enough... I'll certainly keep up with you," he sneered. "Besides. We might all be part of a group, but *I* decide what I do." He thumbed his chest.

Kieran spoke. "Mate, you will do as you're told."

"Hang on Kieran." Jared held up a hand while eyeballing Craig. "If he wants to go that bad, fine. He can go. But I picked the team to go because I know they can keep up. You will carry *your* backpack, which will be filled with what I say, and if you can't keep up, nobody will wait for you. Happy with that?"

"I'll keep up, and I'll be getting what I want. If there's room, I'll carry what you want."

Kieran snorted looking him up and down. "You won't make it to the bottom of the hill mate."

"Righto. Grab some breakfast guys. We leave in twenty minutes," said Jared.

The group dispersed and the chosen few got busy with preparations.

I felt nervous. Looking at these people, they were all seriously fit. I was never a runner at school. Short legs, long body and a slightly large backside in between, I wasn't even someone that *looked* like a runner.

But I had to go. I really needed the books that the doctor's surgery might have, plus the chemists. I could give them a list but what if there is something they don't grab because it's not on the list? No, I had to go and I had to eat first. I started on some rice crackers from my backpack when Amy slid up alongside me with a bag of Carbohydrate Sweets. "Take these. You'll need the energy."

"Thanks, Amy, You're a lifesaver."

Amy shook her head. "Nope, looks like that's your job," she laughed.

Once we were all ready, Jared led the way and we headed off at a quick pace. We climbed up the ridge we crossed yesterday and headed down the other side. We'd been walking across the slope yesterday. Heading straight down, it showed me just how steep it was. There were times when I was sliding on my backside to prevent getting too much momentum and flying headfirst down the hill.

I followed Jared who was constantly looking over his shoulder checking on me. Behind me were Louise, Kyle, and then Craig, but I couldn't look back to see how they were going. I had enough to worry about simply not breaking my neck on this hill. The bomb had left the ground covered in leaf litter, making it seriously slippery. At times it was almost knee deep, so finding footholds was by feel or by chance. By the time we'd been heading down for maybe twenty-five minutes, it occurred to me that I would have to climb back up this!

A short time later the ground levelled out and Jared's pace slowed. "This'll be where the houses start. We'd best stay quiet and try to find a way onto the nearest street."

Another twenty meters on, through some awful regrowth trees, we came to high timber fences with houses behind them. A large dog started barking and came running up to the fence, growling savagely. We kept walking and I'll be honest, I was praying the fence didn't end, and we meet the dog on the other side.

When we finally approached the end of the fence line, we could see it was at the dead end of a street.

"Perfect," said Jared quietly. "Right. Now we head east from here and we should end up at the-" He stopped at the corner.

The scene ahead was like something out of a war movie. The street we were walking onto just *ended* thirty meters away. There was nothing but rubble after that, broken bitumen and pieces of houses, all the way to a set of large buildings about five hundred meters away. The houses on either side of where we were walking were largely intact except for all the windows having been blown in. There were cars parked on both sides of the street and all their windows were also gone. As we got closer, I could see the panels of those cars facing the flattened ground, were crushed and dented.

There were dogs barking from the houses on either side of us and off into the distance, but there were no sounds from the huge pile of rubble... and no people anywhere.

Kyle said, "How the hell are we going to cross that?"

We'd reached the edge of the destruction. Ahead of us was broken ground leading up onto the pile of rubble maybe five meters high. It stretched out kilometres in either direction.

"The bombs are *shaped*," said Jared in awe.

"What the hell does that mean?" asked Craig.

"Look at it. The damage is longer than it is wide. It didn't blow everything out... it just mixed it all up like a rotary hoe. It's designed to cover a specific area. By the looks of it, that area is the bulk of houses. I heard the bombs drop. There was only one dropped here. The others were to the north and south. We couldn't see the whole thing from the top of the hill this morning, so I had no idea it would be like this. This bomb's not like anything we have. By the looks of it, because the shape of the suburb isn't the same as the shape of the bomb blast, there are houses left mostly untouched around the edge."

"So like James said, they're trying to exterminate us?" I asked.

Jared turned to me. "I don't know, Jess. I'm only guessing... But it doesn't look good, hey."

Louise spoke from behind me. "Well either way, I don't think we're in a good place. Shall we keep moving?"

"Yeah, let's keep-" Jared was interrupted by Craig. His voice is a mixture of triumph and sarcasm.

"Hang on, what's your plan here? You gonna 'G.I Joe' your way across that lot?" he asked, pointing at the huge pile of rubble.

"You first," said Kieran.

"Alright guys." Jared held up a hand. "Look there is the ground between these houses and the pile that's relatively clear. We can travel along it until we can hopefully get around the mess... Let's move north." He headed off at a walking pace. "Keep your eyes out for a vehicle of some kind that's not as badly damaged as those" He thumbed towards the wrecks behind them. "Kyle... you're an auto sparky aren't you?"

"Yeah. Why's that?"

"Reckon you could hot-wire a car?"

"What, one of those?" He pointed at the wrecks. "Nah mate, they're all computerised with immobilisers and alarms... I mean with the right tools and a computer, yeah I'll get 'em going, but with a pocketknife? Nah, those days are over... find me an old one, then yeah... I can do it."

"Right. Keep your eyes peeled for an old car everyone. Preferably four wheel drive." Jared then broke into a trot and said, "Keep up."

I did keep up, as best I could anyway. These guys were really fit; they were barely out of breath. But at least I was way ahead of Craig, he was out of wind when he got to the bottom of the hill and still hadn't regained his breath. He'd gotten pretty beat up on the way down too. He had scratches on his arms and face, and one of his knees was bleeding. I guess I should have offered to look at it for him, but I couldn't find it in me.

We'd walked/jogged maybe two kilometres when Kieran spotted a possible car. He saw the roof of an old Landcruiser poking out above a half knocked down timber fence. "Let's check it out," said Jared. "One minute, and that's it. If it looks like a goer then we'll try… If not, I don't want to waste any time here."

Everyone agreed except Craig, he was still catching up and lagged fifty meters behind already. Louise and I hung back while the guys climbed/walked up the broken fence to look at the car. They didn't need the whole minute; they turned around and came back to us. "Missing a wheel," said Jared. "Let's keep moving." And he set off at a trot again.

Craig was still twenty meters away as we set off. His footfalls were heavy and his breathing hard. "Hey!"

"Here we go," said Kieran.

We waited for Craig to catch up and when he did, he said between gasps of air, "What do you think caused this damage?"

"Ahh, just as I thought." Kieran shook his head. "He's a 'have-a-chat'."

"What's that?" I asked and immediately regretted it, knowing it was likely to be derogatory and would only add fuel to the fire between them.

"I've worked with guys like this, we call 'em *have-a-chats*. It's always the lazy bastards who stop you to have a chat about the job. Gives them a chance to slack off or catch a breath while the boss thinks they're still on the job."

Craig just glared at Kieran for the longest moment.

"Plenty of time for this at camp, let's get moving," said Louise, and she set off at a jog.

Kieran was right of course, that's exactly what Craig was doing, but we didn't have time to call him out on it.

We went on for another half a kilometre when Kieran again spotted a car. He had an eye for four-wheel drives. Behind a broken garage door was visible the wheel and mudguard of a car.

"That's an old patrol," he said and jogged up to it while we followed. He dove under the door while we waited outside and his head emerged shortly after with a, thumbs up. "Looks good. Time to work your magic, Kyle." He grinned and the others scrambled under the door.

I was preparing to wait outside when Jared poked his head back out. "You too, Jess. At least we're out of sight in here." I looked behind me and Craig was way back now and walking. *He'll have to work it out himself*, I thought, and I dove in under the door.

Inside was a typical cramped double garage. The car was definitely an old four-wheel drive. But how Kieran knew the make and age from a mudguard was beyond me. Everyone else had set about going over the vehicle, which wasn't something I could help with so I wandered around looking at things. It felt strange to be in someone's house like this. Where were they? I wondered. Would they mind us stealing their car? My eyes were beginning to adjust to the dim light now when I spotted an LED torch on the timber bench. I pounced on it, found the power button, and it worked. *Yay for me!* I thought. *Sorry to whoever owned this, but I need it now.* I used it to look around for anything else useful. I spotted some camping gear. Fold up chairs and tables, which were useless to us on foot. I saw a large camp oven, but when I picked it up, I quickly put it down again. Way too heavy for hiking.

I moved a tarp off some more gear and found a folding camp shovel and an army style aluminium pannikin/water bottle set and a small lightweight backpack. *That'll do nicely.* I shoved what I'd found in the bag and began rifling through things, looking for more treasures. Kyle had worked his magic fast and I heard the engine of the car fire up. I quickly turned around and everyone was climbing into the car. "Let's go Jess," said Jared with a grin. I opened the door behind the passenger seat where Jared was sitting and jumped in beside Louise. Unfortunately, I was sitting in the shattered glass from the windows, but it was safety glass. Worst I'd get is a few splinters.

"Right, hang on folks, I'm just going to drive through this door," said Kyle. "Always wanted to do this." He grinned. The door was a lightweight aluminium panel door, which broke away easily and scraped across the roof as we exited the garage. Kyle spotted Craig still some way back and asked, "Do we pick him up?"

"*Yeah,* we'd better," Jared said as he exhaled loudly.

"I woulda left the lazy prick," said Kieran.

Kyle quickly turned and drove the car towards Craig. When we got there, he turned the car around in front of him. As the car did the U turn Kieran yelled out the window at Craig, "IN THE BACK" and thumbed towards the rear of the wagon.

"Don't want that sweaty, fat prick beside us," he said to Louise and me with a grin. I returned the smile. I actually agreed with him. The cargo door of the vehicle opened and I felt Craig climb in, the suspension moving with his weight. I heard the door slam and we were off.

The car ride wasn't exactly comfortable. We were driving across mostly broken ground and people's front lawns, through fences and over garden beds. At one point the road veered towards the pile of debris and we had to scrape our way between the houses and head through backyards to get around it. As we crashed through one fence we narrowly missed ending up in someone's swimming pool!

We'd gone several blocks like this when we reached the northern end of the rubble pile. It coincided with a street that headed east and we had a brief period of smooth running before leaving the street and heading across people's yards again to round the very tip of the pile. As we travelled south along the eastern side of the pile, things were a little better. There were no houses on this side. Just a road that was once the Cairns Western Arterial, and while broken it was still largely intact. Kyle weaved his way through most of the cracks, occasionally leaving the road to find a way around the worst of it. As we neared the turn off into Redlynch, we saw some damaged cars on the road. They weren't burnt out or accident damaged. Just crushed like someone had driven a monster truck over them.

"What do you make of that?" asked Kyle.

"Dunno," Jared said, peering out of his broken window to get a closer look at one. "But it doesn't look good. Might explain why there's no car sounds anymore."

He was right. We hadn't been hearing the hoon's screeching tyres anymore. The only noises were dogs barking. There didn't seem to be anyone around at all.

"I'm really not happy out here in the open," said Louise. "Let's just get this over with, hey."

Everyone agreed. Kyle had weaved his way through the last of the damaged cars and headed straight for the shopping centre. As he drove around the car park towards the entrance it appeared the front doors had been smashed open, so Kyle actually drove through them!

"Like your *style Kyle*," laughed Kieran.

We all had a chuckle at that one. I even heard a snort from Craig behind me. There were skid marks all over the floor and the bench seats, often found in the middle of the walkway in these places, were pushed violently out of the way and into shop fronts.

"Clothes!" I thought when I spotted a jeans-shop sign coming past my window. But it was virtually empty, looted already. We kept driving until we finally came across a chemist shop. "Ahhh, I think this is your stop madam," said Kyle with a smile over his shoulder.

"It's show time." Jared opened his door.

We all piled out and I went straight for the shelves at the back of the shop. "Can you guys please get all the first aid gear you can find?" I yelled over my shoulder.

"Anything and everything," said Jared to the other guys. "We'll toss what we don't need later."

The shelves at the back were a disappointment to say the least. All the drugs were pulled off the shelves and onto the floor.

I just stood and looked at the mess. "Bugger me," said Jared over my shoulder. "Looks like someone's been here for the drugs already."

"Yeah, but did they have to trash everything they *didn't* want?"

I crouched down and started rifling through the pile. "Open your bag please, Jared." He did as I asked and I started tossing packets of medications in there by the handfuls. Thankfully, they'd left the antibiotics alone. I also found anti-inflammatories, antihistamines, and useful medications like high strength anti nausea tablets, Imodium, and a whole range of anti fungal creams and powders.

I spotted the boxes of contraceptive pills and thought for a moment. *If I get that wrong I could get someone pregnant.* But I grabbed some boxes anyway and figured the other girls could go through them to find their usual one. If it's not there, then they'd just run out.

Next on my mental list were bags of saline for drips and needles. But when I looked, they'd all been broken. I spotted the fridge full of liquid medications and saw it open. *No way to keep them cold anyway*, I thought.

In the rush I couldn't think of anything else I should grab. My mind went blank while I just stood there.

"It's more than what we had before, Jess, it'll have to do," said Jared.

"Ok," I said, before grabbing a few more boxes of antibiotics and shoving them in Jared's backpack. "Let's see what's out here." I headed back out into the shop.

The others worked fast. They had almost completely cleared the shelves, and when their backpacks were full, they'd started throwing stuff into the back of the car.

"Ok, I think we have everything guys. Let's get out of here," Jared said.

Everyone headed for the car and got in.

"Right, now for the doctor's books, anyone know where the doctor's surgery is?"

Nobody did.

"How about we find the directory?" I offered.

"There's an idea," Laughed Kyle and he started the car and drove down the rows of shops. I looked beside me and saw some of the stuff the boys had grabbed. I started going through it and tossing what was useless out the window, Adult diapers, gone, back scrub loofahs, gone, gift packs of soaps and perfumes, I started chucking those when Kieran objected. "Hang on, we need those."

"Really?" I asked.

"I dunno about you, but I've noticed some of us are starting to smell a bit ripe." He grinned.

"We could start with a shower," Louise said, laughing.

"Well yeah, that's another option." He shrugged and helped throw more of them out.

"But keep some soap all the same," I said.

"Righto." He began ripping the soap out of the boxes and tossing the rest.

The car skidded to a stop at an intersection, which opened up to the food court on one side, which already smelt a bit off. The directory stand was smashed up against a wall on the other side, but the information looked intact. Jared jumped out and had a quick look before running to get back in. "It's outside on the Southern side," he said. "If we go straight ahead, it will get us outside and then turn left."

Kyle gunned the engine and did a big wheel spin as he took off. "Sorry folks. Another thing I've always wanted to do." He laughed with a slight maniacal edge. He was enjoying this too much. "I should probably mention that I don't currently have a license, A little misunderstanding about a speed limit...well.... several actually." He grinned at Jared who just laughed.

We raced down between the shops, way faster than felt safe, but I assumed Kyle knew what he was doing, despite not having a license. When we reached the doors at the end of the concourse, there was a car blocking the way. They'd smashed through the doors but were wedged up on the anti ram-raid bollards outside. It never occurred to me that there weren't any on the other door. Kyle started reversing the car back the way we came, very fast. When we got to the food court, he swung the wheel hard and pulled on the hand brake, making the front of the car slide around with a squeal of tyres to make us face the way we'd come. He then released the handbrake, selected first gear and took off towards the way we'd entered. I admit, as scared as I was, it was an impressive bit of driving.

As we neared the open door, Kyle slowed the car to negotiate the wreckage of the doors and Jared put his hand up. "Stop. Stop. Stop," he said in rapid fire.

Kyle immediately stopped and we all heard it, the sound of an approaching aircraft; one of theirs.

"Stop here mate and turn off the engine."

Kyle did as instructed and we were all silent until Craig said loudly. "We should go! Get the hell out of here before they bomb the place!"

"Shut the hell up, Craig, we're listening," said Kieran.

The sound of the aircraft was almost above us. It was moving fairly slowly compared to the other flybys, and we heard small explosions every now and then.

"They're mopping up," Jared said with a coldness in his voice I hadn't heard before.

"What does that mean?" I asked.

"They're going slowly through and shooting anything that moves. It's called *cleaning* or *mopping up.*"

We were all silent then. I guess each with our own thoughts, on what that meant for us. As Jared would say, *it doesn't look good, hey.*

We sat for another two minutes listening to the aircraft, now knowing that each explosion likely killed someone. It was sobering, to say the least.

"What time did the explosions happen last night?" Jared asked nobody in particular.

"Just after dark, maybe six thirty or seven," I said.

"Right and the ones before that?"

Umm. Maybe seven or eight in the morning." I was getting where he was going with his questions.

"It's about eight now, yeah? So roughly every twelve hours we can expect a visit, based on their history anyway."

Craig laughed. "A bit soon ta make a call like that."

"Got another theory, mate?" Asked Louise.

"Yeah. What's your theory? I'd be keen to hear it," snorted Kieran.

Jared sighed. "Guys, the aircraft is gone. I'd say it's safe to go now."

Kyle started the car and drove slowly out. As we entered the daylight, we were all looking around but only saw fresh plumes of dust in the distance.

"Looks clear, Kyle. Let's go. Turn right and we'll go find the doctor's."

We drove out and around to the doctor's surgery. When we got there, it was a shambles. Someone had rammed through the front of it with an old commodore sedan and gone all the way to the front counter.

We all got out and went inside where it got way worse. The place had been trashed. I raced into the first door only to find faeces smeared all over the walls. Every bit of paper in there had been torn up and thrown around. On the desk the smashed computer screen leaning against the wall was full of liquid, presumably urine. It was disgusting. I couldn't fathom why these people had suddenly become *animals* because the world as we knew it had ended. These people live amongst us but until something like this happens, we don't see them. There are parts of humanity I don't really want to understand.

The others tried the rest of the rooms and by the sound of the comments, found something similar.

Kyle came out of a back room holding a kidney tray with some forceps and some bloody swabs with a bullet rolling around in the bottom.

"These any good?" he asked.

"Maybe the forceps," I replied. "But find some alcohol to sterilise them before you touch them."

"I have some of those," said Jared.

"Righto, ditch them, better safe than sorry."

Obviously, things were getting out of hand down here if people were removing bullets at the local doctor's surgery.

I went into the room he'd come out of. It was the procedure room where the doctors perform minor surgeries, like stitching up small wounds. Everything was trashed, but I did find a couple of disposable suture kits and some unopened packets of sterile swabs on the floor. It was better than nothing.

"Did you find any books?" Jared asked me.

"Nothing. Let's get out of here."

"Righto, let's get out of here everyone." Jared headed out the door.

Back in the car, Kyle started the engine and we headed off back the way we'd come. "What about the food?" said Craig from the back, over the wind coming through the cabin.

Jared replied. "We have food. Enough for now anyway and I'm not comfortable out here. There's nobody else around, so what food there is, isn't going anywhere for now. I'm sorry we didn't get what you wanted, Jess," he said, looking over his shoulder at me.

"We got most of it, nothing to be sorry about. We'll just have to try for the books somewhere else."

"What do you need the books for anyway? Thought you knew what you were doing," Craig commented from his spot in the back. He tried for the back seat, but one look from Kieran sent him into the cargo area again.

"Mate, you're starting to piss me off," said Kieran, turning in his seat. "I've had a gut full of your bitching. Give it a bloody rest."

"Guys we're not far from the forest. Just cool it," Jared said from the front seat.

Kieran eyeballed Craig for a moment longer and turned to face the front again, fuming.

There it was. I'd been called out as the imposter I was already. I'm not qualified to treat anyone. What if someone was really sick? What would I do? All those pills we just took. They were prescription medicines! If anyone found out I'd given them to someone, I could go to jail!

I was still considering the implications of what I was doing when we passed one of the crushed cars on the road. I don't know why I didn't see it before, but it was plain as day now. Blood had dripped from under the door and had pooled in a large dark red patch on the road. Someone had died right there. The car was so flat there was no chance of there being a survivor as the roof was touching the floor. They had died and there was no one to help. Tears started welling in my eyes as the truth dawned on me like it really hadn't before. There is no one to help anymore. It could be that we're all that's left...

I let out a small sob and Louise put her hand on my shoulder. "Right, mate?" she asked.

"Yeah, I'm fine."

Kieran turned to Craig and growled, "See arsehole, you made the Doc cry. Now say you're sorry, or I'm gonna grab that extra chin of yours and ram it down your throat."

"I didn't say anything, all I asked was why she needed the books," Craig whined.

Jared asked, "Are you ok, Jess?"

Oh God now everyone is fully aware I'm crying again.

"I'm fine, guys, really, I just saw some blood coming from that car, and it freaked me out that someone had died there."

"There was blood?" asked Kieran. "I missed it."

"Yeah, there was blood, I just didn't mention it in case it upset anyone," said Kyle.

Louise cut in, a little exasperated. "Guys please... Can we just get back?"

There was silence for a moment.

"Yeah. Let's just get back," said Jared.

We travelled in silence for much of the trip back. Each deep in our thoughts about what we found, I guess. The supermarket part of the trip looked like it had been abandoned in favour of gathering medical supplies. It kinda made sense, as we had food, certainly enough for the next week or so. It was everything else we didn't have, homes, clothes, families, medical care. By the look of it we'd have to do without those things for a while. I did miss a hot shower though. I surreptitiously lifted my arm for a quick sniff.

"See... Told you so," Kieran said with a grin.

"Argh... speak for yourself," I laughed. A little embarrassed that he'd seen me do it but enjoying the joke.

When we reached the high fence with the dog behind it Kyle pulled the car in between the fence and the forest and drove another few meters in. "Might want to use the beast again some time, best we hide it."

"Good plan, mate," said Jared. "Righto, let's jump out and have a look at what we have. Try to prioritise what we carry up the hill."

It was after nine now and the day was warming up. I really wasn't looking forward to the climb but there was no other way back to the others. I popped one of the carbohydrate sweets Amy gave me in my mouth and offered them around. Everyone took one appreciatively. They knew this was going to be a climb as well.

Sorting through the haul took some time. They had literally grabbed everything, and the upside was that I could take a little more time to look at things, and see if maybe they could be adapted to use for something else. A 'face peel' I reasoned could maybe work as a wound covering in a pinch. At least it would keep the worst of the dirt out. Leg, shoulder, and arm braces could do the same job as a pressure bandage if we had none.

Our trip into civilisation had changed my perspective; from someone avoiding the worst, to someone accepting that it had already happened and trying to make the best of it. I found it surprisingly liberating. No more tears.

Packs loaded, we set off. The rest of the gear we couldn't carry, Jared said he would send someone down for.

The climb was just as hard as I'd expected, only I was wearing a backpack full of gear that wasn't planned for, weighing on me every step. Jared insisted I leave it behind for someone else to bring up, but that wouldn't have been fair. "I'll carry my share," I said.

Which was all very noble, but I was regretting it after the first ten minutes. This was where the fitness of these guys *really* showed. They had large full packs and made it look easy. Craig fell behind as soon as we started. No surprises there. Last I saw him he was maybe thirty meters away. His face was bright red and he was panting hard and he'd only just started.

I dug deep, determined to keep up and to carry my share. I'd like to say I managed it, but watching the others climb I could see they were pacing themselves to let me keep up. If I slipped, there was always a strong hand to reach down and help me up. I'd like to say as a modern feminist woman, I swatted their hand away and said, "I don't need help, thanks." But I didn't. Truth is this was a hell of a climb, and I was knackered. My legs burned like fire. Out of breath and sweating profusely, I did it pretty hard. Louise was doing it easy compared to me, obviously very fit and used to this sort of exercise.

When I think we were about halfway, we stopped for a rest and a drink. Jared handed me his water bottle, which I gratefully took. I stupidly didn't even think to bring one! I took a swig and handed it back, but Jared shook his head. "Proper drink, Jess."

I took it and had a good few swallows before handing it back. "Thanks," I said breathlessly. Then wiped the sweat from my eyes and tried to smile, but I doubt I managed it.

Craig was nowhere to be seen.

Once I recovered enough, I instigated the return to climbing. I could see they were all waiting for me.

It took almost two hours to climb to the top and back down into the camp.

When we arrived, everyone raced toward us asking about how it went, what news we had and what did we get?

I was still a little out of breath and my legs felt like jelly when I flopped down beside the now cold fire, so I let Louise and the others field the questions. After a while another voice asked a question.

"Where's Craig?" asked Jamie, one of the few who backed Craig when he was trying to become leader. His chubby forearms were covered in small red spots and he was scratching them like crazy. He must have had them everywhere because he kept scratching his belt line as well.

The group went quiet, and all eyes were on Jared.

"He's coming."

"You left him behind?" Jamie asked, and added quietly to the guy beside him, "What an arsehole."

"Screw you," said Kieran taking steps towards the man. "He knew the score. We weren't gonna wait for him... He wanted to go and that was the deal."

"So you left him out there to die because he couldn't keep up?" the man retorted.

Kyle took a step forward with his hands up, trying to make peace. "Hang on you guys, before you get too dramatic, we didn't leave anyone out there to die... Craig is behind us. He was slower climbing the hill that's all."

Everyone went silent for a moment until Jared spoke. "We got quite a lot of stuff and it will take a few more people to go back down and get it. I won't kid you, it's a bit of a climb, but it's in the forest and pretty safe. I'll come with you and show you the way. Any volunteers?"

"I'll go," said Amy.

"And me," said David.

Paula, James, and another guy everyone called Jacko, although I didn't remember Jacko introducing himself yesterday, all agreed to go.

I noticed that neither of Craig's supporters volunteered and I wasn't the only one.

"You guys not feeling well?" asked Louise, looking at Reece and Jamie.

"We got firewood," Jamie replied, a little too defensively.

"That's the firewood?" Louise was laughing, pointing at the pile of wood beside the campfire.

She was right... it was pitiful. Kieran and Jared got more last night.

Everyone scoffed and walked away on the pretence of getting ready to go. But really nobody could be bothered with their pathetic excuses.

When Craig finally walked into camp more than an hour later, he was sweating profusely and the small red dots on his skin stood out like neon polka dots.

I noticed as he approached the camp, he started to limp. Favouring the knee with the scratch. When he threw off his pack and slumped to the ground in the middle of camp... He was breathing heavily.

"So, we all made it back ok then," he said.

"Yeah. Good to see you kept up," laughed Kieran.

"Well, I spent a bit of time looking around to make sure we weren't being followed."

"Yeah, right. That's what it was," laughed Louise.

"Yeah, after you lot did that, trip around in a car stunt, someone had to look after our security. You know they have a car, everyone?" He looked around the group. "We've been busting our arse walking through the bush and they have the keys to a four wheel drive!"

"The what? Keys? What the hell are you on about? You were there. We hot-wired it from someone's garage!" said Kyle.

"Not what I saw. You just walked in and drove out."

"How the hell would you know ya fat prick, you were still dragging your arse down the road!" said Kieran. He was getting up a head of steam.

"You guys have a car? Why don't we just drive south?" asked Jamie.

Jared stood up and with both hands out said. "Calm down everyone. There are some things we need to tell you about using the-"

Craig cut in. "Yeah, I'm sure he's going to tell you all sorts of stories as to why we can't take the car South. Saving it for yourself Jared?" he sneered.

I could see now what Craig was doing. It was a dangerous game to turn everyone against Jared and those who went to get the supplies, but that's exactly what he was doing.

Craig was relentless. "So, where's the food, Jared? Why didn't we get any food? All we got was crap from the chemists for your girlfriend, that we all had to carry up the bloody hill."

A group of others moved into a circle around Jared, all asking what he was up to. When Louise picked up Craig's backpack to make room she stopped. Others noticed and were watching her. She unzipped the top to open the bag and her mouth fell open when she saw what was in it. She paused for a moment looking at Jared and then said to Craig. "Tell us, what exactly did you have to carry back up the hill?"

He snatched the bag back and said. "That's got nothing to do with it. When was Jared going to tell us about the car?" he demanded.

"What's in the bag, Louise?" asked Kieran.

"A packet of tampons... Nothing else. One bloody packet of tampons." Louise walked over to where I sat and tried to pick up my pack. First with one hand, but then added the other hand to lift the weight. She lifted and then upended it on the ground. The boxes of medicines and bottles of cough mixtures spilled all over the ground.

"Exactly who was carrying it all up the hill, Craig?" she asked.

"Where's all the stuff I put in your bag, Craig?" asked Kyle. So far Kyle had seemed placid enough, but he certainly didn't seem placid now. He was keeping his cool, but it looked like only just.

"I was injured and had to leave it behind."

"Injured?" asked Kyle, narrowing his eyes.

"My leg, my knee, you saw me limping into camp, it was all I could do to make it up the hill, so I left all that crap. It was just tampons and stuff. If the girls want them, they can go down the hill and get them themselves."

Well, he didn't do himself any favours with *that* comment.

I heard Kyle say he saw Craig putting on the limp, but the girls tearing strips off Craig drowned him out.

The argument grew and became more heated. Before long, everyone was involved in some way or another; all except Jared, who sat on the ground, leaning against a rock with his hands on his knees and his head down.

There was one other person not arguing. She's easy to overlook as the quiet one but in an instant, she grew two feet in height.

"THAT'S ENOUGH!" Julie shouted over everyone else.

Everyone stopped talking.

"ENOUGH of all this bickering, Christ you're worse than five-year-olds! We are all here in the rainforest trying to stay alive, we don't know where our families are and you're just bickering like school children." She burst into tears, and everyone was silent. A few seconds later she rallied again and continued. "Jared was about to tell us what it was like down there and I want to hear it. So please, sit down and be quiet!" Her use of the preschool teacher voice would have been funny if she wasn't so upset.

Everyone was shame faced, Amy was the first to walk over and put her arms around Julie to console her.

There were a few murmured apologies to her, and everyone sat down to listen to Jared. There were also a few steely glares between people who obviously weren't finished with their arguments, but they still listened to Julie and were quiet.

When they were all seated Jared said, "Thanks, Julie, for reminding us of how we should be behaving."

Jared proceeded to tell everyone what we'd found. Including the crushed cars and how he didn't think road transport was a good idea. He also explained why we didn't go for food as well and why the medical supplies were more important.

By the time he was finished there were some concerned faces.

"Are you saying there's nobody left?" Amy asked, her tiny voice and her eyes wide, it made her look like a scared small child.

"We don't know that yet Amy," began Jared. "But we saw nobody, only dogs. Most of the houses were gone and there were no signs of anyone at the houses that were left. That's all we know."

Kyle said, "James, you seemed to have a few clues about what they might be doing. Might be time you shared them."

Everyone's eyes turned to James who looked quite uncomfortable in the spotlight.

"All I know is how it's often done in sci-fi stories. I don't know if that's exactly what they are doing. I was just saying what I'd do if I was them."

"Ok," Jared said. "What would you do next if you were them?"

James looked around the group and back to Jared. I think he was looking for permission to speak his mind.

Jared said, "I think we need to hear what might well be happening, James."

James nodded and began. "Ok then. Look I've gotta say this is just my theory, I don't know any more than you do. But by the sounds of it they're doing what I expected, if they are... exterminating us that is."

The group was silent, so he continued. "What we know so far is they've cut power and communications; they've cut roads and the airport. Now they've dropped a bomb on a residential area and are pinpointing cars on the road... They are killing people and don't want any to escape is my guess."

There was a murmur amongst the group.

"So they want to wipe us out?" asked Louise.

"Don't know any more than you, but what else are we to think? That bomb dropped here was one of three we heard, yeah?" said James. "I can't imagine why else you'd bomb Redlynch, there's nothing there but people."

Jared said, "I have to agree with James. I've been thinking about it and what they've been doing since this started, seems more like genocide than a military action. Why else would you bomb civilians on purpose? And make no mistake, that bomb was shaped to take out the bulk of the houses."

The whole group was silent, with most just looking at the ground. It was a lot to process, especially if you hadn't seen it firsthand.

"Now we still have to go back down and get the rest of the stuff. I think there's about three good backpacks worth of gear in the car, plus another pile somewhere on the hill."

Everyone looked at Craig who sat stone-faced. Jared continued, "It's a lot of gear for us to carry but I think it's important stuff. We can spread the load among us and from here on, each day's hike won't be as rushed or maybe as far as we're away from the city."

"Where are we going exactly?" asked Louise.

"Good question Louise," said Jared. "I think we should head south, way south. Away from Cairns and major towns. Maybe set ourselves up somewhere with good access to food, water, and maybe some shelter so we can wait this out. If we were near farming land, we might be able to get fresh fruit and vegetables and keep ourselves going indefinitely. With less population, farming areas will be less of a target. Maybe there's people still around down there. I don't know." He shrugged.

Louise nodded. "That actually sounds like a good plan, Jared. I agree we should set up somewhere and wait this out. And you're right. Food we can find. Medical supplies we can't."

I suspect Louise's opinion of Jared just went up a notch and by the nodding from most in the group I'd say the same happened for many. It was a good plan and now having it, seemed to give everyone purpose. Jared didn't need to ask for volunteers to go back and get the stuff again. A group organised themselves and headed off with Kyle in the lead; he must have been tired after the first climb up that hill, I was exhausted! I couldn't imagine doing it again. Kyle just went up a notch in my book too.

Everyone said Jared should stay back and help me organise the medications. I checked Tony's leg that was wounded by the tree branch yesterday and found it looking red around the edges. Left dry it might have been ok, but taking a dunking in creek water and then having the wet bandage on it since yesterday did it no favours. Infection was setting in. I found some antiseptic cream and smothered it before putting fresh bandages on. I made him promise to keep it dry and remind me to keep a check on it.

It was almost noon when they returned with the rest of the gear from the chemists. With much of the leaves gone from the trees it was really hot in the little hollow we were camped in. I could only imagine climbing the hill in the heat of the day. Those left on the hill took the climbers packs when they arrived and gave them water and food. I added the contents of their packs to the pile of gear and kept sorting. I decided to spread out the medications amongst the group. I'd hate for someone to lose a backpack, only to find it was the one carrying all the antibiotics.

Kieran's backpack gave me a laugh. It was mostly boxes of condoms. I picked out a packet of "slim fit" ones and said with a straight face, "Shall I put these small ones aside for *you*, Kieran?"

He burst into laughter and held a finger to his lips. Then he said, "Shhh. They're Craig's, but he was too embarrassed to carry them, so I said I'd do it for him. Don't embarrass the poor fella." He giggled some more and said quietly.

"Nah, honestly I thought they might be useful, waterproof covers or something."

"That was good thinking Kieran. But I'll keep a few aside for you," I smiled.

A New Camp

*The art of medicine consists of amusing the patient while nature cures the disease.' -*Voltaire

The mood in the camp improved greatly from the morning's argument. I think the comments made by James and Jared caused a few people to wake up to our predicament and realise how important we are to each other. I also think having a plan helped us all, in that we weren't lost now. We had a plan to follow.

Craig was sulking, while everyone else was busy around camp, he sat away from the group pretending to be in pain any time he thought someone was looking.

Even his two supporters were giving him a wide berth.

I finally got my trousers dry. I borrowed a sarong from Paula and laid the pants on my tent. The lack of leaves on the trees meant the sun got to them and made them crispy dry in no time. It's a small thing, but it's the little things that can make all the difference sometimes.

One of the guys climbed the next little ridge and found a much better campsite. After a brief meeting, Jared made the decision to move to the new site for the night. It was about two pm, so we had time. Packing up took about an hour; way too slow if we were going to do this often. The trek only took another hour and we set up camp in a nice open area with a running creek close by and a waterfall, just thirty meters downstream. We were a bit smarter about firewood this time and each picked some up along the way.

With our camp set up and a couple of hours of light left, we girls decided we'd have a shower at the waterfall. Paula said I could keep the sarong as she had two, which I was so grateful for. I hadn't planned enough to pack anything like that. They have to be the most useful thing to take camping; they are good for clothing, a bath towel, beach towel, a bed sheet, and even a mozzie net if desperate.

We took turns under the water while the others sat on the warm rocks. It sounds idyllic, but there wasn't a lot of water flow and it was so cold I could barely put my head under it. How creek water gets that cold in the tropics is beyond me, but it does. The showers didn't take long, but we were all left feeling clean and fresh afterwards. It was actually fun, and I enjoyed the bonding with the other girls. There were only six of us and I felt like I barely knew them. That time spent apart from the guys was important to us. It's strange to reflect that while we were laughing and making jokes, the world we left had been destroyed.

When we returned to camp, the boys had a fire going and Jared was boiling water in my saucepan to cool for drinking water.

"Your turn Kieran," I said.

"My turn? What, for a shower? What are ya trying to say Doc?" He pretended to be hurt.

"Not saying anything. But if you don't go for a shower, you aren't allowed to walk upwind of me," I laughed.

Jared laughed and said, "Everyone's got to have a shower, doctor's orders. Besides, why do you think I stay up front, Kieran?"

Kieran roared with laughter.

David joined in. "Well, Jared, as one who has said he'd follow you, I expect you'd better lead the way to the showers or you'll find everyone walking *beside* you."

Jared laughed, "Well, I can take a hint. I'll go for a shower now."

The guy's showers and our dinners went without incident, aside from the almost girlish squeals and swearing coming from the waterfall. Obviously they found the water cold too. The conversation around the fire was light-hearted. Nobody mentioned the invasion or what happened today. I doubt anyone had the energy for it. We were all pretty tired and everyone headed off to their tents early. There were only a few of us left still up. I could have checked the time on my phone but that would have meant pulling it out of my pack and turning it on. I didn't need to know that badly, what I needed was sleep and headed off to do just that. When I'd said goodnight to everyone and laid in my tent, it occurred to me that there might be a good reason to know the time. I crawled back out and asked Jared. "Don't spose you know what time it is, do you?"

"Almost time. Just thought of that myself. Guess we'll see if the theories' right soon."

I crawled back out of my tent and sat beside him at the fire.

"I'd rather not be in a tent if it happens again."

"No, best not, I spose. But you know, I don't expect there is anything left to bomb near here. I doubt we have to worry. Besides, we're on another ridge behind the last one. Did you see the hills when we were in town today?"

"Not really, why?"

"I just noticed the tree damage skipped the valleys and that's why the bomb last night didn't hurt us quite as bad. We were quite exposed for the first ones."

"Well that's good to know. At least we can hide in the valleys and be safe."

"Oooh I dunno about that. It's just a theory. I'd still rather get away from anywhere they want to bomb in the first place."

"So we hike tomorrow?"

"Yeah, I reckon so; and the next few days if we can. Get some miles between us and the targets."

We sat in companionable silence for a while until we both heard distant rumbling.

"Thunder?" I asked.

"Maybe. Guess we'll see soon."

We sat and listened intently in the quiet of the forest. I say quiet, but the forest is almost never silent. A billion, maybe a trillion bugs and little creatures; all calling to each other in earnest. It was *anything* but quiet, but it was background noise to me already. Anything foreign was quickly noticed and the thunder was getting louder and more distinct. A moment later I realised the sound was getting much *closer*; it wasn't thunder.

"Best rally the troops" he said standing up. "OK EVERYONE, LOOKS LIKE THEY'RE COMING THROUGH AGAIN."

Sleepy heads popped out of tents to listen and when they heard it too, they all scrambled out, many were still getting dressed.

We could hear the aircraft approaching.

Jared quickly kicked the burning logs in the fire over to put them out, which left us in complete darkness under the forest canopy.

We all just stood there, listening. In a way it was worse than being surprised by them. Just waiting to see if they would drop a bomb on you was *torture*.

We could clearly hear the aircraft now, but the bomb sounds were small and more numerous than before. *More mopping up,* I thought.

As they passed, the aircraft was a fair way to the east, towards the coast. They dropped very few bombs close to us, but a lot to the north.

In fact, they spent longer there than they had on any other run. They were taking their time now. I gave an involuntary shiver and Jared, who was standing beside me, put an arm around my shoulder and gave a little squeeze. "Gone now, Jess. Might as well go to bed."

I nodded and then remembered it was pitch black. "Yep, might as well go to bed."

I don't remember falling asleep.

The next morning started much the same as the last, *early*. Jared was up and making a racket, I suspect it was his version of a wake-up call, Having gone to bed so early, I was one of the first up and as I crawled from my tent, I saw Jared walking past each tent with his pannikin of coffee held close to their tent flaps. Everyone forgave the noise when they smelled coffee.

"Devious," I chuckled.

He looked up and grinned. "Means to an end. How'd ya sleep?"

"Fantastic. But I must make more of an effort to clear the ground under my tent. I had a few sticks under me."

I grabbed my new pannikin and Jared poured half his coffee into it for me. It was good and just what I needed.

When the last of the faces appeared from the tents, Jared said loudly. "Righto folks, good to see you're all early risers." With a chorus of groans for a response, Jared grinned and went on. "The plan for today is moving south. I'd like to get an early start so the hike won't be too hard, and we can get some distance under our belts. So I reckon we head off in an hour. That should be plenty of time for breakfast and to pack up. Coffee is hot, so get into it," he finished, pointing at the saucepan full of steaming hot coffee beside the fire. The scramble for coffee was funny to watch. Even Craig was there, his pretend limp even worse now, grimacing with every step and a couple of times I'm sure he grimaced at the good leg being used.

The injured leg reminded me to check on Tony's leg with the tree branch injury. Once he'd grabbed his coffee, I asked him to come take a seat on a rock, and I looked at his leg. When I unravelled the bandage, I was greeted with a very angry looking sore. The antiseptic hadn't worked, but I thought as the redness was only surrounding the cut, it could well heal itself if it was looked after. I poured iodine solution on it and smeared more antiseptic cream on the fresh gauze before bandaging it up again. "Is it bad Doc." asked Tony.

"Nah, it's just a bit infected. Keep it dry and we'll have another look this afternoon."

"Thanks Doc, appreciate it." He smiled.

"All good, you can pay the receptionist on the way out." I smiled and stood up.

"Will do, Doc."

When I turned around, I saw a half dozen other faces lined up waiting to see me.

"Looks like the doctor is in," Jared laughed.

I saw them one by one. A couple of minor scratches. A nasty rash on one arm. A couple with dozens of little pimples that weep clear fluid and itch like crazy, mostly around the beltline, but extending to arms and legs as well. I had no idea what they were, but Kieran provided the answer. "That'll be *scrub itch*. I did warn ya mate." He said to the Jamie as he walked past, overhearing the complaints that they itch like mad.

"You recognise these, Kieran?" I asked.

"Yeah, it's like I said to Craig and his mates. Don't sit on damp dead logs in the rainforest. They're little mites that bite ya. Itch like hell."

"How do I treat it?"

"Dunno Doc, I never bothered." He shrugged. "They go away if you leave 'em alone. But if you scratch 'em, they'll get infected."

"So, the mites are still there? Should we kill them?"

"Nah, they're long gone, even before it starts itching. I did read something about it years ago. I wouldn't worry too much about them. It's just a bastard if you have 'em coz they *itch like a bitch*." he grinned.

"Thanks, Kieran."

"Anytime, Doc." He saluted and walked away.

I said to Jamie that he had his answer and addressed everyone in the group. I told them to take on board what Kieran had said.

The next was Paula, who had them on her forearms and she whispered, "On my breasts as well."

Given what Kieran had just said, I asked, "You picked up firewood yesterday Paula?"

"Yeah, we all did."

"Did you hold it against your chest?"

The realisation dawned on her. "Yeah, I did... I guess that was stupid."

"I didn't know either." I shrugged. "Don't scratch them, and if your bra makes it worse don't wear it."

"Ok, thanks, Jess." She smiled.

I actually felt pretty good at that point. I was needed and was able to make things better for them. After all, that's why I wanted to get into medicine and while I wasn't a doctor, it didn't seem to matter to them.

Craig was the last of the *'patients'* and he hobbled up to my rock, putting on all sorts of groans and grunts with effort.

"Left knee." He grunted rudely.

I let it slide and looked at his knee. "Roll your pants leg up," I replied, just as rudely.

When he did so, I noticed it was a little swollen. "Roll the other one up."

"What the hell for, there's nothing wrong with that one."

"Because she told you to," said Kieran from the fire.

Craig exhaled loudly and did as I asked.

Comparing the two knees, I could see that the left was definitely a little swollen, but it didn't look that bad to me. The scratch on it was healing ok. It continued to weep, being on the knee the skin stretches and breaks the scab. Nothing much could be done about it except put some antiseptic cream on it. I dug around in my backpack and pulled out a knee brace the guys had grabbed from the chemists. It was a medium size, and this was clearly a large knee but I told him to put it on. He made a big show of how much it hurt, but he managed to get it on.

"Its cutting off the circulation, it's a stupid idea," he said.

His attitude was starting to annoy me. "Then take it off and go without. It's all the same to me." My comment had a little more bite than I was used to giving.

"You tell him Doc," grinned Kieran.

"Nobody asked you." Craig glared at Kieran before turning to me and growling. "Look, all I want is some proper painkillers. We all know you've got some, so hand 'em over."

"We've got nothing of the sort." I stood up. "The chemists had already been raided. I have some anti-inflammatory tablets which may help, but that's it."

"Thaaat's *crap*," he growled. "You must have got something; you're just saving them for your *mates*. Look, I got you down there to get the bloody drugs, so you owe me. Get 'em now."

Louise launched herself from beside the fire and stood over him. The other girls all did the same and surrounded him. Fists clenched; Louise let him have it. "That's enough out of you. You don't speak to her like that, she's trying to help you, and you're being a prick. She said we don't have any then that's it, if you're a junkie and need drugs then you're all out of luck because the other junkies beat you to it."

By this time Kieran was behind the girls and looked ready to pounce. A few of the other guys had done the same. It was a tense moment until Craig, seeing his situation changed his attitude. "Sorry. I'm just in pain. It makes me cranky."

I bent down to my backpack, retrieved a bottle of anti-inflammatories, and took one from it. I handed it to him unceremoniously, "Take this with food." I turned to the others and said, "Thanks guys." Then I left to pack up my gear in the hope of diffusing the situation. I tried to look busy packing up my tent but watched out of the corner of my eye as everyone slowly went back to what they were doing. I've never been part of a group that would stick up for me like that before and I have to admit it felt good. I was a part of this group and with our newfound *sisterhood,* we girls were going to watch out for each other... It gave me hope for our future.

MAKE SOME MILES

---

*'As to diseases, make a habit of two things — to help,
or at least, to do no harm.'* -Hippocrates

We packed up and headed out early. Jared led as usual, and we slogged it out all day. The morning run for the aircraft happened roughly on time. But as Jared suggested, with nothing left to bomb in this area they pretty much left it alone.

The terrain wasn't as easy as the last trek and it was made worse by the deep layer of leaf litter confetti. There were many slips and by lunchtime I started to get worried that someone was going to seriously injure themselves. When I voiced my concerns to Jared he said. "Not far now Jess and we'll be out of the damaged area. The only way to avoid this is to go up the mountain and it gets really steep up there."

Right as always, by the time we made it to the end of the Redlynch valley and crossed what was left of the river that makes Crystal cascades, the trees were virtually undamaged. But the river had been badly eroded from all the water coming from the dam at once. What we found was a steep eroded bank, dropping up to a hundred meters onto the rocks below, piles of logs and debris were strewn down the river. A crossing here was impossible, so Jared led us east along the river and down to the floodplain, where we left the rainforest and crossed the road. None of us felt safe here in broad daylight and we all kept pace, getting as quickly away from there as we could. We found a place where we could cross the river relatively easily and there were no houses here on the flat ground to worry about anymore. Only mud, at times knee deep and sticky making every step a slow hard slog. By the time we entered the forest again on the other side of the valley, we were all exhausted.

We came across a road heading roughly in the right direction, it was heavily forested on either side so it felt relatively safe to walk along it and we were too tired to do much else. Being late afternoon, nobody wanted a steep climb. We saw numerous driveways leading off the road and houses we could see through the trees. A lot of dogs were barking but we saw no sign of people. Feeling as tired as I was, a house with a proper bed would have been bliss, but I agreed with Jared that it wasn't worth the risk. The clean up operations might include bombing houses not already destroyed. Craig wasn't happy with that at all and voiced his opinion loudly. So loudly in fact that he set off every dog in the area barking madly. He was quickly shhh'ed by everyone. Even Amy told him to be quiet, so once again he just sulked at the back of the group.

When we took the final turn and walked to the end of the road it came to a huge house surrounded by forest, which looked deserted. As we passed alongside it towards the backyard, I stopped Jared.

"I want to go inside for a minute. Just to grab a towel and check the bathroom cabinet for any drugs they may have left. Can we stop here? Just for ten minutes?"

He looked reluctant, but agreed and called a ten-minute break. Most went to the pool and dunked their lower legs in it to wash off the mud from the river crossing- but a few went inside.

The back door wasn't locked, and Kieran went in first with an "Anybody home?" But nobody answered. Inside was a beautiful home, the furniture was all very expensive and tasteful which made me feel very out of place in my muddy wet pants and soggy boots. It smelled so *clean*, with just a hint of some kind of air freshener. It was a stark contrast to how we smelled.

While the others went to the kitchen for food, I went straight to the bathroom and opened the cupboard. I found all kinds of drugs there. Antidepressants were the first I noticed. Three different kinds but I didn't feel they were something I could give anyone, as they aren't something you take a few of. So I left them there and as I rifled through I found a couple of bottles and a blister pack of prescription painkillers! One contained codeine and another bottle of very strong opiates and the blister pack of Oxycodone, a slow-release Morphine. Whoever lived here had serious pain to deal with. I pocketed them looking over my shoulder to check nobody had seen.

Craig's performance that morning had shown me that making it known I had them wasn't a good idea.

I quickly searched for another bathroom and found one off the main bedroom. In here I found little but some paracetamol and ibuprofen, but I took them anyway. On the way past the main bedroom's closet, I had a quick look for anything that may have been of use. Unfortunately, the woman's taste in clothes didn't really suit hiking and camping. The owners were likely a middle aged, professional couple. Plenty of business suits, golf trousers and long dresses but nothing of use to me. I did however spot a large sarong the woman must have used around the pool; I grabbed it and tied it around my waist. I grabbed a pair of thick socks, shoved them in my pocket, and headed back out the door.

Kieran and the others had been busy in the kitchen and in addition to some canned food; they found the liquor cabinet and were sporting partly empty bottles of expensive spirits and a few bottles of wine.

Jared was laughing about it, but he had a slight furrow in his brow when I went and sat beside him. "Hey, good score. Might as well have a couple of drinks tonight hey?" I said.

"Yeah, as long as it doesn't get out of hand,"

"Nah, let them have their fun. Just look at how much booze there is and how many of us there are. I'd say they couldn't get into too much mischief."

He looked again at them and smiled. "Yep, you're right, Jess, not enough there to do much damage, then let's go make camp and have a drink." He got up and began getting ready to go again.

We reluctantly left the house and all it's comforts and made our way back into the forest and up the hill. We walked for another hour, and it was getting dark before Jared called a halt in a bit of a clearing near a small creek. "Alright folks. We'll camp here tonight. All I ask is that we wait till we're all set up before we have a drink. Booze on an empty stomach is not going to do you any favours."

Everyone agreed and there were a few jokes told while they worked, about past experiences with drinking on an empty stomach.

Camp was set up fast, not because we all wanted a drink, it was because we were getting better at this, we were becoming a team.

With dinner done, we all shared the bottles around, each pouring some into our cups or pannikins. The mood was really good and morale in general was the best I'd seen. While we were all exhausted from the hike, the camaraderie kept us all going.

The evening bombing run came and went, with no bombs coming even close to us, so Jared's theory was working so far.

With a few drinks under our belts, we all went to bed rather merry, but nobody had enough to call them drunk.

The next day marked the real beginning of our long trek south. From there on we settled into a routine of hiking all-day and sleeping all night. Hard at first for all of us, but as the days went by, I noticed it was getting easier. I was getting fitter, and I must say leaner, all our packs were getting lighter as we consumed our food stocks and Jared was pleased with our progress. I noticed we were all looking leaner already, especially Amy who really couldn't afford to lose much weight.

The forest went through some dramatic changes as we passed Walsh's Pyramid, a tall cone shaped mountain just to the west of Gordonvale. Here the forest was quite dry and made up of mostly gum trees. It was more reminiscent of the dry forest out west and to the south of Townsville. It also had a lot of Golden Orb spiders that string massive golden webs between the trees. They are a *huge* spider, as big as a man's hand, but quite harmless. Their webs are so strong that you can bounce back off them if you are unfortunate enough to walk into one, so Jared took to holding a stick up high in front of him as he walked.

It took us the best part of a day to get past the dry forest and as we crossed a ridge just to the south it was like night and day. We were back in the cool wet rainforest, even wetter than the forest behind Cairns and it wasn't just the trees that changed. The sounds of birds and insects also changed. Oddly even the sound of our footfalls changed, as we entered the wet forest, they became muffled by the dampness of the soil and voices didn't travel as far. The smell of the forest was also different, the damp, earthy smell of rotting leaf litter with a hint of mould, blocked out almost all other smells.

As we travelled, we were finding it easier to move inland. In the beginning I guess we wanted to be close to civilisation, but as we progressed, I think we were all finding it easier going if we weren't near the edge of the forest. There the disturbances from tree cutting and weed infestations penetrated far from the edge. The vines in particular often made impenetrable walls of green that we had to go around. It was seriously hard going and swinging the machete looked like hard work. Plus, I guess we'd come to feel safe deeper in the forest so keeping away from the edge, didn't need much encouragement.

There were few medical problems to speak of and Craig's knee had all but healed. Although that didn't stop him complaining and insisting on a lighter pack load. As we were all sharing the food and carrying a variety of things that we didn't bring, Jared made a point of making sure everyone carried their share of the load, including Craig.

It sounded very egalitarian, but I caught Jared taking things from some of the weaker hiker's packs and putting it in his own pack... He swore me to secrecy.

Jared wasn't the only one though. On the third morning I saw Louise do the same to Amy's pack and I also found my pack lighter than it should be, I suspect it was Kyle that lightened it for me.

By day four we'd made it all the way to Babinda, and we camped the night behind the big hill overlooking the town. As we were rationing the food heavily already, there was a discussion about whether it would be worth a raid into town to see if there was any food left. We were all getting pretty hungry, and the long days hiking without enough food was taking its toll on both our energy levels and our morale. I'd noticed a few sharp remarks between a few of our group. Just grumpy from a lack of food and being tired I guessed.

I took the opportunity to check on Tony's leg while everyone was talking. When I removed the bandage, the wound looked worse, way worse. It was now oozing pus and it had angry red lines leading up his leg. He had a fever and said he felt weak. This was a serious infection now and I couldn't think of what else to do but use some of the antibiotics we had. I explained that to Tony while I cleaned and dressed the wound. He said it was fine and that he'd remember to take them on time. When I handed him the packet of antibiotics, he took one while I watched and we then both turned our attention to the discussion at hand.

I did want to do a run into the chemists on the off chance they had more than the last one did. But in reality we could only carry so much. Food was the new priority, as we'd get by without more medical supplies.

It was about ten minutes later when I could hear Tony's breathing become noisy and a little laboured. I turned to him and in the fire light, I could see his face looked a bit odd, kind of puffy. I asked him. "Are you feeling ok, Tony?"

"Dunno... I'm not feeling too good, Doc."

I grabbed my torch and shone it on his face. He was bright red, and his lips looked puffy. When I touched his skin, it was like he was on fire. Within moments his breathing was quite shallow, and he was struggling to get breath. "Tony, talk to me. What's wrong?" I asked, a little panicked.

Tony never replied...

When I had time to digest what had happened, I realised he had suffered *anaphylactic shock* from the penicillin tablet I gave him... I GAVE HIM!

Tony got steadily worse until no longer able to breathe at all, he went into shock. Jared and the others all tried to help but they couldn't do anything. He was allergic to Penicillin; he'd never had it before, so he couldn't have known. CPR didn't work, his tongue had swollen and throat closed. We couldn't get air in or out, not enough to keep him alive. We did CPR for maybe an hour, until we were all exhausted and his skin had gone from blue... To cold and grey.

Between the sobs and tears of frustration, I put my hand on Jared's while he was doing chest compressions and spoke. "Please... Jared stop... He's gone."

Tony was gone.

I cried like I've never cried before. Oh my God I'd just *caused* the death of someone... On top of the stress of the invasion, the exhausting hikes in the rainforest, tired, dirty, and inconsolable, I just cried.

Jared and the others did their best, but they couldn't take away from what I'd done. It was my fault.

The next day saw the very first funeral I'd ever been to. The boys were up at dawn digging a grave using the folding shovel I'd picked up on our way to the chemists.

It had to be a fairly shallow grave as the digging wasn't easy. Under the thirty centimetres of soft rainforest humus in which everything grows, there is the hard clay soil full of rocks. Folding camp shovels are really no match for it.

I just sat in stunned silence by the fire, nursing a coffee Jared had handed me. He laced it with some of our precious sugar and a large nip of some whiskey he'd saved from the lot we'd picked up in that empty house. I really didn't taste it.

Julie and Amy walked me up to the grave where we laid Tony to rest. None of us were religious and nobody knew if Tony was, so the prayer was a fairly cobbled together affair. We all said a few words and the guys filled in the grave. It turns out that Kieran had done a bit of wood carving in his spare time, so he made the cross and carved Tony's name and death date on it. Nobody knew when he was born.

Afterwards, nobody had much to say, I guess everyone felt their own grief over his loss, or maybe they were just sad about witnessing a death. I don't know. I just sat staring into the fire, not really knowing how to move on from this point. I'd been sitting there for hours when Jared handed me some lunch and sat down beside me. "How ya doing, Jess?" he asked softly.

"I can't do it, Jared, I can't."

"You can't hold yourself responsible. How were you to know he was allergic?"

"I gave him the tablets that killed him, Jared." I turned to look at him. "Have you any idea what that feels like?"

"No... No, I don't, but I know you can't keep blaming yourself for it. I saw the infection too, he needed antibiotics, or he was going to die… You don't need to be a doctor to recognise sepsis."

"It's my fault he got that; I must have left something in the wound because I didn't clean it out properly."

"Oh, you mean while you were concussed, trying to pick pieces of wood out of a leg wound in a war zone you mean. Come on Jess, nobody holds you responsible for this. You did your best and that's all we could ever ask of you. Were lucky to have you at all, look how many of us you've helped so far." He looked up at the others around camp and said." Hey everyone, how many here has Jess helped?"

There were hands up everywhere.

"Doc helped me," said David and he walked over to where we sat and took off his shirt. "See Doc, that rash, on my arm, gone thanks to you and that cream you put on it."

Amy walked over too. "If you hadn't told me to keep my burst eardrum dry, I wouldn't have thought twice about getting it wet. I could have got permanent damage or an infection in my head… Thanks, Jess." She smiled. One by one the others came up and showed me what I'd fixed in the short time we'd been travelling together. The last one, Paula who in her usual unabashed manner, showed me her arms that were now almost completely clear of the scrub itch and then lifted her top to show me her breasts were no longer itchy. "It was you that worked out what caused those itchy spots on my boobs and told me to leave my bra off… best thing I ever did. I'm not putting it back on again either." She grinned.

Kieran stepped up and began undoing his trousers.

"I don't need to see it, Kieran," I said, shielding my eyes from the likely cured tinea he swore me to secrecy over.

Kieran laughed and gave me a big warm smile. He then leaned forward and said quietly, in the most sincere voice I've ever heard him use.

"We need ya,, Doc." And then he grabbed my head in both big hands and kissed me on the forehead.

"We need ya, Doc" was chorused around the camp. Tears streamed down my face.

"Thanks, everyone."

I meant it. My confidence was in tatters, but they'd reminded me that I could at least help my friends with the little things that mattered to them. And they *were* my friends now.

CLEAR THE DEAD WOOD

'Demagogue: one who preaches doctrines he knows to be untrue to men he knows to be idiots.' -H.L. Mencken

Later that afternoon when we were preparing for dinner the whole group froze when we heard "Cooee" from up on the nearest ridge. I saw Jared do a quick scan of the camp, "Where's Louise?" he asked.

Her head popped out of her tent. "I'm here."

"Well, if we're all here, then that's not one of us...I guess I'd best answer them. Hide the food and any valuables." Jared then returned the "Cooee."

I admit it was a bit exciting to hear other people. We were starting to think we were the only people left.

When the other group came down the hill, they were all smiling and waving. There were eight of them. Four of them were just kids of maybe seven to fourteen years old, the other four were two women and two men carrying rifles.

"Hey, how's it going?" asked the man in the lead. He was in his forties and dressed like a farmer including the wide brimmed hat.

"We're good, how about you?" Jared returned the friendly tone.

"Yeah, we're all good. Just heard the female voices and thought this might be a friendly group to visit.

"Of course, welcome. Where ya headed?"

"We're headed for Cairns."

"Wow, that's going to be a bit of a trek with the little ones, where are you from?" Jared motioned them into the camp. "Please, come on in guys, were happy to see some other human faces,"

"Thanks, mate, yeah we're about a half hour's drive south of Babinda, but it took us three bloody days to get here."

The rest of the new group filed into camp, and everyone came out to welcome them. We all sat down to swap information. It turns out they were sugar cane farmers. The two men were brothers and their wives and kids who have relatives in Cairns, they had decided to head up there to get away from the bombing. Jared looked at the others and me before he spoke. "We've just come from there five days ago. We're heading south to get away from the bombing too."

The two men looked at each other. "How bad was the bombing? I mean it was pretty bad down here, just wiped out all the roads, most of the towns and now they're starting on the houses. They bomb any cars on the road, we were all packed up in the Toyota when we heard what was happening so we decided to leg it. It can't be as bad up there."

"All the same up there mate. Whole suburbs are gone, dams burst, roads destroyed. And all that was maybe four days ago. I'm not sure it's going to be an improvement for you, I'm sorry." Jared shook his head.

The other man swore under his breath and his wife grabbed his arm with a frightened look on her face.

Jared said, "Look it's already getting late, why don't you guys camp here with us tonight, there's plenty of room and we can tell you everything we saw. Maybe you guys can tell us some local information about further south."

"Thanks, mate but we really should be making tracks and we wouldn't want to impose," the man said, before his wife spoke quietly in his ear." Let's stay here Jim. The kids are tired, and so am I."

He looked thoughtful for a moment and then he looked at the kids who were sitting on the ground in a circle chatting to Julia and Amy about their travels.

"Yeah ok." He sighed. "Thanks mate, we'd like to camp here tonight."

"Great, well, pitch your tents anywhere you like, we've got plenty of wood so no need to get any. Make yourself at home." He smiled.

"Thanks mate, we will." The man called Jim stood and shook Jared's hand and then the adults went to set up their tents.

Jared turned to me and said quietly, "They're walking into far worse than they left I think, and with four kids."

Kieran must have overheard. "At least they have guns. Mine are all still in Cooktown."

Jared turned to him. "Yeah I don't have mine either, but I doubt they'd be much good against those aircraft."

"Nope, but I'd make short work of those dogs that have been following us." Kieran winked.

I was about to ask Kieran about the dogs when Julia spoke across the camp. "Hey Doc, you might wanna look at this arm." She pointed at the youngest girl's arm. Her Mother must have heard and said quite urgently. "Is one of you a doctor?" She began walking toward us.

"I'm not a doctor, I'm a third-year pharmacy student."

"Oh...well maybe you'd know what that is on her arm?" She looked hopeful and called the little girl over.

After Tony's death the night before I was in no frame of mind to be treating anyone, but the worried look on the mothers face when she showed me the arm made me give in. The girl's arm had a red, swollen area that covered most of her bicep. It looked sore and I bet it was itchy.

"She's wearing gloves to stop her scratching it," said her mother.

"Yep I bet it's itchy, that was a good idea." I then asked her every question I could think of EG: Has she ever had it before, when did it show up, did she touch anything, changed her diet?

By the time all the questions were answered I was confident I knew how to treat it. The process was reassuring to me. I needed to be sure of what I was doing, I needed the confidence that surety brought with it. I dug around in my bag and found some topical hydrocortisone cream, which I then rubbed on her arm. The little girl smiled when I finished. "It feels better!"

I handed the tube to the mother and told her, "I suspect she's brushed up against something in the forest, a few of us have had similar. Put that cream on three to four times a day until it clears. You can use that on similar rashes that you guys get along the way. Be careful to follow the directions carefully and wash your hands after applying it. Don't let her touch the area and then touch her face, ok?"

The girl's mother agreed and thanked me; she even offered to pay for the tube.

"It's fine, we stole it anyway," I laughed. She looked a little surprised until I explained how we came to get it.

"Is... Cairns really that bad?" she asked.

"Yes. We can only vouch for the areas we could see, but they were pretty bad. I'm sorry."

"That's ok, thanks for telling us." She returned to putting up the tents.

Kieran stood and placed a hand on my shoulder. "Nice one, Doc." He gave my shoulder a squeeze before letting go and heading off to start the fire.

I guess I was playing doctor again. Of course, handing someone a tube of over the counter cream is nothing like fighting to save a man's life... And then losing.

But it looked like I'd found my way forward... to some extent anyway. And all it took was a little girl with a rash.

We all enjoyed dinner, it was so nice to meet some new people, we'd been in the bush for just under a week but already it felt like a lifetime. I really hoped they didn't go to Cairns; it would be mayhem back there. Not to mention the trek we'd just done, they would have to do it in reverse with the little ones, which would have to take two weeks at least until they get there. That's an awful long time for the kids to be hiking. The little one I treated, being so tiny, she couldn't afford to lose much weight.

After dinner and the kids were in bed, Jared had the map out and was showing them where we'd travelled and camped. They had their own map, which I recognised (with some satisfaction) was also a 'topo' map and they were discussing at length their planned route. It closely matched ours, but they were planning on doing more walking outside the forest. Along the headlands of the cane fields, something our group had discussions about on several occasions. As we've moved south, away from the city it made more sense as it's more sparsely populated. But back when we were near Cairns it seemed riskier as we assumed Cairns to be the target. But from what these guys have been saying about bombing raids in their area, it seems the cities are not the target...*People* are the target.

I went to bed early and left them to talk, I was till a bit of a wreck over Tony's death and I needed some sleep.

When I awoke the other group had already up and gone.

"Left before sunrise," Jared said, handing me a coffee. "I tried to convince them to come with us but they were determined."

Craig's head poked out of his tent. "You invited them to join us without asking the group?"

"Yeah, I did."

"Don't you think that's a group decision? I mean what are they bringing to the table? A bunch of kids to look after?"

By this time everyone was up and very interested in the conversation.

"They're good people. What do any of us bring to this group other than being good people willing to look out for each other?" Jared pointed out.

"Well that's crap. Everyone here has a use and isn't a burden on the others. As soon as someone is a burden, they should go."

"There but for the grace of God go I," said Amy quietly behind me.

"What the hell was that?" asked Craig with a sneer at Amy.

She shrank in size. I could see it in an instant, he's her bully and she's an easy mark, he knew all it took was a glare to make her feel small… Well, I'm not Amy.

"It's John Bradshaw, what he said when he saw others on the gallows. What that means here is that any one of us could be considered a burden. I came with hardly any food. Jack came without a tent, and we all came without a clue. We are all burdens on each other and we carry the burden of others because we are part of this group. That's what makes us strong," I said proudly.

"Her," he said pointing at Amy. "She's not even one of the group."

Well, that pushed my buttons. "Amy is far more part of the group than you'll ever be. In fact, how long were you in the group for? I don't remember ever seeing you at the drinks nights, or online."

"I was there, just didn't make a show of it. Look I came fully prepared and I'm not a burden on anyone. I have a right to be a member of this group."

"Fully prepared?" asked Louise. "You hit me up for food as soon as we got to the first ridge that first night."

"And me," said David.

"And me, when we made camp!" said Peter.

"I do my part. More than *the 'Doc'* anyway." He said using air quotes. "All she does is make us go get piles of crap we can't eat and then she hands out pills that may or may not kill you."

Kieran launched himself at Craig so fast I barely saw it. Jared tried to stop him but Kieran was too fast. He punched Craig in the face so hard I heard bones break. He hit the ground hard and then Kieran proceeded to give him two more bone crushing blows before Jared got to him and hooked his arm through Kieran's as he was lining up for the third. Several others who were not quite as fast were also making their way toward Craig with similar intent. Louise, led the charge with an almost war-cry of, "You bastard!" She let fly with a kick to Craig's ribs, which connected with a sickening whack. Jared dove across the now unconscious Craig to protect him from more blows. "STOP!" he yelled. "THAT'S ENOUGH!"

They did stop. But they weren't done hurling abuse at Craig who wouldn't have heard a thing. When they'd calmed down, Jared got to his feet. "This is not how we solve problems."

Out of the corner of my eye I saw movement between the trees on a nearby Ridge. It was the families who must have seen what happened. The man, Jim, saw me looking and just shook his head then turned and walked away. That hurt more than what Craig said. They were coming back to travel with us but seeing what we would do to one of our group, obviously decided they would face the worst, rather than be with us.

Jared was bent down looking at Craig, whose face was a bloody mess.

"That prick deserves more Jared," said Kieran.

"Maybe, but this is not how we go about it mate." Jared was angry but I could see disappointment in his face.

Louise, still wild with anger, stood with her fists clenched. "That bastard has to go, he does nothing but tell others to do the work and complain about everything, and I'm sick of his perving on us girls. He sneaks extra food but refuses to carry his share."

"He's taking extra food, when was that?" asked Kyle.

"I've seen him do it a few times, he takes two lots and puts the extra packet inside the other while his hands are in his backpack, to make it look like it's just one packet. That's why he sits away from us when he eats, so nobody sees how much he has."

There was a murmur of derision through the group.

"Why didn't you tell me this, Louise?" said Jared.

"I assumed you knew -that everyone knew, it was so obvious."

"I've seen it too," Amy said. "He told me not to say anything. He scares me and I didn't want to make him angry, so I ate less to make up for it. I'm sorry, I should have said something."

Louise and Paula walked over to Amy and hugged her.

Kieran shook his head sadly. "Jesus, Amy, there's nothing of you to begin with, and you're doing without so that bastard can take more!" He turned to Jared. "This pricks gotta go."

"That may be... But like I said, not like this. We're not going to become a pack of dogs all turning on one of the pack, just because nobody likes them. I've seen what that can do to someone. We're better than that and when he comes to, we'll ask him about the food... Jess, I know what he said, but could you take a look at him? He doesn't sound good."

I walked over to check on him. I swore no Hippocratic oath, but still felt it my duty to care for everyone, even if I didn't like them.

He was flat on his back and his breathing was fairly normal, but he was gargling through the blood from his smashed nose draining down his throat. I asked Jared to help me roll him over on his side so the blood drained out his nose instead of down his throat. But we needed David to help. It worked and he was soon breathing better. He was starting to come around now and looked dazed. Jared handed Craig his water bottle and he took a drink. His now flat and swollen nose, still streamed blood, and it ran down his chin and onto his chest.

"You saw that, Jared," he started. "That was an unprovoked attack. What are you going to do about it? I want him kicked out of the group."

Jamie, one of Craig's supporters found his courage and spoke. "Yeah, you've all been bagging him but he." He pointed at Kieran. "King hit him for no reason."

"Hardly *no reason,* and it wasn't a king hit," Louise said turning to face the man. "He knew it was coming and he deserved it."

Jared raised his hand. "Hang on guys, let's not get into all that yet. Craig, I hear you've been taking extra food, is that true?"

Craig looked at Jamie. "Tell them what you saw! That mongrel hit me and I didn't do anything to him."

He pointed at Louise. "Yeah, I saw it, he just king hit him and then that bitch kicked him while he was down-,"

"LIKE I SAID," Jared interjected loudly. "I want to know about the extra food. Craig, have you been taking more than your share?"

"You don't understand the question you ask," Craig said, as though he were quoting a great philosopher.

Everyone groaned and Kieran said, "Don't give us that crap, answer the bloody question."

"My share? I've been carrying three times what most of these chicks are carrying, it takes energy to carry all that weight."

"The weight you're carrying is *you,* ya fat prick," laughed Kieran.

Jared held up his hand again. "Let's keep it on topic. We all have our share of weight based on our size. I can assure you Craig, that those girls feel just as loaded as you do."

"But unlike you, we do it without complaining," Louise said to a mixture of laughter and applause.

Craig wasn't done defending himself. "I'm a big man, I need more calories per day than the rest of you. You'll want a big man around when things get serious, and it takes food to maintain one."

The laughter from the group erupted like canned laughter from a bad sitcom from the nineties. I swear, even his supporters were laughing.

It probably wasn't the reaction he expected. It was just so preposterous to think that the group, in any way, considered him as someone we'd rely on when things *got serious*.

Jared finally spoke in the silence that followed our laughter. "Well, I think we need to set up some boundaries for everyone to follow. From now on we all only get food based on size."

We were all stunned. Had he heard anything that was said?

"You must be bloody joking mate," said Kieran.

"No, I think what Jared said is fair." Craig nodded.

"You would," Louise said. "This is crap, this guy steals from us, bullies one of the smallest in the group, says horrible things about Jessica, and you say we should give him more food! Seriously? Is that what you are saying?"

Jared held his hand up yet again but this time it didn't have the effect it usually had.

Several people started at once, they wanted to know if that was what Jared was planning? If he could really let Craig get away with what he'd done. Before long everyone was talking at once.

I have to admit, me included. I couldn't believe what he'd just said. I was watching him lose his leadership, protecting someone who has tried to undermine him from the first day.

Kieran stepped into the middle and put both his hands up to silence everyone. It worked.

"Hang on guys, Jared has been a good leader to date, and I think we need to hear what he has to say... I hope for his sake, he has something to say." Kieran looked Jared in the eye.

Jared sighed. "Look I know some of you are upset, I understand, but we can't behave like animals when one of us goes astray. What Craig did was wrong; he shouldn't have taken more than his share of food. But I see his point, so we adjust and move on."

Well that didn't improve anything at all. Everyone started yelling at once. I couldn't believe Jared had this so wrong! I strode over to him and grabbed his arm. "I need to talk to you." I led him a few paces away. Everyone was still yelling so I put my hand up and they went quiet. Wow that felt way better than it should!

I spun him around to face me and spoke face-to-face (well face to chest, due to his height) with Jared in a quiet, but very firm voice. "What the hell are you doing? Never mind; stop doing what you are doing. I don't care if you think it's right, what you are doing is wrong and it's tearing the group apart. *Fix it.*"

"I don't *know* how to fix it, Jess, but we can't just kick him out-"

"Yes we bloody *can*," I hissed. "This isn't the cub scouts, this is life and death, we rely on you, and that arsehole is just walking all over you."

I looked around at the faces all looking at us. "If you aren't careful, it might be *you* that gets kicked out. Wake up to what's going on here!"

"I'm trying to do the right thing here, Jess, I just hate all this arguing, we have to-"

"Jesus, don't you understand what's-... Never mind, I'll talk to them."

I turned and walked back to the group. They were all talking animatedly amongst themselves, and I raised my hand. They stopped talking and focussed their attention on me. I've heard the term 'drunk on power', I understand it a little now.

With my heart racing, I began, "Right, everyone, have breakfast and pack up, we'll be leaving straight after we've eaten. We'll head onto town and see what we can find." I paused momentarily and then went for broke. "Craig, Louise will help you pack your backpack, it will contain only what you would usually carry and no more, you and anyone else who wants to go with you, will head off in whatever direction you like... But it won't be with us."

A loud cheer erupted from the group with a lot of smiles until Craig spoke. "Who the hell do you think you are, quack? You don't tell me what to do, if anyone's going to take over as leader... It'll be *me*." He thumbed his chest and began to get up.

Kieran came and stood beside me. "Lady's spoken, pack your stuff and piss off."

Craig glared at Kieran but thought better of a physical challenge that he knew he'd lose.

My heart was racing, I'd never done anything like that, and I hoped nobody saw it was all bluff. I've never really been in charge of anything, and I must admit it felt really good to make others do as I say. But that's not why I did this; I could see it was all going so very wrong, I understood what Jared was trying to do... But he was wrong this time... We had to clean the wound and that meant removing the source of the infection... Craig.

The group all started getting breakfast prepared and after a couple of minutes, Craig finally stood up. He held his hand up, but nobody stopped what they were doing. He cleared his throat and said in a booming voice. "Right, anyone who wants to leave this ridiculous group I'll be leaving after breakfast. I won't be going south like these idiots; I'll be heading north along the cane fields where there will be less climbing through the bush. The bombing has stopped so obviously the aliens have lost the war. Back in Cairns there will be more food and the authorities will have things under control. Anyone with me will be ready to go in thirty minutes."

"You really think the authorities will have fixed things?" asked Paula.

"Of course they will, it's been a week now, there will be places to get food, accommodation, they will probably house us in the resorts while they rebuild. We'll be living on free room service while these idiots are living like animals in the forest. Come with me and I'll show you." Craig puffed out his chest.

Kieran couldn't let it slide. "You must be joking, if anyone believes that crap they deserve what they get. Let me guess you're all gonna ride up there on Unicorns?" he laughed.

Louise shook her head. "Paula - don't believe that, he knows it won't be like that up there. He's lying to get people to go with him."

Jared had returned to the group. He looked sad and just stood beside me looking at the ground.

Questions were thrown at Craig by several members of the group, which he answered with more and more fanciful dreams as he got into the swing of it.

One of the guys, Jack, asked me, "Why are we going south then if Cairns is better? You and Jared have been dragging us through the forest for a week and for what? What's down south that you two want? Those other people are heading to Cairns, *they* know it's going to be better. Why are you lying to us?"

I couldn't believe he so quickly became convinced by Craig's lies. I was stunned and couldn't speak. Nobody's that stupid *surely*.

Heated accusations of us lying to them started flying across the camp with equally heated rebuttals by several of the group, including Kieran.

I turned to Jared. "You have to say something."

"Nope, this was your idea...And if they're dumb enough to believe Craig, they are welcome to go with him."

He was right. I started this. My little brush with power went to my head and now it was threatening to split the group. This was precisely what Jared was trying to avoid and I'd blundered on in and made it happen. I felt so stupid.

Craig had sat back down with a smug look on his face and let them argue now. He'd planted a seed and now people were coming up with their own ideas of what might be back in Cairns. One of them even suggested there were most likely buses heading north and that they should stick close to the road. Another took that and went on further, suggesting they actually walk on the road in case one comes along. "It'll take no time to get to Cairns that way. Even if we walk, we'll be there by tomorrow night. And if a bus comes, we'll be there in an hour."

I thought I knew a little about human nature but this situation just blew me away. They'd been given a little ray of hope and they followed the source without question. Wilfully ignorant of all they knew and had seen, they grasped these lies with both hands rather than face the bleak reality.

I'd read about cancer patients spending all they had on quack cures like vitamin C injections, in spite of scientific proof they don't work. I could never understand why. But right in front of me, I was seeing it firsthand and I *still* didn't understand them.

The argument raged on around Jared and I, neither of us saying anything. What could we say? To say that in reality we had no idea what was going to happen to us all and that we were just looking for a place to hide, would have just added fuel to Craig's fire. Craig offered hope; we offered possible survival and a bleak future... And no room service.

By the time the argument finished, half our group was going with Craig, including Paula. "We'll be taking half the food too," Craig said with a smug smile directed at me. One of his followers asked, "Why do we need it? We'll be in Cairns tomorrow; it'll be heaps easier if we aren't carrying all this stuff." There were a few others that agreed, and they began emptying their packs. The smile faded from Craig's face momentarily. He hadn't expected that, and it was my turn to have a little smile.

"We'll take it anyway in case we're delayed, better safe than sorry. Besides, this lot won't need it, they won't survive out here long enough to eat it." His smug smile was back. "Leave all the quack's crap here though, it'll just slow us down."

Paula came over to me carrying all the medical supplies from her backpack. She looked apologetic. "Here you go, Jess, I wish you were coming with us. It'll be better up there."

"Paula," I shook my head. "It's all lies and I wish you weren't going. But if you must go, please take those things with you. Or if you like, I'll make up a kit you can use."

"Nah I'll be fine, you guys will need it more."

"Look, at least take these," I said, handing her some antiseptic and topical hydrocortisone. "Use that on scratches and that on rashes, ok?"

"Ok, Doc, I'll take them... Thanks." She smiled warmly.

I hugged her hard and then she turned and went back to her backpack.

As they were ready, Craig's new group were assembling in front of him. He was in his element. Like some self styled General he was all puffed up with self-importance and barking orders at his little band of troops.

The thing I found most distressing was the attitude many of his group were showing towards us. It had become them and us, and we were now almost the enemy. These were people I thought of as friends an hour ago, we were all a part of one group, helping and supporting each other. Now there were sideways glances and glares.

I guess it marked the complete fracture of our group, even before they'd left.

When they were all ready to go Jared finally spoke up.

"Everyone, I'm sorry to see you go, especially when I seriously doubt what you've been told." There were a few comments from Craig's group, which Jared ignored. He continued, "If any of you change your mind you will be welcomed back. We'll be heading south as you know probably down to Etty Bay or Mission Beach. The forest goes down to the coast there, so we can maybe fish and get shellfish to live on till things improve. Come find us if you want to."

Craig laughed. "Yeah well, have fun with that, we won't be back."

Paula said, "I'll send someone to come rescue you."

One of the guys who also didn't now hate us echoed the sentiment. "Yeah, we'll tell em where to find yas."

And they left... It was a sad moment. Our group was now less than half the size. Of all those who went with them, I wished Paula had stayed. She wasn't very bright but had an almost childlike honesty that was endearing. I liked her and I knew I'd miss having her with us.

But as I looked around our little group, aside from Paula, I think we kept the best of them. In our group now were Jared, Kieran, Louise, Amy, David, James, Peter, and myself. That made a total of eight out of our original twenty. But that also meant eleven less mouths to feed. As we were getting short of food, that meant that if we could find a little, we had some hope of it sustaining us.

BABINDA FOOD RUN

Wherever the art of medicine is loved, there is also a love of humanity.'-Hippocrates

We were all quiet for the first hour of our hike into Babinda, but as we walked, conversations started and by the time we made it to the outskirts of town, our spirits were somewhat restored.

The little township was like most of what we'd seen. Aside from dogs barking, it was all quiet and most of the houses were flattened. Not like that shaped bomb that destroyed Redlynch, but more like the cars on the highway. There was a stench to this place; that of death and rotting things. At times I had to hold my shirt up to cover my mouth and nose. Blowflies swarmed everywhere and tried to get into our eyes and mouths. I was used to bush flies at home, and they were annoying enough, but these were the big green bottle blowflies that create maggots in rubbish bins. You just know, whatever they've been eating isn't good.

Jared led us into the main street, which was largely intact aside from a lot of vandalism, several crushed cars and more of the terrible smell. James spotted the supermarket sign, and we all made a beeline for it. I'm sure the others were just as keen to get out of here as I was. The entrance was smashed, and it smelled awful but it was a different smell. This was rotting food, which made sense given the fridges and freezers had no power for a week.

Kieran volunteered to head in for a look and he darted off into the dark store. He was back a few moments later shaking his head and breathing hard. He must have held his breath. "Nothing in there," he gasped. "All gone except what's in the cold store…And I don't think we want that."

"Then I reckon we should just get out of here," said Jared. We all agreed and headed back up the main street heading west which led to the mountains. The chemist and the doctor's surgery had both been burned out. I assume it was vandals on the first day or so after the bombing started. There was really nothing this town could offer us, so a quick departure was the best option.

As we got to the end of the street, where it had become residential again, I saw a house across the road that was still intact. And after a double take, I realised there was someone sitting on the front verandah!

I pointed them out to Jared who said, "Well let's go say hi." We crossed the street towards the house and a man in his fifties wearing a dirty flannelette shirt stood, with a beer in one hand and a rifle in the other. "Nothing here for you, keep walking."

"Mate, we're not after anything, just saying hello," Jared told him.

"Well in that case, *hello*… Now keep walking. I've had a gut full of people coming through looking to steal everything."

"There are others?" asked Jared. "We've been in the forest; we don't know what's been happening"

"It's all turned to crap is what's been happening, gangs of thugs driving into town with ute's, stealing everything not nailed down. They burned the chemists down... The pills I needed were in there. All gone now; old doctor Jacob's surgery all burned down as well."

"What pills?" I asked.

He fixed me with a suspicious glare. "Blood pressure and heart," he said. "You going to tell me you have them?" he asked with a sardonic laugh.

"No, I'm sorry we don't."

"Nah I thought not. Anyway, you might as well bugger off, there's nothing left in this town and what I've got, you can't have." He lifted the rifle and laid it on the handrail.

"Righto. Thanks for the info, we'll leave you to it," said Jared and we walked away down the street.

"Jesus! I'd kill for one of those beers," laughed Kieran.

"You and me both," Jared said. "It even looked *cold*. Tell you what though; it makes me think more about houses out of town. There might well be more food in them than the supermarkets."

David laughed and said, "Just as risky as going into towns, plus the added bonus of maybe getting shot."

"Yeah there is that, but we can check to see if anyone's home before we go in."

Everyone agreed that it was a better idea and Jared pulled out the map to look for roads with possible undamaged houses on them; the ones that were not clustered together to make one bomb enough to take out many houses. It was a good plan.

We turned left down one road and followed it out of town. It felt strange to be so out in the open, but with the bombing runs stopped, it made some sense to take a road instead of hiking through the forest. Besides, the mountains here were much steeper and it was quite difficult hiking. Nobody minded the change.

We found a few houses along the road but they were all either bombed or ransacked.

We were maybe ten kilometers along the road when Jared stopped at a driveway, which wound its way into the rainforest. He waved me over and on the letterbox was written *Dr B Jacobs.* "Didn't that guy say the doctor's surgery belonged to an old doctor Jacobs?"

I couldn't remember, but several of the others were convinced that was what they'd heard. "Might be a chance for your books, Jess," Jared said with a shrug.

I didn't want to be reminded of the whole 'doc' thing. I was pretty happy just being one of our now smaller group. I hadn't even thought about my responsibilities as their medic. "Can't hurt to ask, I guess," I said.

We followed the driveway up and maybe a kilometre up we could see the house, quite a grand colonial style with a beautifully manicured lawn. When we left the trees and entered the open lawn area, I spotted an old man with a grey beard digging in the lawn. He had his shirt off and was swinging a pickaxe.

"*Hello,*" Jared called loudly, startling the old man. "Are you Doctor Jacobs?"

The man dropped the pickaxe and picked up a single barrelled shotgun, which he then pointed at us.

"There's no drugs here, so you're wasting your time," he yelled back.

Jared said quietly to us, "Stay here guys, let me go talk to him. Kieran and Jess, come with me."

We approached the man slowly with hands outstretched away from our bodies.

Jared spoke when we were about ten meters from him. "We aren't looking for drugs."

The man then said, "Well I'm not treating anyone either so you can leave."

"We don't need treatment either," said Jared, stopping. I was hanging back behind the guys. I admit I was a bit scared of the gun. I looked at the hole he was digging and saw it was in the shape of a grave. He was burying someone.

"What do you want then?" he asked, even at this distance I could see the suspicion in his expression.

"We're looking for books... medical books."

The old man gave a fairly sardonic laugh and said, "Ahh you want to treat yourselves eh? Those books without the proper training will likely kill more of you than not having them."

"We have someone with training," Jared then looked over his shoulder at me.

Kieran said, "Come up here, Doc."

"She's a doctor?" asked the man.

"I'm a third-year pharmacy student," I said, now standing beside Kieran.

"Jesus, with that training and my books you'd definitely kill someone."

That stung and I looked at the ground. He was right. Kieran put an arm around my shoulders and pulled me to him.

"Ahh... It's already happened," said the man, looking intensely at me.

I nodded.

"What happened?" he asked. His voice had lost a little of it's edge.

"Anaphylactic shock from a penicillin allergy... I think," I replied, my cheeks heating.

He was quiet for a moment looking intently at me, before his shoulders slumped and he said, "Well as you can see I'm busy." He motioned to the hole.

Jared said, "Can we help you with that hole, Doctor?"

He thought for a moment and said, "I'd appreciate that, yes... It's for my wife." He then looked at me and said, "Well, you'd best come up to the house and tell me about it... just you, Miss. The rest can stay here." He slung the rifle over his shoulder and grabbed his shirt from the top of a shovel he had stuck in the ground.

Jared whispered to me, "I don't know if-"

"It's fine Jared," I replied and headed off.

The doctor walked slowly towards the house. When we reached the verandah, he opened the screen door for me, and I entered the house. He filed in behind me and while leaning the shotgun up against the wall he said, "Right, come on into the office... So you lost one, you'd better tell me about it."

Once we sat down in his very comfortably furnished office, we introduced ourselves and I told him everything about Tony's death, from the first injury to our performing CPR. He may have been old, but his piercing eyes told me he was still as sharp as a tack. He listened without a word; his intelligent mind was picking the information he needed from what I said. A skill he would have learned after years of listening to patients tell him their problems. While I tried to keep it brief and use medical terms when I knew them, I'm sure it was a chore for him.

"I just wish I knew more, I could have saved him, but instead I killed him," I said.

He was quiet for a moment, just looking at me and then he said, "Look, I don't do absolution. I deal with matters of the flesh not the spirit. But I will say this... He was dead the minute the branch hit him. With a pair of tweezers and no local anaesthesia there was no way you could have found all the pieces. And as for an allergy to penicillin; did he tell you that?"

"No, he said he'd never had penicillin before. I had no other way to treat it, so I had to give him the amoxicillin."

"What makes you so special?" he asked bluntly. I was a little taken aback, and he continued, "I've been a doctor for over forty years, and I can't tell who's allergic to what, just by looking at them. And treating anaphylaxis on the ground in the rainforest; you had adrenaline?"

"No."

"Crash cart? Team of trained staff?"

I could see where he was going with this. "No. I didn't have any of those things," I said

"And you're taking responsibility for his death? Look... They say you're not really a doctor till you've lost one. You're fast tracking your career...you can't save them all. Learn from it and move on."

"But I'm not a doctor. Should I have treated him at all?"

"Ha, I'm not about to give you permission to treat people if that's what you're after." He sat back in his chair. "But given the circumstances I can see why you need to. That group you're with. Are they making you do it?"

"God no, they're good people. I'm just the closest thing to medical help they have. And I want to help them. I just don't know what I'm doing, and I'm scared of making things worse," I said.

He sat forward with some enthusiasm. "Well, that's a good attitude to start with. *Primum non-nocere...First, do no harm...* Heard of it? It is an important thing to remember when treating others. What that means for you is you must treat only what you have to, and to the best of your ability and knowledge. Given your lack of training I would suggest surgery is beyond your abilities." He smiled. "When it comes to treating people, you must consider what *will* happen if you do nothing and what *could* happen if you treat them. Do you understand?"

"Yes. I understand what you mean."

"Good. And at least you have a clue about your potions, I'm sure they teach you well these days and I want to say this, when I started my medical training my mentor Doctor had only just stopped practicing bloodletting."

"I've heard about it," I said.

"It's true, some were still doing it up to the middle of the twentieth century. That man gave me his favourite book, which he himself used as a student. It detailed how and why to blood-let on patients. You can see how far we have come in medicine. The three years you have studied have likely given you more academic knowledge than an experienced doctor a century ago would have possessed. But be not scornful missy, what they learned they have passed on, you are standing atop the shoulders of giants. Your knowledge will grow with experience and will come in time.

"But you need to cut yourself some slack or you'll be a basket case in no time. The way things are going, you *will* lose more." He gave me an intense look to make his point. "That, I can promise you and some of them may even be your fault. I'm certain never intentionally of course, or from negligence, but it will happen. You just need to take a lesson from each that you can move on with and grow in your knowledge. That's really all the advice I can offer."

"Can you come with us?" I blurted out... It was a long shot.

"Ha, I'm seventy eight. I'm way too old to be traipsing through the bush with a bunch of young people. No, my time is done now." He said with a far-away look out the window, before rousing himself and continuing.

"I'll tell you what. After I bury my wife, I'll be going away. Come back this afternoon and all the books you'll need will be on the dining room table. Take them and use them well. In fact, take anything you or your friends need. I won't be needing it, there is a wine shelf in the kitchen pantry. Help yourselves... but do me a favour, there are two, *very* expensive bottles of wine in there. Do them justice and try to pick which ones they are." He gave me a mischievous smile.

"Oh and no one is to enter this room when you come back. You must promise me that... Leave an old man his dignity," he said, returning his gaze to the window.

A moment later he turned to me suddenly like he'd just thought of something and said very seriously. "Then *never* come back to this house, it won't be safe for people to enter for a long time."

I promised and we got up to leave the room. My eyes had fully adjusted to the dark and as I turned, I noticed a syringe in a disposable kidney shaped bowl. The syringe was full of a clear liquid and there was a small brown bottle beside it.

"Don't tell your friends I have that," he said. "It's all there is and it's my only way-" His voice cracked and choked back a sob.

"I won't mention it. And they really aren't interested in drugs," I said. "Are you sure you won't come with us?"

He shook his head. "I'm sure, I'm about to bury my whole world. Forty eight years we were together, and she died in my arms last night from a heart attack." He paused to gather himself before continuing. "There's nothing left for me in this world, what's coming next for those who stay, is famine and disease. I'm too old to survive it anyway."

He led the way out onto the verandah where we could see the guys were taking turns at digging. He'd left the rifle leaning against the wall. The boys were going hard at it and the hole was nearly shoulder height in depth already.

"Can we help you bury your wife, Doctor?" I asked softly.

He said nothing for the longest time and then finally said, "I'd appreciate that yes... I'm not a young man anymore."

The hole took another half hour or so before the guys decided it was six feet deep. They were all glistening with sweat and covered in red dust.

"There's a hose over there to wash off if you like, boys," said the doctor. "It's gravity fed creek water so best not to drink it. There is tank water out the back if you want to fill your water bottles."

The boys went and hosed off and when they were presentable, four of them followed the doctor inside to get his wife's body. I followed to help where I could. We found her lying in a king sized four-poster bed, looking peaceful with her hands clasped together, her hair brushed, and make-up done. She could have been asleep.

He gave me a sad smile. "She would have been horrified to be buried while looking a mess," he said by way of an explanation

Jared asked in a respectful tone. "Would you like us to wrap her in a sheet Doctor?"

"Um, yes…Yes please, I wasn't sure how I was going to do all this on my own," he replied.

"Well we're glad to help," I said, placing a hand on his bony shoulder.

The guys wrapped her in a bed sheet the Doctor supplied, and she was gently laid to rest in her grave.

It was my second funeral in two days, but at least I didn't know this woman.

The guys were amazing. They treated her and her husband with such respect. I was truly proud of them and when the last of the dirt was piled on the grave, each of us paid our respects to the Doctor and left him to his grief.

When I shook his hand, he said to me in a conspiratorial tone, "Remember our agreement. Come back in two hours, nobody enters that room, help yourselves to whatever you need, but never come back… OK?"

"I remember Doctor. I'll do as you ask and thank you." I hugged him. I'm not usually a hugger, but it felt like the right thing to do.

We all left and walked back down the driveway. As soon as we were out of sight everyone hounded me for details on what was said. Jared asked about the books.

I told them the plan, that we would come back in a couple of hours and what we needed would be on the table.

"Why didn't he just give them to you now?" Kieran asked. He hadn't understood what I'd tried not to say out loud, so I said, "It's just how he wanted to do things." And left it at that.

With nothing else to do we killed time snoozing in the cool shade of a raintree at the start of the driveway, until it was time to head back to the house. The tree was huge, its massive branches spreading out from a trunk at least two meters wide. It made for a great shade tree while we waited.

Our visit was brief, and I wanted to keep it that way. I'll admit part of me wanted to open that door. I wanted to lay him to rest with his wife, but I'd made a promise and I wouldn't break it. As he'd said, there was a stack of books on the dining room table that were all I could hope for. Alongside them was an old school black 'doctors bag' that contained all the things an old school doctor needed. It also contained a note from the Doctor.

Dear Dr Jessica.

This bag served me well for my forty years of caring for my community. I'm sure it will serve you just as well for your caring future.

Good luck.

Yours sincerely.

Dr B Jacobs. MD

A tear rolled down my cheek. I ran my hand over the bag and found the engraved plate at the top with Dr Jacobs name on it. I was proud to have this bag and resolved to do it justice.

Everyone went through the house looking for anything useful. As agreed, nobody went into that room. The guys found the wine rack and I told them about the wines to look for, which they saw as a challenge.

The fridge, to our astonishment, was chock full of food. And it was still working! The Doctor had a solar battery system on the house, and it still had power. While we had a meal fit for a king, we had to do it away from the house. I couldn't take my eyes off that door. Kieran grabbed the Doctor's shotgun only to find it wasn't loaded. He searched the house looking for the ammunition but only found a box containing one very corroded round of birdshot in the garage and said, "One willy round is all we've got." He showed me the shotgun shell and its powdery green coating all over the brass base.

I had to ask. "What's a willy round?"

"Well, when they're all corroded like that it's a question, will he or won't he *go off*," he said with a grin.

Before we left, one of the guys discovered a drinks fridge on the back patio with a dozen cold beers in it. This, beyond a doubt made everything worthwhile for the boys... And if truth were told, us girls were pretty happy about it too. A cold drink of any sort was a welcome sight and I like a nice cold beer. We found an esky and emptied the fridge-freezer into it. It wouldn't stay cold long, but for as long as it did, we had proper food. A lightweight skillet from the kitchen meant we could fry meat, which we all craved and by unanimous vote we doubled Amy's share in an attempt to put weight back on her. She was dangerously thin, and she got any illness, she had nothing in reserve.

We made camp at the base of the driveway and drank our beers and wine in honour of the good Doctor and his wife. In case you are wondering, I think we found one of the expensive wines. It really was *very* good.

The next day we set off to head further south. We stayed on the road and made good time covering a fair distance but still not seeing anyone. There was talk of maybe stealing a car and travelling faster, but fear of being made flat by an alien bomb soon killed those ideas.

The road eventually headed back towards the highway, so we took to the headlands of the cane fields, which kept us close to the safety of the forest. There weren't many houses on this stretch and what we did see; maybe two out of three were bombed. Why they bombed some and not others was a topic of much discussion. James's theory was that they bombed the ones where they saw humans. "Maybe they had a light on or were seen outside or something."

It made some sense so we resolved to be invisible and avoid houses should the bombing runs start again.

We did see the aircraft a few times. But they were travelling way up high and at phenomenal speed so we assumed they must have just been passing through.

Trek South

'If you pick up a starving dog and make him prosperous he will not bite you. This is the principal difference between a dog and man.' –Mark Twain

Dogs barking were an ever-present noise, but I noticed that now we were in a rural area, the type of dog barking was different. Unlike in suburban areas with small housedogs, these were often big dogs. Early on the second day as we passed a run-down farmhouse a massive tan coloured dog came running out at us. I'd seen these types of dogs in the back of utes driven by pig hunters. But they were caged and under control. This was on its own and it meant business. It was barking and snarling about five meters from us.

"Stand still," Kieran said as he slowly handed the shotgun to Jared and unclipped the hunting knife on his belt.

He took a step forward and yelled. "WHAT ARE *YOU* DOING?... *SIDDOWN*!" He paused and said... "I said *SIT DOWN*!"

The dog stopped barking and looked unsure. "SIT!" yelled Kieran.

It did as it was told and sat down.

"Good dog." He said in a gruff but calmer voice. "Right, now go home." He swung his hand in the direction of the house with a pointed finger. The dog looked at the house, and then back at Kieran. "I said *HOME!*" He pointed again at the house. The dog looked reluctant, but it slowly headed back to the house, looking back at Kieran every few paces.

"Jesus! Kieran that was impressive, how did you know he'd listen?" I asked.

Kieran replied without taking his eyes off the dog. "That coulda' gone either way Doc. That collar he was wearing is a pig-hunting collar. They're tough dogs and usually only respect a strong hand... Don't worry, it was all bluff...Did ya see the *size* of it? I was crapping myself." He turned and grinned at me. We all laughed at that, more a release of tension I think.

We set off again and I noticed Kieran occasionally looking behind us. I followed his gaze and saw the dog following about half a kilometre behind us.

"Yeah, he's following us, Doc," he said.

"That could be a problem," Jared said.

"Why would it want to follow us?" asked Amy.

"Because it's lost its owner and figures Kieran will do," Jared told her.

Kieran nodded. "Yeah, well, I spose he'll replace the others that were following us, they went with the other group when they left."

"I've been meaning to ask about that, Kieran. What do you mean?" I asked.

"Well, there's a mob of dogs that has been following us since Redlynch. I suspect they've been eating our food scraps and poo."

"Gross," Louise and Julie said almost in unison.

"Yeah it is really, but I think they're lost pets and they're hungry. Maybe they've hooked up with some feral dogs that are afraid of humans, so they don't want to approach us. "

"They were following us?" Louise asked.

Amy said, "That's creepy."

Kieran chuckled, "Yep, I think so. And yeah, I spose it *is* a bit creepy Amy. That's why I kept asking everyone to throw any food scraps in the fire and to bury their poo deep. Nothing to eat, gives them no reason to follow us."

"Unless *we're* something to eat," said David.

"Yeah well, we're less likely to be on the menu if they aren't around us. But the ones who weren't careful with their waste, all went with Craig. And that guy behind us will lose interest if he doesn't get a feed."

Well, the dog didn't lose interest. He followed us for the next two days. He would occasionally disappear for an hour or two; Kieran said he was probably hunting. But he would always return to be the same distance behind us.

On the third day we passed a house set back in the forest and three blue heeler cattle dogs raced out and bailed us up. They surrounded us. I looked behind and there was a fourth, a crossbreed blue heeler with maybe a bit of bull terrier in it. These dogs were fierce. We all stood back-to-back while they growled and barked, occasionally one would lunge forward snapping its jaw at us, then step back a little. But each time they did this, the circle had closed a little more around us. Before I knew it, the big dog that had been following us was closing the gap. My immediate thought was he was joining the other dogs, afraid to take us on alone but happy to join a pack.

Kieran tried the commands he'd used before on the cattle dogs, but when he did, two of them lunged at him from both sides and almost managed to separate him from the group. A bluff wasn't going to work with these dogs, and he almost got a nip on the leg for trying.

With our one shotgun shell, Kieran tried to take out the leader. He was larger than the others and was leading each of the charges at us. Kieran aimed and fired, but all it did was make a less than spectacular fizzing sound and produced a lot of white smoke. I guessed that answered the 'Willy' question.

The dogs seemed to be focusing on the smallest in our group, Amy.

Jared reached across Amy's chest with his left hand and pulled her behind him into the centre of our circle. It worked a little, the dogs lost their focus on their chosen prey, and it threw them a little while they chose another. Unfortunately, the next smallest in our group was me. They kept lunging either side of me, maybe trying to force me to run. I'd never been so terrified in my life. These weren't just barking farm dogs that barked out of fear; we weren't a threat to them; they were actively hunting us for food!

All of a sudden one of the cattle dogs lunged at me. Kieran kicked it in the ribs hard and it went tumbling away.

The big dog had finally arrived and he ran at the tumbling dog at full speed, knocking it flying with a yelp; he then pounced on it and with one bone crunching bite to the neck, he killed it. He then rounded on the other dogs that had lost all concentration on us and were barking savagely at the big dog.

The lead cattle dog lunged at him and then retreated towards the others. The big dog then charged at the dogs causing them to scatter in all directions. They all ran about five meters and turned to bark again, but the big dog was right behind the slowest of them, a bite to the back and a toss of his great head sent it flying with an awful yelp. The fight was over in seconds. The cattle dogs were fast, but no match for the power and sheer lack of fear in the big dog. They all retreated back to the house they came from.

When it was over, the big dog simply looked at Kieran for a moment and sat down. His face wore no expression, and his mouth was closed. He appeared to be waiting for something.

"Good onya mate. Good boy," Kieran said.

The dog's expression changed, his tongue lolled out the side of his mouth and he began panting, his expression was almost a smile. Kieran patted his knees and the big dog went to him with his head hanging low in a submissive posture.

He sat in front of him, and Kieran patted its head, carefully at first and then progressively rougher and more familiar while the dog's thin but muscular tail, wagged back and forth on the ground, kicking up a small cloud of dust on the driveway.

It seemed as though we now had a dog. I was still quite scared of him, and Amy was too. He was a massive thing that easily weighed more than Amy and I combined. Kieran said he was a Bull Mastiff cross. Amy laughed and said she thought it might be crossed with a horse.

He had slack jowl skin so drooled continuously, he smelled worse than a mix of working dog kennel and dead cane toads, but he'd just saved our lives, so we figured we owed him.

There was much discussion about how we were going to feed such an animal, but Kieran said we shouldn't worry and that he thought it might be the other way round.

With our newfound protector trailing along we headed off again, still shaken but unscathed.

The next morning the big dog proved his worth again. We were walking along a sugar cane headland when the dog spotted a group of small wild pigs dart out of the forest and run into the canfield. He took off after them, with Kieran having dropped his pack and the useless shotgun, in hot pursuit. The rest of us just stood there, unsure of what to do. None of us knew how to hunt pigs. We could hear the dog occasionally barking and Kieran's voice talking to him, but we had no idea what was going on. About five minutes later there was an awful squeal and more barking and then silence.

A few moments later we saw Kieran emerge from the sugar cane about fifty meters away with a dead pig about a meter long over his shoulder, the dog beside him and a big grin on his face. All three were covered in blood.

After Kieran deftly cleaned and gutted the pig, we had roast pork that night, and I can tell you it was the most amazing thing I could remember eating. Cooked to perfection it was crispy on the outside and juicy on the inside. We all had the juices running down our chins. The guys made a makeshift spit with a tree limb and took it in turns to rotate the pig, who was minus its head. That belonged to the dog.

Kieran said he didn't normally eat the pigs he shot up Cape York because they're full of worms. As omnivores they will eat anything, which includes dead carcases they find, and they are known for parasitic worms. But here in the forest they live mainly on fruit and plant roots so are generally worm free and excellent eating.

We gorged ourselves and I was pleased to see Amy going for seconds. Her face was filling out again and she was looking healthier.

Listening to the dog crunch his way through a pig's head all night was not going to work for me, and I made a point of this to Kieran, who promised he'd take him away to eat his dinner in future.

The bird sounds were different here in the wetter forest. One night we heard a bird quite close to camp which made a *he-he-he-heeee* sound. It was like some hillbilly from an American movie was laughing at us! We all looked at each other and it was Julia who said. "That's a Red Necked Crake."

"Ha-ha, it's a what?" said Kieran.

"A Red Necked Crake... It's a bird."

"Well it certainly sounded like a redneck," laughed Kieran. "You're not just making that up?"

"No, that's really its name."

On the whole, medical issues were very few for now and I put that down to not travelling in the forest. It was our protector, but it came with problems, like the constant insect bites, rashes and cuts which were fast depleting our stocks of creams. I didn't know when we might be able to get more. If ever... It made me wonder how anyone survives in the rainforest without our modern medicine. It wasn't just our own indigenous people who lived in the rainforest. Many cultures have done it for millennia; what we were going to need was some of what they knew.

I spent any spare time I had reading the books Dr Jacobs gave me. They were heavy and I was so very grateful to those who volunteered to carry them, which was pretty much everyone as there were many books. They contained a wealth of knowledge and were invaluable to us as a group. If I really was all the medical care we had, I needed to lift my game.

First Contact

'If Aliens visit us, the outcome would be much as when Columbus landed in America, which didn't turn out well for Native Americans.' -Stephen Hawking

We bypassed Innisfail on our way south. It was just too far across open ground to get there safely, so we all agreed that we would push on. We were already getting braver, instead of following the tree line religiously, we were now going from point to point and skipping kilometers of walking up valleys and back down again, only to wind up a short walk across open ground from where we started. We weren't blasé about it. If there was a creek or line of trees, we would follow it, so we had cover if needed.

But we were making seriously good time this way. Until we were halfway across a stretch of open ground, maybe two kilometers either way from the forest and we heard vehicles on the north-south highway, which was close by at that point.

Stupidly, my first thought was buses coming to take people to Cairns, but I quickly dismissed that rubbish and mentally cursed Craig again. But we were all curious as to who they were, to be so brave driving up the highway like that. *"Maybe we've won the war!"* I thought in a flash of excitement.

"Everyone, get into the ditch," said Jared.

We were walking along sugarcane headlands and there was a deep drainage ditch alongside us. Fortunately, at this time of year it was dry, so we all scrambled down into it.

The sound was louder now, and we could tell it was a convoy of trucks. We were slightly elevated above the highway, so had a good vantage point to view them as they passed. Jared peered over the tip of the bank and said, "They're our trucks!"

We all clamoured up the side to peer over the edge. Yep, they looked like our army trucks.

"If they're ours then we must have won!" said Kyle. And he started to climb out of the ditch.

David grabbed him and pulled him back. "Hang on mate, we don't know that yet."

Jared said, "Good call. We don't know if it's our guys in those trucks, it's common for an invading force to use enemy vehicles."

James added, "While I doubt they play by the rules we're used to, it makes sense that they probably didn't bring everything they'd need. Ground transport like heavy trucks probably don't fit into spaceships all that well."

The trucks were just a little too far away to get a good look into the windows. We could see shapes but couldn't tell who, or *what* they were.

I counted fifteen troop carrier trucks and maybe two-dozen four-wheel drives. They were soft-top Jeep style with the tarps on them so we couldn't see into them either. It was frustrating to say the least. If they were our guys we were saved! If they weren't and we went running down there... Well judging by the bombing, I expect they wouldn't be friendly.

Jared spoke. "Look guys, I don't think we should show ourselves; I have a bad feeling about it."

"But if they're ours we could be out here for nothing," Louise said.

"Yeah, I know, Lou, but look, those were troop transport, not supply trucks. If they were coming to help the population after a war, wouldn't they bring more than troops?"

James laughed. "There is absolutely no arguing with that logic Louise, Jared's spot on. There'd be medical trucks and semi trailers full of food and water. They wouldn't rock up empty handed... And besides, I doubt Far North Queensland was an important enough area for the Aliens to only bomb here... I imagine our Army would have their hands full with the rest of Australia, it'd be months before they got up here to help."

There was no arguing with James's logic either. I imagined for a moment what somewhere like Sydney or Melbourne would look like after what they did here. A few guys with utes stealing things would be the least of your worries in a major city. It must have been horrific for any bombing survivors.

We laid low until we heard the last of the vehicles pass into the distance and climbed out of the ditch to continue on our way. We'd walked maybe ten meters when we heard the aircraft coming.

"Back in the ditch and stay still!" yelled Jared.

We all dove in and lay as flat and still as we could, but nobody told the dog that. He was at the top of the ditch and started barking at the aircraft as it approached. The dog's movement must have caught their eye as they slowed down over us for what seemed like an eternity and then sped away to the north.

The ship was an awesome sight. We'd never seen one up close. It really did resemble one of those American stealth bombers, but a bit chunkier. It was a dark colour, but I challenge anyone to say what colour it was exactly. It seemed to change constantly. Not like bright pink or yellow, but subtle shades of dark colours.

The noise was phenomenal. A high-pitched whine that pierced your brain like a stiletto knife and you *felt* the sound more than heard it. It was quite different when you were close to them.

When it was gone, Jared said. "Sorry everyone, I never thought about air support for their troops. That's my bad."

James was almost excited. "Did you see that thing? It was awesome!" He dropped his pack and rummaged around for a notebook and a pencil. He sat down and started sketching the aircraft. He worked fast, and the sketch was surprisingly good.

"We really should be moving," Jared said.

"Yeah, I know, but I need to do this while it's all fresh in my mind, we might need this info at some point," James told him.

"Would this help?" asked Amy, handing him her phone with an image of the aircraft showing.

"What a legend, Amy," said James, totally surprised. "It never occurred to me that someone might still have a charged phone... Can you show me this again later?"

"Of course. I got a heap of photos so hopefully it will help with your drawings."

He jumped up and gave her a one-armed hug and then packed his notebook into his backpack. I'd never seen James excited;

sarcastic and aloof was his norm and I must say it made a nice change.

We climbed out of the ditch and continued on our way to the protection of the forest. We jogged the stretches without cover, feeling more vulnerable than ever now. I felt a sense of relief when we broke though the weeds and into the protection of the trees. The earthy damp smell was just like we left it, at least here the understory was open and the walking was relatively easy. Not like walking out in the open but better than the vine-covered trees to the north.

When our eyes adjusted to the gloom, we hiked for the rest of the day in virtual silence. I guess everyone was deep in their own thoughts and probably it was all the same things I was thinking about. The aliens, where we were going, what our future might hold and maybe even about family and friends we may never see again or about our lives I'm sure we all missed.

I have to admit that I did miss my life. It felt a little like we'd been on a nightmare holiday and were ready to go home now. But of course, we couldn't, maybe not ever.

Stop thinking about all that Jessica, I thought to myself. *It's not going to do you any good.*

I was right of course. Letting my mind dwell on things wasn't healthy. I needed to focus on the here and now.

Jared's voice broke the silence when he said, "Anyone else think we've been quiet too long?"

There was a laugh from pretty much everyone and, "Hell yes." Was the general consensus. Jared must have read all our minds or maybe he was thinking the same. I guess he's not immune to all this.

We all started chatting about nothing in particular and everyone's mood improved, including mine. The day finished alongside a wide slow creek that left the forest about fifty meters downstream and continued on between the cane fields. It was a picturesque spot with a nice flat area amongst tall trees and a warm, gentle breeze was flowing up the stream from the cane fields. We set up camp and the guys rolled some large boulders around to make a shield for the fire, so it couldn't be seen from outside the forest. With the fire started, we all sat down to relax a little before dinner. As had become his habit, Kieran's dog stood guard. And unfortunately, where he decided to sit was upwind of us ... The smell was just awful!

Jared leaned towards Kieran and said "Mate... You know I love ya and all... But we have to talk about ya dog."

Kieran roared laughing and said, "Yeah, I know... I hear ya mate. Just not sure about how to bath him... I dunno how he'll take it."

"I'll help," Louise said, as quick as a flash. "Seriously... He reeks!"

There was a chorus of agreement and offers of help.

"I'm sure we can all spare just a little shampoo," I offered.

"Sounds like a plan," Jared said. "It's a bit cold for him now, especially since he doesn't have a towel. But tomorrow, before we leave is as good a time as any... For now though Kieran, any chance of asking him to move downwind?"

Kieran laughed and got up. "Well, I'll try mate, but you may have noticed he pretty much does his own thing, he just chose me to go along with."

After much pulling and cajoling the dog did finally move, not all the way mind you, but far enough so he was no longer up wind.

When a dog is as big as he is, maybe eighty or ninety kilograms, and who kills things for a living, everything he does is on his terms.

Just when we were all getting ready for sleep, we heard a cat calling from the forest. Well, kind of a cat, but a little like a baby crying. It was creepy!

"That's a Cat Bird," said Julia, matter-of-factly.

Kieran laughed loudly. "Oh come on, *now* you're pulling our legs. Ha."

We also could hear dogs barking in the distance.

"Let me guess, those are *Dog Birds*?" he laughed.

Julia wasn't going to take the bait. "It's a Cat Bird," she said flatly,

I had to ask. "How do you know Julia?"

"I like birds," she replied with a tone that said the discussion was over.

We didn't ask anymore.

I went to my tent exhausted as always, but for some reason that night I'd looked up at the roof of my tent. That was when with the light from the fire, I saw the silhouette of *huge* spider. My heart skipped a beat. It was a huntsman spider that would have easily been the size of a man's hand. No, I'm not exaggerating. I lay there frozen, I'm not that scared of spiders, but this thing could turn anyone into an arachnophobe, and if I reached out, I could have touched it! The worst part was, in the flickering light; I couldn't tell if it was on the outside or inside of my tent! I listened for the others, thinking I could just ask someone to check for me, but everything was quiet, there was nobody still at the fire that I could call on. I was going to have to deal with this myself. I slid the zipper on my sleeping bag down as far as my arm would reach. Then I spread my knees to make the zipper continue to open towards my feet. I got it maybe three quarters of the way down. I slipped a foot out and fumbled around with my toes to feel for the zipper of my tent. When I found it, I undid the zipper as far as I could and put my other foot in the hole and spread the zipper. So far so good, the spider hadn't moved, so I felt a little braver. After much wiggling I managed to get my body halfway out of the tent, never taking my eyes off the spider. When my backside was laying on the leaf litter it occurred to me at that if the spider was on the outside, I'd just done all this for nothing. But I pushed that aside and undid the zipper very slowly the rest of the way with my hand. With enough room now, I took a deep breath and quickly rolled onto all fours backing out of the tent as quickly as I could and jumped to my feet.

"Well that's an interesting way to get out of your tent, Doc," Kieran said from beside the fire. He'd been sitting there, poking the fire with a stick and watched the whole thing, without saying anything! "If you're going for a wee you probably want to keep that zipper done up in case that big spider decides to climb in there with you," he chuckled.

The next morning after we packed up, it was bath time for the dog. We still referred to him as 'the dog', as he didn't answer to anything we called him. All we could tell was he had some reaction to words with a 'B' at the start. It was one of the topics of conversation the day before. We all tried to think of dog names starting with 'B'. It was hilarious, but fruitless.

We lined up on the bank of the creek, shampoo bottles and soap in hand. It made sense for all of us to have a bath at the same time, and it was suggested that if we did, he might take the whole idea better.

The guys started it. They stripped down to their undies and waded in. We girls followed suit and before we knew it the dog was in too. If anyone had said two weeks ago I'd be bathing in my underwear with a bunch of guys, I would have thought them mad. But I did, and I didn't really give it a thought. It's alright for someone like Louise, who has a figure most men drool over, and two weeks of hiking has done her nothing but good, but for the rest of us, we don't do it easily. It was different with these guys, as we'd become close. We'd hiked, eaten, slept, and even toileted within a stone's throw of each other through all this, and being undressed in front of them didn't matter a bit. Besides, one advantage of having girls like Louise and Paula around is that once they strip off, I become invisible.

With my saucepan in hand, I took a breath and headed for where Kieran was standing knee deep in the water, holding onto the dog's collar. As I filled the saucepan, the dog saw me and knew immediately what I was up to. Acting like it was a game, he bolted straight over Kieran, knocking him flat, and he ran around us in the water. We were all trying to call him closer, but he wasn't having any of it. He just kept running around us barking until he wore himself out, and he stood there on the opposite side of the creek with his tongue hanging out, looking at us.

We were all soaked from the splashing, so we gave up and decided to just have our baths, figuring at least *some* of his smell would have washed off. When we were all busy washing ourselves, he must have figured the game was over, so he just flopped down with his head and neck above the water. Over the next few minutes, he slowly crawled his way along the bottom to end up alongside Amy. She was also sitting in the water and looked nervous. "It's all right Amy, he's not going to hurt you... It looks like he wants to make friends," Kieran said.

Amy reached out and patted him on the head tentatively, and then withdrew her hand. The big dog didn't move but turned towards her panting, his tongue out the side and that *almost-smile* on his face.

"Maybe he'll let you wash him, Amy?" laughed Kieran.

Amy had her shampoo bottle with her, so she poured some into her hand before throwing the bottle on the bank and began washing her hair, then she reached over with her soapy hands and did the same to the back of the dog's head. It worked!

Louise went and sat beside the dog and did the same thing, before you knew it, he'd stood up and let all the girls shampoo him from front to back. He just lapped up the attention. Louise reached under and undid his collar, which he was *very* interested in; God knows what he could smell on it. She gave it a good scrub while Amy washed his neck. Each time Amy gave his neck a good scrub, the dog's hind leg would start paddling in the water, which was seriously funny.

After a couple of minutes of scrubbing, Louise stood up with the collar in hand and yelled triumphantly. "It's Bruce!" The dog's ears pricked up immediately. Yep, that was his name; Louise had found it written inside the collar under all the dirt. We all cheered and the dog, now known as Bruce, got all excited again and took off around us all splashing and barking. The whole thing was actually a lot of fun, and it was some great bonding time with him.

The upside is, he now smelt a whole lot better. Still not great... But better.

I have to say I also felt a lot less nervous around him now. I'd seen him behaving like a stupid puppy so some of his *tough guy* facade was gone. I think Amy felt the same, later that day I saw him brush past her, and I saw her hand come out and give him a stroke as he went past. It was a small, but significant gesture.

Late that afternoon, Kyle and Amy weren't feeling well. Kieran said he felt a little off but was ok and Jared called a halt for the day at a nice spot alongside a creek, just in case. Lucky he did as by dinnertime all three said they didn't want to eat, which didn't bode well. I instructed them all to drink plenty of water and rest. By maybe nine that night, both Kyle and Amy began throwing up, not just a little sick, but violently, almost projectile vomiting. With their stomachs empty, it was a case of the law of diminishing returns, after the bile came up, they simply had nothing left to give but the violent contractions continued. The diarrhoea began which was equally as severe with gut wrenching cramps and a complete lack of control, whatever they had it was a pretty nasty bug.

Kieran was still a little under the weather, but his system seemed to be coping with it so far.

I tried to get the other two to drink but there was no way anything stayed down before it was violently ejected. David joked with Kyle about his vomiting. "Keep going mate, one or two more and you'll get that lung up."

Kyle tried to laugh but groaned instead. "Nah I think that's already come out the back end mate."

But as it kept going and I think David was getting as concerned as I was. The vomiting didn't stop. Amy simply didn't have the reserves to cope with this kind of illness, after a day's hike she would have already been dehydrated, so the vomiting and diarrhoea quickly took her to *severe* dehydration.

I wanted to give them some anti nausea medication but there was no way they could have kept it down long enough to absorb even a little of it. By maybe two or three in the morning, Kyle's vomiting had started to subside. He was able to take in and hold down some water, long enough for him to have absorbed some of it anyway.

Amy on the other hand was now in a pretty bad way. Her breathing was rapid, as was her heart rate; she was also beginning to get quite vague and confused. This was getting serious. We'd moved her onto a sarong near the fire so I could see better and as we did so, David made a suggestion.

"You know, Doc, on the boats if someone is too seasick to swallow a tablet you have to stick it up the back passage."

"I can't see why that wouldn't work," I replied. "But nothing is staying in there either really. I don't know how long it would take to be absorbed. She's getting dangerously dehydrated, but without an IV drip, I don't know how to get fluids into her."

David thought for a moment and said, "You know a yachty once told me a story about a family who sunk out at sea and ended up in a life raft for like a month, and the mum, who was a nurse, gave them all enemas with the crappy rainwater that had been contaminated with salt n stuff. Saved their lives apparently."

"Of course! Jesus, David you're a genius!" I exclaimed and raced over to give him a hug.

Again, I'm not a hugger, but it was very appropriate given he may have saved Amy's life.

I turned to the others and said, "I need a hose and a container of water as quickly as we can."

The others scrambled to find something, and I went to Amy's backpack to get some electrolytes. From my studies I remembered that the absorption of water in the rectum was a form of osmosis. The body naturally does this to remove water from the faeces before it's expelled. You needed salts and/or sugars, for the water to be absorbed through the wall. It had to be the right mix, which I had no idea about. Too much or too little and it doesn't work. I vaguely remembered it was nine grams of salt per litre of water to make saline but given where we were and the equipment we had, mixing it accurately was unlikely.

I found a sachet of electrolytes and decided to take a punt on it being pretty close to right once diluted properly.

Jared pulled a clear hose from his backpack. It had a rope running through it and the hose was there to make it more comfortable as a handle. It was about ten millimetres in diameter and maybe four hundred long, perfect. Amy had a few pouches of high-energy soups, which held about a quarter of a litre and the hose fit the nozzle with a bit of effort. Keen not to waste the high-energy soup, as Amy would need it later. I got Jared to empty it into his pannikin and fill the pouch with boiled but cooled water. "As close to body temp as you can get," I said.

I spoke to Amy, to tell her what I wanted to do, but she wasn't responsive, she was just still dry retching with her eyes closed. My decision was made for me. *Primum non-nocere.* What would happen if I did nothing? Amy was going to die.

She could hate me for it tomorrow, but for now, I had to do what I had to do.

David helped me position her on her left side with her right leg bent up, it seemed to be the easiest way and it would point the rectum downwards and hopefully hold the water in better.

With the pouch filled with water and electrolytes I attached the hose and stopped. I couldn't insert it dry. "I need some sort of lubricant," I said. Everyone scrambled to look for something and it was Louise who suggested antiseptic cream. "That'll do," I said holding out the end of the hose. She found the tube and squeezed some on. I took a deep breath and went for it. I had to time the insertion between her stomach contractions as she tried to vomit again and again.

The hose went in fairly easy, and I was careful to make sure it was past the sphincter muscle, but not too far.

I won't lie, it was messy, but at that point it was absolutely necessary. It was spat out twice before I finally got it into position and I asked for some tape to tie the hose in place in case it slipped out, then as I watched with some satisfaction, the pouch slowly emptied.

It didn't take long before I asked for the pouch to be refilled. I didn't know how much to put in there, or what would happen if I over did it but I figured a litre would probably fit ok in the large intestine, so I'd stop at that and wait for any improvement. I asked for one of the anti nausea tablets to be crushed and added to this second pouch. My crack trauma team was an absolute marvel and couldn't have been more helpful. I asked... They delivered.

This pouch went at about the same rate, and when it was empty, I had it refilled with a crushed paracetamol tablet for her fever.

The third didn't go as fast, so I handed it to Louise to hold up and just watched Amy closely.

I listened to her heart rate with the stethoscope. Talk about imposter syndrome, I felt such a fraud using the doctor's stethoscope, but I actually knew what I was looking for and miraculously after about fifteen minutes, I heard it. Her heart rate steadied and her breathing improved. She was dry retching less and some of the colour was returning to her face.

It was working! The third pouch emptied and was refilled. It had been about thirty minutes since the first pouch went in, so that was about three quarters of a litre in half an hour and her large intestine seemed to be full, as she was taking it much more slowly.

Her condition was really improving fast and I considered whether I should stop the treatment but decided to keep going until she was able to sit up and drink herself.

At about the forty-five minute mark she started to become responsive, and I told her what I'd done.

"You stuck a what, where?" she asked, quite vaguely.

"I'm sorry Amy but it was all I could do," I said.

"It's ok," she said and drifted off again for a moment before stirring and reaching back with her hand and groping aimlessly trying to remove it. I took her hand to stop her getting a hold of the hose.

"Not yet Amy. Just a bit longer, wait until you can drink for yourself ok."

She grunted and drifted off again. She didn't stir for another fifteen minutes, but when she did, she was vastly improved. I explained again what I'd done, and she just giggled before realising everyone else was there. "You guys saw!" she said groggily.

Everyone laughed.

"It's ok Amy, I was discrete," I lied.

I was purely concerned with saving her life. Her modesty was not even in the picture for me, but she didn't need to know that.

I gave everyone the one-sided head movement to ask them to look away while I removed the hose. Once removed, I turned to Kyle and Kieran while holding it up. "How are you guys feeling?" I asked.

They spoke over each other quickly. "Nah all good thanks." "Fit as a bull, could hike all night."

I laughed. "Cowards."

I had no problem getting anyone to drink after that night. All I had to do was say, "You're looking dehydrated," to make anyone chug half a bottle of water.

Jared carried Amy down to the creek and I washed her off, which she complained about, but it really had to be done. When we brought her back, we sat her between Julia's knees so she could lean back against her chest while Julia leaned back on a rock. She was able to drink small sips of water before resting her head on Julia's arm and dozing again.

The whole ordeal had been pretty taxing on her physically and she looked exhausted. The others were well on their way to recovery and strangely, Kieran only had a very mild case of it. He said he'd, "Had a little spit" earlier but he was fine, I suspect he's got the immune system of a tank.

"Doc, I've had every tropical bug there is, if there's one I haven't met, I probably know its cousin well."

I had to laugh at that, as he was probably right, he may have already met the cousin of this bug and it's given him some resistance to it.

As for where it came from, it remains a mystery. All three had eaten different meals, were drinking different batches of boiled water, and hadn't shared cooking or eating implements. Why they got it and nobody else is a question I simply can't answer. One of the mysteries of the forest I guess.

I ordered all drinking water chucked and fresh water boiled. I reminded everyone about hand washing with soap after toileting and to be careful to wash hands before eating. That's all I could do.

When I went to the creek to wash up, the water was freezing but I had to brave it and I told myself there was a warm fire to return to. To my surprise, on my return I was greeted with a big hug from Jared with a kiss on the forehead. "You just saved Amy's life...You're amazing Jess," he said.

One by one, the others came and did the same, each with something nice to say.

I can't tell you what that felt like, Amy's recovery was thanks enough for me, but that show of support from all these people I'd cared about... Well ok, I got a bit emotional.

▼

We spent two more days camping there. I wanted Amy to be one hundred per cent fit before we asked her to start hiking again. She was much improved, but her clothes looked like they were still hanging on a clothes hanger. She was stick thin and her face looked gaunt. She had the heart of a scrub bull, but the physique of a sparrow and I really needed to make sure she gained some more weight.

To try to build up body fat, instead of eating larger meals which was hard for her, I asked that she eat more often. I suspected that wasn't the last stomach bug we would encounter, and she really needed something in reserve for the next one. With that in mind, I cleaned the hose and packed it away for future use, at least until we could find something more suitable.

When we set off on day three, the hiking was fairly easy; I think Jared was pacing us to suit Amy. We were hiking for a couple of hours when we heard a vehicle outside the forest. It wasn't the first one we'd heard since the convoy came through, but it was the closest.

We crept down to a small ridge and peered through the foliage to see what it was. We could see a house about three hundred meters away and the vehicle, an army Jeep pulled up to it. A man came out of the house holding a rifle, which he was pointing at the Jeep. Two figures got out of the car holding sticks about a meter long. They were Lizards! Just like we'd seen in online videos, they were similar to us but with bizarrely long legs and arms with a very short body. They wore a belt across their chest, but nothing else. The passenger lizard simply raised his stick to waist height and WHOOMPH. The man was blown several meters backwards and lay still. Bruce barked at the noise causing the Lizards to look up. Kieran did his best to keep the dog quiet, to the point of holding his mouth closed which Bruce didn't like. He kept trying to shake Kieran's hand off while whining.

The passenger went into the house, at the same time a woman came running out the back door holding a child in her arms and heading for the forest. My heart leapt into my mouth with worry for her. We heard two more muffled Whoomphs before the Lizard emerged at the backdoor and fired at the woman. WHOOMPH, and she fell to the ground. He walked back through the house, emerging at the front door, walking past the body on the ground without giving it a glance, he got back into the vehicle, and they left.

We all leapt to our feet to go down there but Jared stopped us. "We can't all go blundering in there. The Lizards might be watching. Jess, you'll have to go in case there are survivors. Kieran, wanna go or stay here and I'll go?"

"I'll go," he said. "I'll grab any weapons they have too."

"Right, the rest of us will make our way down to the edge of the forest at the back of the house. Let's go."

Kieran bolted off down the hill with me struggling to keep up. When we reached the bottom, I went straight for the woman with the child and Kieran headed for the house. When I reached her, I saw she had burst both eardrums and the child had burst one, but amazingly they were both breathing! She'd fallen partly on the child, which was a little girl of maybe five years old. I pulled the woman off her and felt for any broken bones in the child, but she seemed fine. The woman was dressed in shorts and an old T-shirt, which had ridden up her back to reveal red, inflamed skin. I noticed the same swelling on the child's lower legs and a little on one arm. When I remembered she was being carried with her legs either side of her Mum and her arms around her neck, it made sense that whatever that weapon was, it had hurt the child too.

It was our first actual sighting of the aliens; we'd seen them online and on television but never in person. And we'd just watched them kill someone in cold blood.

The child started to regain consciousness and was whimpering a little. I tried to soothe her but as she began to fully comprehend what was happening, she started crying. She looked for her mother and when she found her, she crawled over and began telling shaking her mum's shoulder and saying, "Mum, wake up, Mum!"

I tried to explain that her mum might sleep for a while longer, and then realised everything I'd said, the child probably didn't hear. Aside from the blown eardrum, her good ear would be ringing loudly.

I spoke up and she jumped with the realisation I was there. I did my best to calm her, but she was quite fearful of me.

Her mum started showing signs of waking up, so I focussed on her for a moment. I waved to her with a smile to show her I was there and then showed her my black doctor's bag. She nodded vaguely as though she understood, and I grabbed the small torch from the bag and when she sat up I checked her for concussion. I didn't need Jared to confirm this one. She was severely concussed. I tried to check the little girl, but she was having none of it. All she wanted was Mum, so I didn't press the point.

I heard Kieran approach from behind me and of course his shadow, Bruce. The little girl took one look at the big man and his enormous dog and squealed, trying to bury herself in her mother's neck. I thought that was a pretty fair response and discounted any major brain trauma.

"How are these two?" he asked, smiling at them.

"Concussed but they'll recover. What did you find?"

He said nothing, so I turned to look at him and his expression said a thousand words.

"Best get the others down here if it's safe," I said, returning my attention to the mother and daughter.

"Will do, Doc," he said and called the dog to come with him as he walked away.

I smiled at the little girl and remembering to speak loudly I said, "He's just a big cuddly bear really."

She kind of smiled slightly at the mention of a cuddly bear but was still very suspicious of me.

The mother started to come round fully and became quite upset. She was starting to remember what happened and began asking questions, ones I didn't have an answer for. Like what happened to Jason and Karen. I didn't know who they were but guessed they were inside. She tried to get up, but I stopped her. She obviously wasn't hearing well so I made hand gestures that told her I had to check her and her daughter out. I needed to buy more time before the others arrived.

I pulled out the stethoscope and checked both mother and daughter. I wasn't listening for anything in particular, I truly didn't know what I'd be looking to find, but they submitted to it and that was all that mattered.

Out of the corner of my eye I saw Jared and the others approaching. "These are my friends," I said. "They are good people."

The woman nodded like she understood.

Kieran must have filled Jared and the others in on what he found, as everyone seemed to have a job to do.

A few sat with me making a fuss of the little girl, while the others went into the house. The woman was still talking about Jason and Karen, none of the others said anything, but their avoidance of the subject told me as much as Kieran's expression did. I told her the guys were inside and they will do what they can. Well, that was the wrong thing to say. She suddenly leaped up off the ground to go and find Jason and Karen.

I tried to stop her, but I couldn't.

With her little girl in her arms, she ran back to the house where Jared met her at the door. I followed but was a few paces behind. Jared's face was all the woman needed to see, she stopped abruptly in front of him and then burst into tears. I caught up and hugged her, trying to console her in any way I could. She was distraught.

The others had caught up too and walked the woman away from the door, so I had the chance to ask, "Is there anything I can do in there?"

He just shook his head and said. "No, Jess, nothing can help them... We'll wrap them up and start digging graves. Is she going to be ok?"

"She doesn't know anything yet, but she can guess, she's quite distraught. I'm not really qualified for this."

"None of us are. We can only do our best," he said, before he turned and went back inside.

I went back to the woman, Julie had the little girl in her lap, hugging her and rocking her back and forth.

The woman looked at me and asked. "Are they... ok?"

I shook my head. "I'm sorry."

She let out a wail and started sobbing uncontrollably. It went on for another minute before she asked. "And Bob... the man... is the bastard dead?"

I didn't know what to say. I assumed he was her husband.

"You mean the man out the front?" I asked, a bit unsure.

"Yeah, tell me that prick is dead," she said angrily.

"Yes, he's dead," I said.

"Good, I hope he *rots* out there."

It was pretty clear I didn't understand who everyone was in this household, and I didn't want to upset her further by asking. I figured it would all make sense at some point.

I got up and went to find Jared but he was already on his way to find me. "We've found some shovels; we'll start digging on the other side of the shed so she doesn't see," he said quietly.

"I think the guy out the front isn't family. She hates him and I'm not sure he should be buried with the others," I told him.

"Well, that's interesting...Makes some sense, he's a lot older than she is. No idea on what the story is?"

"Not yet. But she hopes he rots out there."

"Oh...Well I'm happy to respect her wishes, one less grave to dig I guess." He shrugged.

I had to ask. "What happened to the ones inside?"

He paused and looked at me before answering, finding the right words, or really not wanting to say I couldn't guess, but he eventually said simply. "They killed the other two kids, Jess."

"Oh my God," I said feebly.

Past his shoulder I saw the other guys start coming out the door and they went straight to the rainwater tank around the side of the house. Their hands were bloody and their faces grave. What a terrible sight it must have been.

I'd never seen anything like that, and the others were dealing with it while we were outside. Of all the people I could have ended up running with, I was so glad it was our group.

I went back to the woman and her child. I felt I had to be doing something useful, while the others were dealing with such horror. The child seemed to be recovering; I doubt she fully understood what had happened. The mother on the other hand was almost becoming catatonic. She was barely responsive when I spoke to her. I think the emotional shock was just too much for her. I checked her pulse and it was normal, so at least she wasn't going into physical shock.

I told her, as gently as I could, that we were going to have to bury the people inside. It was met with more wailing which upset the little girl who had started to settle with Julia.

There was no other way that I knew; I had to tell her what was happening. I was certain she knew of course, but each time it was spoken out loud, it made it all the more real for her.

It was awful for all of us.

The boys started digging the grave. They dug one wider one instead of two and took it in turns on the shovels. Determined to do our bit we girls each took a turn but we just slowed them down. Feminists to the bone we may be, but they were stronger and more practiced at using a shovel than we were.

When the grave was finished the boys brought out the bodies to a fresh wave of wailing from the woman. They'd wrapped them in sheets and quilts as best they could, but the blood had soaked through, and they were an awful sight.

The funeral service was better than the one we gave Tony. We took a lot from the one we gave Dr Jacobs' wife, so made less of a mess of this one, but I was already seeing far too many funerals as far as I was concerned.

As per instructions from the woman, we left the man out front to rot. I was certain there was a story to be told about that but left it for another time to ask her.

With the funeral over we convinced the woman to come with us and I finally found out her name. It was Carol and her daughter was Kinshasa. Well Kieran decided that it was a mouthful, so called her Kini. It stuck and the mother didn't mind, as her brother and sister called her that.

We'd grabbed what we could from the house, which really wasn't much. I suspect they would have been in real trouble in a few days when the food ran out anyway.

Kieran grabbed the rifle and found a box of bullets to go with it so he was happy. It was a high-powered hunting rifle, capable of bringing down a pig and that meant more food for all of us.

Once we were organised we headed off. Hiking through the forest was now a lot slower with a five year old and after an hour or so she was tired and grizzly. She'd had a pretty traumatic day so it was agreed we'd make camp when we came across a good spot.

When we did find a campsite, it was alongside a small creek strewn with boulders and a nice flat area beside it. The boys found a tent for Carol and her daughter in the shed, so they had somewhere to sleep, and they shared a sleeping bag.

I noticed during our hike that Bruce was quite intrigued by the little girl. He rarely took his eyes off her the whole time we were hiking. To a point where I got a little worried about whether he saw her as *bite-sized*. When we were sitting around the campfire that night, he gradually worked his way around to sit beside her. I watched him closely and motioned Kieran to do the same. She was just staring at the fire, lost in her own thoughts, I guess. Bruce wasn't doing anything either, he was just sitting and looking at the fire. After about fifteen minutes he craned his neck to steal a sniff of her arm and then sat bolt upright and motionless, pretending like nothing had happened. Both Kieran and I chuckled at the sight.

Kini glanced at him but did nothing. A few minutes later he bent down and ever so gently, licked her hand where it rested on the rock.

She squealed and giggled, pulling her hand back and Bruce's tail wagged like crazy. She put her hand back and a moment later, he did it again to even more giggles.

It seemed Bruce had won another heart and the next morning the two were inseparable. No matter how hard the hiking, Bruce was there as a hand hold for Kini. It was amazing to watch this massive dog, be so gentle and caring to such a small person.

Often, she would piggyback on one of the guys' backs to save her legs, someone would take the guys pack and he was able to carry her for some distance, before someone else took over. We tried sitting Kini on Bruce's back and he thought that was just great, but Kieran voiced concerns that if Bruce spotted a pig, he might bolt with Kini aboard, so we scrapped the idea and went back to piggybacks.

Kieran was another challenge for Kini. He was the big scary guy she saw when she first came to. It took almost all the first day before she would go anywhere near him. I could see Kieran was hurt by it. He'd mentioned before that he had a heap of nephews and nieces he loved dearly. He obviously liked kids. But by day two after a few jokes and games with Bruce, he was a rock star in her eyes and she couldn't get enough of him and Bruce.

Having Kini with us was such a breath of fresh air for us all, she was such a delight to be around, and I'm certain she stole a little of each of our hearts.

Carol, her mum, was still quiet and a mere ghost of a person, wracked by her grief at having lost two of her children. I suspected it would take some time before she felt remotely normal, if ever.

A couple of days after Carol and Kini joined us they'd gone chasing freshwater prawns in the creek in the afternoon.

Jared and Kieran started discussing the alien weapons and what we knew about them. "They seem to be limited by range," Kieran said. "The first shot was to that guy, he was maybe five meters away and killed him stone dead. The shot that hit Carol and Kini was maybe ten, twelve meters away and only knocked them out, giving them both bruising and burst eardrums"

"I guess the ones in the house were close range," Jared said in a solemn tone. There was a quiet murmur of agreement from David who had also gone in there.

Louise grunted with frustration and said, "What is it with you guys? Why won't anyone say what was in there? You guys being heroes and protecting us poor defenceless women from bad things? Give me a break. You don't need to protect-"

Kieran stood and said, "I kill and gut things for a living, Lou. I'd have happily skipped what I saw in there, any day." And he walked away.

When Kieran was out of earshot Jared said, "Kieran couldn't wrap them up on his own. He included as few people as he could, because he didn't want anyone else to see it. He wasn't protecting you because you're weak… he was protecting you because he cares. He had the bodies covered before we went in. He told us not to look at them."

I could see Jared a bit angry with Louise for making him relive it. "You want to know what he saw? Really?"

"Yes," she said with a hint of trepidation.

"Right, anyone who doesn't want to hear this go for a walk."

Amy, Julie, and a couple of the guys left the area. When they'd gone, he began.

"Ok, Kieran told me about it. He had to vent, and I listened. One of them had a hole through the middle about the size of a basketball; he used his hands to demonstrate the size and placement of the hole. "It was almost cut like a serrated biscuit cutter, he could see the kid's insides as plain as day, and it was spread all over the wall which is what I saw. She was maybe ten years old."

I could see speaking about it was upsetting him, but he went on. "The other one had its head and neck cut off." He drew a half circle from shoulder blade to shoulder blade. "Same size hole just in a different place. That one put a hole through the wall and sprayed blood all over the room, even the ceiling fan. It was a boy, maybe twelve. Now, these were kids, Louise, not nameless adults... Little kids! Kieran said he could see the terror still on the girl's face!" He swallowed hard and continued, "You should *thank* Kieran for sparing you that sight... and pull your bloody head in."

He got up and stormed away, presumably to cool off. I'd never seen him that kind of angry before. I guess everyone has their limits.

Arguments were rare amongst our group, and this was the most heated I'd seen. Louise deserved what she got, and to give her credit, she took it on the chin. She was quiet for some time after that, and she later apologised to both Jared and Kieran.

Most of the next day went without incident until we climbed a ridge close to Tully and smelt wood smoke. Bruce's ears pricked up and he left out a deep woof. Kieran had been working with him on being quiet, and it seemed to be working, but not always.

Then I heard it too, I could hear kids playing.

Jared decided we should go down into the valley and say hi. It was nearly time to camp anyway; Kini was tired and needed rest.

As we got closer, Bruce took off in the direction of the sounds and Kieran tried to call him back. I heard the voices turn to frightened and there was a male voice giving orders. Jared yelled out, "It's ok he's with us!" He and Kieran jogged ahead and plunged through some thick scrub. By the time I got there, a very unhappy looking man held Bruce and the two guys at gunpoint. There were about a dozen people there including men, women, and children. It looked like a permanent camp with large tarps strung up and a fully swept dirt area around the campfire that consisted of big rocks placed in a circle.

Kieran had hold of Bruce's collar, Jared was explaining that we were friendly, and the dog is harmless.

When Carol came through the bush one of the women yelled, "Carol!"

"Beverly! How are you?" she replied.

The woman brushed past the man with the gun and embraced Carol in a big hug. She began to chat excitedly about when she'd last seen her and what she'd been doing since then. The man lowered his gun.

Introductions were made and the man with the gun was Greg, he was unofficially the leader of the group of families.

All the kids began to emerge again and eyed Bruce warily. Kini just stood beside him with her arm slung over his back, unsure of what to do next, so Julie took her hand and said, "Let's go make some friends." They walked over to the other kids and Julie went into full preschool teacher mode. She really was amazing around the little ones.

Greg told Jared that their supplies were low, but we were welcome to stay if we brought our own food. He also said they were pretty much living on native tubas and bananas they raided from a nearby farm.

When Kieran heard that he said, "I'll be back shortly, where is this farm exactly?"

When Greg told him, Kieran dumped his pack on the ground, slung the rifle over his shoulder, and took off with Bruce leading the way.

Carol mentioned to Beverly that I had medical training. I'm thankful she didn't call me a doctor, but that meant I was busy for the next two hours with a long list of ailments that were thankfully, easily treatable.

I was just finishing up with the last patient when there was a commotion at the far end of camp; Kieran was back with a pig over each shoulder. "Can't come to a party empty handed," he grinned.

He was an instant hit with these people who hadn't seen meat for weeks. They'd run when the bombing started and hadn't been back. The bombs hit the dam on the Tully River, and they just made it out in time, before the town flooded. The following bombs meant going back was pointless. When I thought about how long it had actually been, I guessed it was about three weeks since the invasion. It felt like months. I could have turned my phone on to check, but I really didn't need to know that badly.

After dumping the pigs Kieran was breathing hard and sweating profusely. That must have been a real struggle to carry two pigs like that all the way back, and he looked exhausted, but pleased with himself.

He was covered in blood, so one of the women took him to where a black poly pipe had been set up to supply water under gravity feed from the creek; they had temporary showers set up with taps for each of the two cubicles made out of tarps. It was an ingenious set up really and showed they had little intention of moving.

The pigs were put on to roast, in their raids on the banana farm for fruit, they'd also raided the machinery shed for lengths of steel and were well set up with campfire implements.

Bruce got his obligatory pigs head and bones to chew on when we were done.

It was an interesting night getting to know these people. I got into a conversation with Beverly and Carol and found out that the guy, Bob, was some loser that just moved into her place, pretty much at gunpoint about a week or so after the bombing started. He'd made himself at home and he'd eaten most of their food, he was starting to get ideas about Carol and that's when the Aliens showed up.

As I listened to the stories from others in the group of what they'd lost, I thought about my family and hoped they were ok out of town on our cattle property. Being fifty kilometres out of town in a remote area wouldn't make them much of a target, at least not for now.

Compared to these people we'd had it pretty easy and much of that was thanks to the group we'd formed. Since Craig left it had been pretty good. I missed Paula but on the whole, we had a complete group. I didn't know what Carol's plans were, we never asked as she had enough on her plate. In the conversations we'd had I'd grown to like her, and Kini has become a real favourite for all of us. They were welcome additions to our world, and I hoped they stayed with us.

The next morning I was fortunate enough to have one of the other group's members show me which plants to dig up to get the tubas and how there are many ways to use bread fruit if we came across a tree in someone's yard. At least we could have something resembling vegetables, which we were all craving.

Kieran took a group of men to the banana farm to show them how to catch pigs, so it was a fair exchange of information, and judging by the hand gestures he was making when he returned, he was also passing on information about the alien weapons. That was something relevant to everyone.

The next day was time for us to go. Carol decided that she'd stay with these people, as there were other kids and someone she knew. We understood, but nobody was more disappointed than Kieran. He'd grown quite fond of Kini and she felt the same. There were tears from the little girl as she parted with Kieran and Bruce. The big dog took being hugged and kissed with his usual calm, gentle way with her. He had a bit of a fan club with the other kids as well and they all took turns hugging him. He didn't understand what was going on, but he smiled and wagged his tail with all the attention.

With our goodbyes said, we left to head towards the coast. We'd all kind of lost track of *why* we were heading to Mission Beach in the first place. I guess it was a destination when we had none, and now we were almost there. I have to be honest I was a little excited, having spent weeks walking to get there.

One of the reasons Jared chose this place was that aside from crossing a few roads, we could go from the mountains to the coast, without leaving the forest. With the Lizards tripping around in cars now, we simply couldn't afford to cross large stretches of farmland anymore.

This was our first real stretch of flat land forest and the change was dramatic. We were used to the hills with mostly open understory and easy going. But by halfway we were into paperbark swamp areas, with their frustrating undulations underfoot which are caused by the wet season floods, leaving deposits of clay as sediment. It was dry now being mid September, but the mosquitoes and sand-flies were just maddening. The sand-flies were tiny little black dots that left a red welt the size of a five-cent piece. They particularly liked my ears, and they must have glowed red by the time we were done hiking for the day. They burned like they were on fire! I ended up wrapping my sarong around my head, which was hot, but at least kept some of them out. Everyone was doing overtime on the machete, each taking a turn and almost all had blisters by the late afternoon. The blade was maybe sixty centimetres long and I struggled to even swing it properly, let alone do anything useful. I tried it but there was a real danger of me doing myself an injury, both in my wrist and arm, or one of my legs on the follow through from a swing that often didn't connect. I handed it back after a couple of minutes to a very relieved Jared who said with a smile, "It's a big, heavy blade for small wrists, Jess. Don't feel bad. You're built for *smarter* work."

I didn't feel bad, he was right. Amy was also excused from that job, but Louise and Julia made us girls proud.

The weather was already warm during the day, and down here in a dry swamp, it was even hotter. There was no breeze, only what we made when we walked, which was very little. Much of what we walked though was undergrowth, so it made for very slow going.

By the end of the day, we were exhausted and ready to camp, but the idea of camping in this mozzie-infested swamp didn't appeal to any of us, so we pressed on.

There was a full moon, which rose just after dark, so we had some light to walk by, and being dark, we decided it was safe to walk on the road. Jared adjusted our course to meet with the road into town. And it was a blissful release to step out onto the road and feel the cooler night air.

We made much better time on the road, and by midnight we'd camped beside the town water supply tank, near the outskirts of town. It was on a hill overlooking the houses and when we climbed the ladder to the top of the tank, we could just see the ocean and Dunk Island in the moonlight. It looked so beautiful, especially because we'd walked so far and been through so much to get here. There were hugs all round as we quietly celebrated our achievement.

It wasn't the most secure campsite, so we decided to skip the campfire and just go to bed. We tucked our tents in the bush behind the tank and slept like logs until the sun came up. As always, Jared was up early, but he didn't have the fire going and coffee ready as usual.

When I came out of my tent he said quietly, "Good morning, best we stay quiet. I've had a look around, we're pretty exposed."

I nodded and began quickly packing up my tent. The others started to rise and Jared said something similar to them, so everyone packed their gear quietly and got ready to go. No dinner last night and missing out on coffee and breakfast this morning was a rough welcome to Mission Beach.

But when we emerged from the trees to cross the road, we saw the azure blue waters of the ocean and it was all forgiven.

Once across the road we followed a ridgeline that ran along the back of the town, well it was one town, called Wongaling Beach. Mission Beach was made up of four villages; the northernmost one was Bingil Bay. To the south of that are North Mission Beach, then Wongaling Beach, and lastly, South Mission Beach.

In truth, from the village of North Mission to the south, it's all the same beach, twelve kilometers of palm fringed, yellow sanded tropical beach. All with a view to Dunk Island just four kilometres off the coast and the rest of the 'Family Islands' extending to the southeast. It really was so beautiful.

The ridge was easier going than the swamp and the old logging tracks were at least flat ground. But we were all getting hungry so by mid-morning we decided to stop for something to eat. "Did anyone else notice we passed a big supermarket?" Kyle asked when we all sat down.

"Yeah, we did, I was thinking we'd find a good place to camp for a while and then do a raid on it tomorrow," Jared said.

"That sounds like a plan," said Kieran. "But chances are it's been cleaned out like Babinda. It's been what, three-four weeks since the bombing started? It'll have been cleaned out for sure."

Maybe," said Jared, "but it won't hurt to try, there's a chemist next door too, you never know what we'll find in there."

David spoke up with a mouthful of banana. "We need some fishing gear, hand lines will do, and a cast net. I'll feed us with that."

There was a chorus of "Hmmm seafood," before Jared said, "Right, well let's see what we can organise, everyone's got a boat around here, one of those might have something."

Once we'd finished our brunch we set off again. As we walked the ridge we came across several houses, some bombed, but some intact. We checked the intact ones but found just empty houses. They were beautifully maintained, but nobody was home, or had been home for a long time. They were just empty.

"Holiday homes of the rich and famous," said Jared. "Maybe visit once every two years, so there'll be no food in them."

We continued on, occasionally using one of the driveways of these places to save some time before heading back into the forest. Along the way we saw a couple of houses down on the flats that had been bombed but had boats in sheds and yards, so we decided we'd come back and check them for gear. At this point we just wanted to get somewhere we could make camp and relax.

Eventually we came to a good place, one that would do for now anyway. It was between two ridges with a flowing creek and close to the town jetty, jutting out into the ocean.

"Right," said Jared. "Let's make camp here and we'll work out what to do next."

We all flopped down. While today had become overcast, the days were quite warm now and the going in this coastal rainforest was tough. The wait-awhile vine was brutal. It's a plant that grows on the edges of clearings in the forest. It has a spiny stem and from the top, it sends out long tendrils with backward facing hook-like thorns about five millimetres long. They grab you as you walk past and if you don't stop, they will either cut you or break off in your skin. They tear your clothes and threaten to take your eye out if you brush past them. Running through them is like running through barbed wire. I spent a half hour with the antiseptic cream treating everyone's cuts and the blisters on their hands. Feet were the other worry; our boots were often wet and never got a chance to dry. Wet feet all day were starting to create problems. Tinea was the least of them. The wet skin is soft and easily torn, making blisters, which bled and invite infections.

Being the first time we'd actually camped with a plan to stay, I ordered all boots off and socks washed in the creek and dried by the fire. If we had to move, at least we wouldn't be hobbling on bad feet.

I also felt an itch at my waistline that was kind of strange. It *felt* strange. I took the opportunity to take a look and saw a red swelling and a small black/brown dot in a crater in the middle. Yay… it was a tick, but what made it worse, it was a paralysis tick. While feeding on a human or animal they secrete a toxin that affects the nervous system. While not very often lethal in adult humans, tick paralysis can make you very sick. I grabbed some tweezers and removed it, being careful to pull it straight out, so it didn't leave the jaws in the skin. I felt around for more but found none.

"Ok everyone, I've just found our first paralysis tick, we all need to check ourselves to see if we have any."

"What do they look like?" asked Amy.

I hadn't thought about people not knowing what they were. Where I lived with cattle and dogs, we all grew up knowing.

I showed her where I took the tick out and explained what it looked like and how it felt when you had one. She screwed up her face and showed me an itchy spot just at the back of her armpit. Yep, it was a tick.

I removed it and showed it to her, so she knew what to look for. Jared had one on his beltline, so Amy took a look at one still attached. Everyone else assured me they knew what to look for.

"So, are you from here or Brisbane, Amy?" I asked. I couldn't believe I actually didn't know. I remembered her dad lives in Brisbane but of all the things we'd chatted about, where she grew up wasn't one of them.

"Yeah, I grew up in Brissy. Dad wanted me to come up here to study because he likes it up here."

"But you get paralysis ticks down there, how did you not know about them?"

"Oh, I'd heard of them I guess, but never seen them. We didn't go anywhere you'd get them when I was growing up. Mum was from Thailand and hated the country; she never wanted to leave the city. If we went on holidays we went to cities and sometimes on boats, but never camping."

"Never camping?" I asked, astonished.

"Nope, never been camping. Sad isn't it," she laughed.

"But you never said anything Amy. You must have been totally lost when we set out."

"Yeah, a bit, but I just watched everyone else to see what to do, Kyle helped me put up my tent the first night, so after that it was ok."

"You're amazing," I said to her, and it was echoed around the group from those listening to the conversation.

"Not really... I actually like it." She shrugged and gave me a smile.

With the camp set up there was little to do but snooze the afternoon away and get clean in the creek. It felt strange to have nothing to do. We'd gotten used to hearing, "*Get some food into you... bit further to go today*" from Jared.

But he was fast asleep with his feet hanging out of his tent.

Kyle and Julie were away from the camp in deep discussion about something. They'd been spending a bit of time together lately. I thought I detected a hint of romance, but I have no idea where they would find the time, or the energy.

With nothing to do I pulled out the books to study. I was reading the more advanced ones now. _Symptoms and diagnosis of major illnesses_. Serious stuff I wasn't remotely qualified to use, but it was so interesting. I kind of regretted not doing the work and going to med school. I guess I was rebelling against the assumption I would become a vet, so we could *keep it in the family*'. What that meant was Dad wanted a free vet to call on. A Doctor wasn't much better, but a pharmacist? Not much need for one of them on the farm.

The day of rest came and went and after dinner we all went to bed with big plans for a sleep in.

It must have been around midnight when I heard the first drops of rain hitting my tent. It started gently and soon became a steady drumming on the nylon. I wasn't overly concerned, my tent was a good one and new, so I went back to sleep. But it didn't stop. I awoke after sunrise and it was still raining. I unzipped my tent flap and looked out. Across the camp I could see Jared and Louise's tents, both of them were looking back at me. We waved to each other and shrugged. What were we to do? We had been lucky so far to have no rain at all, but now it was here, we weren't prepared for it at all. We had nowhere outside our tents to sit without being in the rain.

I got dressed, happy to notice my clothes were still dry. *That'd suck if it leaked,* I thought. I was about to go outside when I thought better of it. These were my only dry clothes. In fact, they were my only clothes. So I took them off again and headed out in my underwear. The others saw me and did the same. We all met in the middle of camp, around our now very dead fire, and just laughed.

"What do we do now?" I asked over the sound of the rain.

Already soaking wet with water running down our backs causing involuntary shivers, we all shrugged. Jared grabbed the machete and said, "I'll be back." Before walking off towards the coast. David and Kieran went with him. Poor Bruce, having slept outside looked very miserable, he trailed along behind them.

I busied myself with my folding shovel, digging little trenches around each tent to keep the water from running under them. Kieran had a little stream running under his tent, so Louise and I moved it to a better spot. How we were going to have a fire in this weather was a mystery. What wood we had was now wet beyond any hope of a fire.

When the guys came back we were huddling under the best shelter tree we had around us and getting cold. They were carrying palm fronds, lots of them and set about making a shelter using a couple of long logs wedged between trees. The palm fronds laid across the logs on top of each other; with their stalks all at the top did an amazing job of keeping the water off. It wasn't a big area, maybe three meters by three but it was enough for us all to squeeze into and have a small fire for cooking. Of course, we needed some dry wood for that and that wasn't something anyone had ideas about…except me. Those books we've been carrying all had extra pages in them that weren't needed. I didn't care who published it or the author's credentials; those pages were coffee and breakfast.

I set about tearing the useless pages from a handful of books to get a fire started. We managed it but it wasn't easy, and it was almost lunchtime by the time we'd made coffee. We huddled together under our slightly leaky, but pretty effective shelter to drink our coffee.

Then the rain stopped as quickly as it started.

We all sat there for a moment looking out before Kieran broke the silence. "You can't be serious."

We all burst out laughing.

Mission Beach

*'Friendship is unnecessary, like philosophy, like art...
It has no survival value; rather it is one of those
things that give value to survival.' -CS Lewis*

It turned out Mission Beach was all we'd hoped for when we found some fishing gear in a boat outside a crushed house. David was happy and he set off for the beach to see what he could get. The rest of us decided to check out some of the houses to see if there were some tarps or something we could use. We'd learned a lesson from our cold wet morning and thought we'd best get set up for rain now we were semi-permanent camping. The clouds had cleared, and we heard aircraft do a few fly overs. There were a couple of explosions, but they were a long way off, so we were fairly relaxed.

We couldn't find any tarps, but we did find some short sheets of corrugated iron that we could use so we carried them back to camp. They made a great extra shelter area and those with leaky tents dragged them underneath. If it rained again at least we were a little prepared.

David returned to camp in the afternoon with a big mackerel fish for dinner, so he was certainly the man of the hour. Any change from what little was left of our dry food and pig, was a welcome relief.

The next morning we all headed off to the supermarket to see what was left. It was decided to try walking along the forest close to the beach to see if it was easier going than the ridge. It was to an extent. We were able to duck out onto the fourteen-kilometre long beach sometimes to avoid the worst of it and duck back in when we heard aircraft or vehicles. At one point a vehicle actually drove along the beach so we headed inland quite a bit to avoid them.

When we came across a creek we had to cross, which meant a knee-deep wade, Kieran refused. The creek was maybe five meters wide and full of dark water and a greenish scum floating on the surface. The trees arched over the top blocking out much of the sunlight.

"No bloody way guys, too crocy."

"Too what?" asked Louise.

"That creek *reeks* of crocs. No way I'm wading through that... Nup, we go around."

"Can't be more than knee deep. What crocs are going to live in there?" Peter asked.

"Anything up to five meters mate," Kieran told him.

"No way." Peter still looked dubious.

"Yes way, I hunt pigs around this kind of water all the time and I've lost a dog a year for the last three years to crocs. Down on the coast the aliens aren't the only kind of lizard we have to watch out for. You see water around here; you steer clear of it."

And he set off up the stream.

Peter called after him, "But we can see the bottom, we'd be able to see a croc."

"You'll never see the one that gets ya, Pete," Kieran said over his shoulder. He wasn't stopping to entertain any more discussion on the matter, and I took his resolve as a good reason to take him at his word. Maybe he was using this creek as an example to educate everyone, or there really was a good chance there was a croc in it, I didn't know and like everyone else, I just followed him.

When we rounded the top of the waterhole, we came across what looked like a track cut by someone else. It looked well used so we followed it and made much better time than cutting our own. We were maybe fifty meters along it when we had our first encounter with a Cassowary. I'd never actually seen one before; I was struck by how easily they move through the forest. They are a flightless bird, shorter than an Emu but much heavier, with beautiful red and blue colouring on its neck and glossy black, coarse feathers.

"Just stand still and let it pass," Julia told them all. The bird stood with its head held high and fluffed its feathers up. It was startled and immediately on the defensive. The bird stamped its huge feet with its three toes, the middle being over a hundred millimetres long. It can disembowel a person with one kick of its powerful leg. With us all standing still, the bird slowly calmed down and after a moment it headed off into the forest. Within seconds its black feathers just blended into the shadows and it disappeared. We all breathed a collective sigh of relief.

"You know those feet are almost exactly like the Velociraptor dinosaur feet," said Julia.

"I'd believe it," said David.

We continued along the track, which emerged at a housing estate that had been flattened by one of those shaped bombs. There were no undamaged houses on the edge of this one and whoever had cut the track, had cut a hole through the fallen trees to get through. Faced with a pile of rubble we followed the track for a while, weaving in and out of the damaged forest until we came to the main road. From there it was open with nothing but a few buildings and a six metre high statue of a Cassowary for cover. We could see the large concrete walls of the supermarket a few hundred meters away and decided to make a dash for it.

As we rounded the corner of the building, we could see the doors hadn't been smashed in, they were open. We bolted in to get under cover. Inside we stood with our backs against the wall panting and waiting for our eyes to adjust. We were standing in a large entrance with a Cafe off to one side and a very empty bottle shop on the other. The doors to the supermarket were also open but written on the glass in red paint were the words

"Only take what you need. Please leave some for others."

"Bloody hell, that's different," said Kieran.

"Reckon...let's go see if anyone actually read that and took it to heart," said Jared.

When we entered it was very dark. I'd brought my torch and shone it around. Yep, it looked like everyone had read it. There wasn't much left, but it certainly wasn't all gone.

"Let's see what dry food is left, guys. I'm going to see what tools and rope and stuff is there. Jess, did you want to check out the first aid stuff?" asked Jared.

"Yep. I saw a sign for a chemist shop at the end of the building we could check out too."

"Excellent, meet back here in five," he said and headed off.

We all met back in five minutes as agreed. Each with a few packets of something, Amy had found some dried peas and cans of tinned fruit which made my mouth water at the sight of it.

I'd found a few things like a box of sticky plaster and some iodine, a couple of bandages and gauze dressings. I also grabbed a bottle of vinegar and a small bottle of bleach for sterilising things. What I did find that was total bliss was some new undies and a pair of socks!

I took that message on the glass to heart. It was a completely different mindset from what we had, this small town had it so right. Looking after each other wasn't for just those in your group.

We had a fair bit of stuff left from our raid on the chemists in Redlynch. With our reduced numbers we had plenty, but I was still keen to check out the chemists to see what was there.

We put our stuff in our backpacks and headed out, a quick dash down the outside and we got to the chemists.

The front door had been smashed in. I guess community mindedness doesn't extend to druggies.

Inside, however, was in reasonable shape. The opiate drugs were of course gone, but most of everything else had at least a few left. Knowing this was here and likely to stay that way, I didn't try to stock up. I grabbed some tinea cream and some antiseptic cream. Both of which we needed, but everything else I left.

As we left the chemists, lead by David, he suddenly stopped causing a few of us to walk into his back in true slapstick comedy style. Looking around him I saw a man in his fifties, wearing grubby blue work shorts with no shoes or shirt, but with a shotgun pointed at us.

"Bin doing some shopping?" he asked.

"Yeah, just grabbing a few things we were short of," Jared replied, walking around David to face the man.

"Well let's see, turn around mate," he said. Motioning for Jared to turn around. Jared did as he was told. The man took a step forward and grabbed Jared's backpack and felt the weight.

He nodded and spoke. "Good to see you people doing the right thing."

He lowered his gun and added. "Seeyas." Before walking off around the side of the building.

"Now that's the most dedicated shopping centre security guard I've ever seen," Kieran said, laughing.

We left the supermarket and headed further south for a bit, just to see what else was around. After crossing an open paddock, we came across a school, which had the main building crushed, but the rest were intact. Across the road were Police, fire, ambulance, and emergency services buildings, all crushed. We decided to head towards the beach when James told us to stop. He'd wandered down between some buildings and found a small amphitheatre with whiteboards set up in a semicircle. On a couple of them were titles written, that said "<u>Lost and found.</u>"

And under that were people's messages looking for family members. There were so many it was heartbreaking. Lots listed names of people with "We're OK" But some of those had a red "X" written beside them. Someone was trying to keep this updated.

Jared and the other guys were focussed on one board in particular. "<u>Things we know.</u>" was its title.

Under it was information written in different handwriting for anyone to read, such as:

"Tully hospital gone, all the doctors were there."

"They don't bomb in the rain."

"Bombing runs are random now, stay safe everyone"

"Don't change anything. That's the things they bomb."

"They bomb boats, no reef trips anymore."

"No army jeeps when it's raining."

"Has anyone seen them at night lately?"

"This is what happens when we don't respect Mother Nature, the universe has spoken."

I didn't quite know what to make of that last one.

Kieran mumbled something about hippies and drugs as he started writing down what we knew of their weapons. It was definitely useful information and he signed it, as "Jared's group" while Jared wasn't watching.

"We'll come back here fairly often; I think it could be very useful," said Jared as he was walking out.

Just as we were leaving, we heard an aircraft and we had nowhere to go. There was rainforest across the road, but it was too late to make it. We had to just sit tight and hope they didn't choose this building to bomb. My heart was immediately racing; it was an awful feeling that reminded me of the first couple of days. I didn't miss that.

We heard some bombs, but none were close to us and when it was gone we breathed a sigh of relief and headed off towards the beach, with an ear out for vehicles.

We were exposed for this stretch and none of us felt good about it, especially when we stepped onto the beach and looked to the north and south. Kilometers of beach with palm trees and calm blue water stretched away as far as you could see in each direction.

The islands off the coast looked so idyllic I wondered if we could just live out our lives on one of them, safe from all that was going on around us. But lack of a boat was going to make that difficult and there'd be nowhere to run once you were on the island.

Jared decided we should head north, back to the camp to offload and maybe look through a few sheds for tarps on the way.

The trip back was uneventful; no vehicles meant we made much of the trip on the beach staying close to the trees, which made it a lot faster. Before too long we'd made it back to camp, fully expecting to be able to just flop down and start eating some of the things we'd just picked up, we were disappointed to find one of the bombs were dropped on our camp!

It had hit the roofing iron and crushed the tents under it. Some of the others showed damage, including mine, but were still intact. Of the tents that were destroyed, Kieran's and Julia's were beyond repair. The poles were shattered and had torn the material so bad that there was little that could be salvaged. The rest of the tents could be patched to make do.

"Well I guess that's what they meant on that whiteboard about not changing anything," said Jared. We all agreed.

"Lesson learned, but at least we weren't in them," James pointed out.

"Yeah, it could have been worse. But how do they know something changed?" asked Louise.

"Probably satellite or aerial photos, compare the images to look for changes. They're looking for people, it's a massive job to bomb every house on the planet, they bombed the major clusters, and now they just bomb the places that have changed... That would indicate people are alive there. It was probably the roofing iron they saw through the trees." said James.

It was an ugly thought. Yet more evidence their plan is to eradicate, not dominate.

"So why don't they just use thermal cameras to find people?" Amy asked.

"I think that maybe they don't have them. If you think about it, they're cold blooded. A thermal camera is useless to them so maybe they never developed the technology." James shrugged.

"So anyway, now we have a housing problem," said Jared. "Someone's going to have to share. Any volunteers?"

All those with complete tents put a hand up.

"And that folks, is why I love each and every one of you," said Jared, smiling.

Everyone laughed but we all knew what he meant.

I said. "Look, mine is one of the bigger tents, Kieran can bunk with me."

Given how much time Julia and Kyle were spending together it was obvious that she would move into his tent. She could have moved in with me but that meant Kieran moving in with someone else. He was a big guy, and all the other tents were just too small to take him and someone else.

It was settled, Kieran would bunk with me.

We tidied up the camp and got settled in for the night, hoping it wouldn't rain. We obviously needed to find another campsite. That was going to be tomorrow's job.

Dinner was amazing, fish and rice with peas and a banana as dessert. Sounds boring, but after what we'd been eating it was awesome!

Bedtime came and Kieran and I retired to what was now *our* tent.

I've mentioned before that Kieran was a big guy, but I never really appreciated *how* big until I had to share a small tent with him. No matter how far he pushed himself into the side of the tent, I felt like he was taking up most of it. I climbed out for a wee in the middle of the night and tripped over Bruce who was curled up at the door. This really wasn't my cup of tea. Plus, he smelled like a guy, not saying I smelled like roses, but I guess I was used to my own damp sweaty smell and guys smell different, not necessarily bad, just different. In the close confines of a small tent, it was almost overpowering. We were going to have to think of something better.

The next morning we had coffee and discussed our next move. We had to find another campsite, one with some kind of shelter for when it rains.

"Something with fly screens would be nice, these bloody March flies are driving me mad," Louise said as she slapped another one off her leg. The rain brought out the Marchies and they were savage. Those and the mozzies were driving us all mad.

"You know we could live in a house if we don't change anything," suggested Julia. We were all silent for a moment while we considered the idea.

"That's a big risk," said Jared.

"How about this for an idea, the info on that board said they aren't bombing at night. Have we heard any at night for a while?" asked James.

We all agreed that we hadn't.

"Well what about we stay in the forest during the day, sleep in a house at night, and be gone by sunrise each morning?"

There was a long pause while everyone thought about that. The idea of sleeping in a bed seemed like an impossible dream. Oh, how I missed a proper bed! But being anywhere near houses had become ingrained in us already as a dangerous idea.

Jared spoke first. "I think the idea isn't all bad, what does everyone else think?"

"I think it's pretty risky," said Kieran. "But by the look of it, so is camping. If we choose the right house, one that has forest up against it so they can't see us coming and going... and we change nothing... Maybe it can work. The wet season is coming, it's gonna get bloody wet for camping."

There was a murmur of agreement. It was a good idea, there were loads of houses like that around here, and if we changed nothing, it was probably less risky than camping.

After a brief discussion it was agreed that we would look for a house today and I must say it was exciting. It was a little like house hunting for a dream home you got for free, but to be honest a bed was top of my priorities, anything else was a bonus.

Jared checked his maps and decided that Bingil Bay was most likely to have something to suit. But it was a long walk to the supermarket, and it was also a long walk to where David was fishing. Our current campsite was pretty close to ideal, so we decided to search locally. In hindsight, we could have split up and covered more ground, but the idea was never raised. I guess we all felt safer together.

By lunchtime we'd found a suitable house, but by the looks of it, someone was already living there. It was strange to think there were others doing the same things we were.

We came across one place that had a solar system with batteries and a fridge that worked! James was concerned about being in a place with power. "There is a good chance they have sensors for that, ok for a visit but I think we shouldn't stay here."

It was funny how we'd all kind of taken on roles we were not really qualified for. James was settling into 'Alien expert.' I was 'Doctor,' Julia was 'Therapist,' Kieran was 'Hunter,' Jared was 'Leader,' David was 'Fisherman,' and the others were still developing theirs, I guess.

The house had food in the fridge but on closer inspection it was fresh, someone else's food. I tore a page from one of my exercise books and wrote a note.

Hi, We see you have found this working fridge too, we haven't touched your food. Do you mind if we put some things in it as well?

Thanks.

Jessica

Jared's group.

The "Jared's group" was Kieran's idea. I left it in the fridge held up by a sauce bottle.

We moved on and agreed we'd check back tomorrow.

Two doors down we found a suitable house. It was ideal. It had a long steep concrete driveway leading up to a two storey; timber pole frame house nestled in the forest. There was also a running creek beside the house where we could get water. There were four bedrooms, two of which had single beds and best of all; it had a working gas cooktop!

Louise came running out of the bathroom saying, "It has a toilet!"

We all laughed. It was such a foreign concept already.

"I wouldn't expect it to work," said Jared. Just then the toilet flushed, and Amy stepped out.

"Seems to," she said with a shrug.

Our new home was all we had hoped for. There were metal storm covers already in place over the windows, so we didn't need to worry about being seen when inside. Jared reminded us all again of the importance of not changing anything.

"Leave nothing outside, move nothing, and only go out when we have to. We come from the forest, and we leave by the forest, no exceptions. We come here at last light, and we leave at first light. All agreed?" he said.

We all agreed.

The excitement of having a proper sleep in a bed had improved everyone's mood and we went in search of buckets to fill the toilet and use for drinking. Kieran said the toilets might keep working because the house is on a hill. "If it's on town sewage it'll go down hill, at least till the system blocks up. If it's on a septic system it'll keep working, we just have to fill the thing with water each time."

That was all I needed to know. We had a toilet!

We found a heap of buckets in a garden shed a few houses away. We were all careful now to leave everything as we found it. If a door was open, we left it open and vice versa.

As night fell, we returned to our house, each filling a bucket on the way past the creek.

Kyle spotted a large rainwater tank under the house, he tapped the side and found it was full, so we had plenty drinking water. A quick hunt around and he found a hose, which he shoved onto the tap at the bottom of the tank and turned it on. "That's our showers taken care of." He smiled as the water ran from the hose.

With the number of us, and the number of beds, someone was going to have to share. Amy and I volunteered to share a double, Peter and Julia the other double and the rest took single beds.

"Don't you want to bunk with me anymore, Doc?" Kieran said, pretending to be hurt. "I thought we had a real thing going there. You know like a romance book, "The Hunter and the Doctor in the wilds of the Jungle." I read one of them once. Holy hell it had me blushing! I want some of that!" he said, eyes wide.

We all laughed, and I couldn't stop laughing long enough to give him a comeback... Sometimes he just cracks me up.

Dinner was awesome. Jared and Peter cooked. David had opted to go fishing in the afternoon and caught two large Mackerel, which we fried up with some rice and dried peas. It was too much for one meal, but we gave it a shot. We all took turns in the shower and sat down just before bed with a small glass of wine we found in the cupboard. It was so nice to feel civilised for a change, all sitting in chairs or on something, not squatting in the dirt. I found some clothes in the wardrobe and borrowed a nice summer dress, which was a size too big, but it was nice to have a change from my grubby clothes.

So, fed, showered with fresh underwear and fresh (albeit a little musty) clothes with the prospect of a bed for the night, I felt like a new woman.

Some of the others had borrowed clothes as well; it was so strange to see them dressed in something different!

Kieran, true to form, came out in nothing but a very small sarong and said, "All the nice dresses were already taken."

Seriously, the sarong was the size of a tea towel, and he wore no underwear!

Sliding into a bed was sheer bliss, I don't remember going to sleep, and I awoke while it was still dark to the sound of someone in the kitchen banging about. I got up and got dressed in my normal clothes, I figured I'd leave the dress for when I was here, and it kind of made it more special.

Jared was making coffee by torchlight and *not* trying to be quiet, "Good morning, how'd you sleep?" he asked with a smile. He was always annoyingly cheerful in the mornings, but this time I could match his enthusiasm. I felt great and told him so.

The others were soon up and after I had some cereal I found in the cupboard (no milk, just dry) and my coffee, I packed up and was ready to go. We dropped into the house with the working fridge, and I found a note in reply to mine on a completely empty shelf.

Hi Jessica,

You are welcome to use the fridge as well,

I've cleared a shelf for you and there's room in the freezer too.

Please don't stay in this house, there are plenty of others around and whatever you do, don't change a thing outside. Be careful not to get seen coming here.

Best of luck.

Jane.

Davo's clan.

It was so nice to get this note, it showed there were good people around, and they were willing to help each other out. I didn't feel like we were so alone here.

We spent the day foraging for fresh food, David went fishing, Kieran took Bruce to see if they could get a pig and the rest of us looked for veggie gardens and new clothes to wear from the undamaged but abandoned houses. We did ok too; winter is the time to grow veggies up here, so we found some with all manner of yummy fresh food. Oh, how I craved a proper salad. We found plenty of clothes to replace our seriously grubby ones as well so really, it was a successful morning.

Kieran caught up with us by lunchtime with a wallaby over his shoulder. "Loads of these around, we certainly won't starve here," he said with a grin.

I wasn't overly excited about eating a wallaby, they were just too cute, but food is food. Amy was not keen at all but promised to try it.

I'd brought plastic bags from the house for anything we found, so Kieran hung the wallaby in a tree and made short work of skinning it and then cutting it up into portions for the plastic bags. I'd grown up watching people do that, so I could see he was fast and efficient, a real pro.

Amy watched in fascination, slightly grossed out, but fascinated by the process. I forget sometimes that not everyone grew up on a farm where this was commonplace. On our cattle property we killed all our own beef and how I missed that life. I missed Mum and Dad too. I wondered how they were going through all this. Mum would have things organised I'm sure and she'd be barking orders at Dad and the workers on what she wanted done. I was lucky growing up with a mum who was strong. My parents had a real partnership; they each had their area of expertise and respected each other.

When we headed for the house that night I dropped into the fridge house and put a fair bit of wallaby and the Barramundi David got into the freezer. I put a large portion of each on the other person's shelf with a note that said, "Thank you!"

So that night's dinner was the best yet. Wallaby stew with vegetables. A meal fit for a king as far as we were concerned. Kieran made what he called *camp bread.* to have with it. They were a kind of flat bread cooked in a frypan and it went so well with the stew we all demanded the recipe.

The next three weeks pretty much went by in the same way. We may have been a bunch of people struggling to survive, but I think we were gaining weight.

We'd met a few others in the area; they were all really nice and just doing their best like us. The guys had started giving away some of the food they caught to those not able to hunt or fish, as we had plenty to share.

Our medical issues were few and far between, I have to be honest I was in the best health I've ever been in, and I think everyone else was too. Lack of processed food, I guess.

OLD FRIEND

'Of all possessions a friend is most precious.' - Herodotus

A few people had begun to seek me out for medical help. I wasn't overly excited about that. Treating our group was one thing, treating strangers was another matter. But there really wasn't anyone else they could go to, so I gave in.

One afternoon we were walking in the forest when we heard a *"Cooee."*

"That'll be the cooee bird," said Kieran, grinning at Julia. She gave him a good-natured thump in the arm.

"Oi... you Jared's mob?" said a man, approaching us through the trees.

When he was close enough, we saw it was our 'shopping centre security guard' from weeks ago, walking towards us.

"Yep, that's us," said Jared. "What can we do for you?"

"You'd best come with me, got someone looking for you," he said.

We followed him, I assumed it was another medical call; they came in all ways these days. We walked maybe a kilometre through the forest on a well-worn path to a rough camp he had set up and to our surprise, as we rounded some large trees, we saw the camp and across the campfire was Paula!

She looked a mess, covered from top to bottom in mud and when she stood up, she was completely naked!

I went to her and in spite of the mud, hugged her so hard. "How did you find us and where are your *clothes*?" I asked.

"Bloody bastard Craig took 'em," she said.

She was greeted and hugged by everyone, and Kieran took off his shirt to hand to her. She took it but said with a shrug. "It doesn't really bother me, I've been like this for weeks, so I don't mind much anymore, just got cold at night and the bloody mozzies gave me hell, that's why the mud," She said, motioning to her mud caked body.

We thanked the man and took her to the house, it was a bit early, but there had been few aircraft the last few days due to rain showers so we risked it.

We cleaned her up and she told her story between mouthfuls of fish and veggies Julia had prepared for her. I was treating the multitude of cuts and grazes all over her when she told me they never actually made it to Cairns

"Night we left, that bastard Craig reckoned since I was a girl, I should do all the cooking and cleaning up. I told him to get stuffed so him and his mates took my clothes, said I could have them back when I knew my place, or could spend the trip to Cairns being useful as something to look at... Bastard."

"Why didn't you just come back? You were so close," I asked.

"He said I couldn't and that they'd chase me if I did."

"That bastard, Paula."

"Yeah, so anyway I didn't give in. I just made my own food and after a couple of days they stopped making jokes about me being naked."

"How did you get away?"

"Well, a heap of trucks came up the road. Craig said they were our Army. He still wouldn't give my clothes back, said the army boys would want something to look at. Anyway, we were close to the forest, so I went looking for something to cover myself with, and all of a sudden the Lizards got out of the trucks and were shooting Craig and his mates. I ran and I didn't stop running till the next day. I was so lost until I saw the ocean. Then I remembered Jared and you saying you were going south to Etty Bay or Mission Beach. I've been to both places, so I knew where they were, sort of. You weren't at Etty bay coz there's nothing there at all now, so you had to be here."

"Jesus, Paula! You walked all this way on your own? What did you live on?" I was totally amazed.

"Yeah. On my own... I got pretty lonely, Jess" She had a sad look. "I ran into a couple of blokes who decided I had to stay with them, but I knew what they had in mind, so I ran again. They fired their rifles a couple of times, but they had no hope of catching me. When my food ran out, I was catching the fresh water prawns out of the creeks. They were pretty gross raw, but I got used to it.

"I had to drink the water, Jess, I know you said not to, but I got so thirsty and couldn't boil it, is that bad?"

I laughed. "I think it's fine Paula, if you get sick, we'll fix you up. For now, you just need to get some rest."

Kieran was happy to give up his bed and slept on the lounge. Paula slept till after lunch the next day, but fortunately it was still raining, so we felt safe enough to just stay for the night and let her take it easy.

Our friend Paula was back with us, underweight with a multitude of grazes and some nasty cuts that will take some time to heal, but in remarkably good condition considering what she went through. It rained solid for the next three days in fact, so we all got to relax a bit. We found some board games in the cupboard and played them till we were sick of it. We talked and laughed, and I guess just hung out together, it was such a nice time for all of us. Paula regained her strength and fit right back into the group like she'd never been gone. The only difference was, while she was never shy before, she would now often not bother wearing more than underwear after a shower or when getting up in the mornings. I wondered a little if maybe the ordeal hadn't affected her, but I figured she'd just decided no clothes was easier. The guys got used to it and before long, nobody really noticed.

Dr Jess

The best way to find yourself is to lose yourself in the service of others.' -Mahatma Gandhi

The days became weeks and the weeks turned into months. We kept wandering around the area exploring during the day, we'd begun to know it well too. Cassowaries were an almost daily encounter now and we'd gotten to know them individually by the different shaped 'Casque' on their heads. We could tell in an instant which ones to avoid. The large females were often the grumpy ones. Fortunately, they'd gotten used to us and knew we weren't going to feed them, so they pretty much left us alone.

We'd gotten to know where most of the people were living as well, which helped our feeling part of this community. My fridge 'pen pal' and I kept leaving notes, which were nice, but one day she stopped replying. I watched the food on her shelf go bad; I kept throwing it out as needed and checking the other things, never taking anything, and always hoping she came back. But she didn't, I was sad about that, even though I'd never met her.

The medical cases continued to arrive. Dr Jacobs was right... I have lost people. I can't believe how casually I'm saying this, but it has almost become a regular occurrence. Bombing victims are carried in often, there is little hope of saving them because their injuries aren't just from the crush of their roofs, but they also have massive internal injuries. If they survive the bomb, they all have hugely distended abdomens, which upon inspection, their internal organs feel like mush. They never survive long, minutes at best.

Almost all the regular patients arrived at night, which was strange to start with, but I got used to it and I guess it was just safer for them. Kieran often played secretary and his favourite thing was using his best posh English accent with, "The Doctor will see you now." Which meant the first thing I felt I had to say to the patient was, "I am not a Doctor."

I recently had to give a man in his sixties 'Beta blockers' for his heart and I agonised over it. This wasn't treating infections and removing fishhooks, this was serious modern medicine. But his heart rhythm was dangerously compromised, to the point of it being debilitating, he was getting angina and was out of breath. As always, I fell back on Dr Jacobs' advice about "do no harm" and only treated what I knew for certain was going to get a *lot* worse if I didn't. Messing with heart medication is not something I took lightly and fortunately the dosage I gave worked on the first try. A concern I passed onto the man was that there was only so much of this medication left in the pharmacy and that he needed to try other ways to reduce his blood pressure before we ran out of it. An easy thing to say, but admittedly a hard thing to do, given our circumstances.

It was a reminder to me that we were eventually going to run out of everything. Our focus had been on surviving the day, the week, and the month. But since we'd settled in, I'd started to think a little more long term. We really needed to learn more about natural medicines before we ran out of the conventional drugs.

Jared suggested that house visits or another location to set up, might be safer for us than having everyone come here.

I agreed, the numbers were increasing, and it meant a steady stream of people coming and going from the house on most nights. It was only a matter of time until we were discovered. So we went in search of a house we could use. We found one soon enough, it was a granny flat out the back of a bombed house on the hill overlooking the central town of Wongaling Beach. From the air it would have looked like a shed, but inside it had been decked out with two bedrooms and a lounge.

There was an old logging track that made the rainforest access to the rear easier from the north and the south.

We put the word out that I would be there from sundown until nine every night and it was soon known as the *'Doctors'* by everyone locally. Being an easy half hour walk from our house there was always someone who would come with me. Usually it was Amy, Kieran, and Bruce as a minimum. Bruce always guarded the door where he figured he was in with a chance of a pat from the people passing. He was a different dog these days, gone was the stoic, aloof killer dog. Now he was far friendlier with everyone and insisted on pats all the time. Kieran curses us for spoiling a good hunting dog, but I think he likes the new Bruce as much as we do.

Often several of our group came and I always appreciated the help when I had a busy night. I eventually asked Kieran to make me up a sign that read, 'I AM NOT A QUALIFIED DOCTOR.' Which he did happily, but then added another on the bottom that said, 'I'm a gifted amateur.' He refused to put up the first one, if I wouldn't have the second, so I gave in.

Amy was proving to be an amazing help and was an exceptionally fast learner, she began acting as my nurse, getting details from the patients and making notes for me, but had also started studying the books and was constantly asking questions which I encouraged. I didn't like being the only one with medical knowledge as if anything happened to me, there really wouldn't be anyone else. Within a month I was able to have conversations with her about patients and she was capable of offering surprisingly informed opinions.

I'd begun keeping records of patient's illnesses and any medications I'd given them. I found this invaluable as the number of patients was growing and I could only remember so many. Word had spread and people were coming from all around the district, some walking for as long as several days to come see me. It was madness really that there really wasn't anyone else in this whole area to help them, and that they would travel so far to see *me*, an unqualified and inexperienced health professional who worked for nothing. Although I will admit, the few who have brought me chocolates were instantly my favourite patients.

Our drug supply in the chemist's shop was finite and I put the word out via my patients that we needed more, and could they please raid the chemist shops, bathroom cupboards of empty houses or just bring medications they no longer needed.

The people came through; within a week we had nearly filled one of the spare rooms in this shed with medications and supplies. I decided it was too risky to store it all in one place, so kept some of the most commonly used drugs and supplies and asked the guys to break it into smaller stashes and spread them around a few places. Amy set to work cataloguing what we had and made a record of where each drug was stored and how much of it we had.

Amy announced one day that she'd turned her phone on and found it was a week until Christmas! I couldn't believe it had been over four months since all this started... And yet it felt like a lifetime.

It was stinking hot and threatened to storm most afternoons, but frustrated us daily by not raining properly, just sometimes a heavy downpour that threatened to wash us all away before the sun came back the next day and the humidity doubled.

March fly season had peaked but they were still in full swing, there was simply no avoiding them if you were outdoors unless you were neck deep in water, then they tried to bite your head.

Bombing runs were still regular when it wasn't raining, and while we hadn't seen Lizards in jeeps for a couple of months now, we remained vigilant. There were a few groups that had set up camp on Dunk Island, they used the existing buildings but weren't careful with their fires. Most days we could see smoke rising from the trees and about a month ago the Lizards bombed them. We've seen no sign of life on the island since.

Instead of just hiding and being thankful it wasn't us that got bombed; we were now actively going out afterwards to look for survivors, and we weren't alone. We most often met others doing the same and we teamed up to bury the dead.

It appeared that in spite of at one point thinking we might be all that's left, we've found ourselves being part of a community of survivors. I estimate there are maybe four or five hundred here locally, with many more pockets still living around small towns to the north and south. But having said that, the numbers were steadily dropping. Between the Lizards and the nature of the survival situation, it was hardly surprising more would die.

I should mention a conversation I had with a patient yesterday who came in with some nasty infections he had in injuries he got while running from Townsville. I thought Jared and the others would be keen to hear what he had to say, since we hadn't had word from outside our area, so I sent Kieran to go get him.

When Jared arrived, the man told us that Townsville was overrun with the Lizards. "There's hundreds of them, they took over the army barracks and are using it as their staging post. Every day they send out trucks and jeeps that head out of town. The airport is where they keep their planes."

"Are there survivors?" asked Jared.

"Yeah, but not many, not like here. We're living like rats, running around getting what scraps we can find. Some people have formed gangs... I was glad to get out of there."

"What happened to the army?" asked Jared. "Where are they? Lizards took over their barracks, so what happened to the troops?"

"They dropped bombs on them, I've seen the mess they left. The troops were getting ready to fight back, but they flew in and just bombed the crap out of them, then they dropped Lizards onto the ground, and they went in and killed what was left. They had no ammo in their guns to fight back. They hadn't been issued yet. They never even got off the base."

"But how can that happen? When the government knew they were coming?" asked Jared, appalled at what he was hearing.

"I dunno mate. I dunno how it happened. But it did. The smell coming out of there is something else I can tell you. Doesn't seem to bother the Lizards though, they've camped up there no worries."

"How many aircraft do they have?"

"I dunno mate, they're always coming and going but I'd say maybe three of the smaller ones and one really big bastard. It's huge, but never really goes anywhere. It just sits there hovering just above the ground."

Jared thought for a moment and then asked, "Is there anything else you can think of that we might want to know? I mean you've been watching them, and we don't know anything about them yet. Can you think of anything?"

"Not really mate sorry, if I think of anything I'll let you know."

"Ok, mate, anything you remember will be great," said Jared, before turning to me. "I expect it's going to rain tomorrow Jess, so we'll at least have a quiet day."

The man said. "Hey, that's something I should mention. They hate water. I saw one of them was standing beside a tarp that had a puddle of water in the middle. A gust of wind lifted it and the water got on the Lizard, all down one side. He danced around hissing and carrying on, trying to rub it off, the water left a mark on its skin!"

"Well, that's interesting," Jared said. "Do you think it hurts them?"

"I dunno mate, maybe more like stings or annoys them, but it certainly didn't like it."

"It might explain why they don't come here when it's raining, but why it would bother their spaceships is a mystery," said Jared.

"Oh the little ones aren't spaceships."

"Sorry?" asked Jared.

"Yeah, they're just planes, they're always pulling them into the hangar when it looks like rain. Me and another guy went to the airport to see if we could find some food and got a close look at them. You'd reckon they'd have more security, but it was pretty easy to get close, the doors on those planes don't have proper seals or anything, and we saw into one of them, it's just empty inside and the side panels don't fit real well. It must leak like a sieve when it rains."

"Excellent, well that might be something we can use at some point, thanks for the info."

"Hey, no problems, hey there was one more thing, they don't do much at night, I don't know if they can't see well or what it is, but they always have heaps of light everywhere and never go out of it."

"Well, that's also very interesting. Keep it coming, and thanks again," said Jared, shaking the man's hand.

It seemed we finally had some real information on these invaders. I didn't know what we could do with it, but at least we knew we were safe at night and when it was raining. When we told Amy, she told us her uncle had said his team had found what they thought was the alien's home planet. It was a very hot and extremely dry planet and because of the increasing prevalence of solar storms from their sun in the last few decades, it had most of its atmosphere stripped away.

It fit the story perfectly, they had adapted to an increasingly dry and hostile environment, but when the solar storms started, they had to find somewhere else to live. I imagined that they must find earth cold and wet in comparison to their home planet.

Christmas day came; unfortunately it was a clear sunny day with no chance of rain so there was little socialising with other groups. Kieran had managed to find a couple of bottles of scotch and one of rum, so we all sat in a creek and had a few drinks to celebrate, well more than a few. We were all quite merry by the time we went back to the house for dinner. As had become the norm Paula stripped off as soon as she entered the house. We all had a delicious dinner of fish and some of the last of the veggies for the season followed by some amazing fruits picked up from a tropical fruit farm outside town. We then relaxed in the lounge room together chatting.

At one point Kieran went to the kitchen and Paula walked past him. I overheard Kieran say, "Jeeze, Paula, when you walk around like that, I never know which way to look!"

She stopped, turned to him and said, "You can look at *me* if you like... Unless you don't want to."

Kieran replied with a laugh, "No, I *want* to... don't worry about *that*. Just didn't want to offend."

"Good, and I'm not offended," she said, and continued on her way.

I may well have witnessed the mating ritual of the Cape York male, because by New Years Eve, there was another bed shuffle, and I lost my place in the queen bed. It reminded me of the guys I grew up with out west, where *'You're alright'* was the utmost praise for a girl and if they added, *'You'll do,'* it was tantamount to a marriage proposal.

So anyway, in the bed shuffle I took Paula's bed, Amy took Kieran's place on the couch; which was at her insistence. It made sense as she actually fitted it. And we were all happy with the arrangements.

I was so happy for Kieran and Paula, they were two of my favourite people in the world and it was so nice to see them happy together.

I was surprised that more pairing off didn't happen sooner to be honest. At uni it would have happened in the first three days, but I guess we all had so much more to think about. I was happy on my own at that point, I really didn't have time or energy to put into a relationship, and there wasn't really anyone in our group that fit the bill for me anyway.

Alien Dissection

'The only source of knowledge is experience.' -Albert
Einstein

Around the middle of January, we had a stretch of
ridiculously hot and humid, but clear weather. The
bombing runs increased, and we had a few Lizards in jeeps coming
to the area. Unlike other times we'd seen them, these ones were
wearing suits with some sort of breathing apparatus on their faces.
We didn't know what to make of it to begin with until Jared
remembered what the Townsville man had said about the Lizards
hating water. "If they hate water then it makes sense, they aren't
going to like humidity," he said.

We were perched on the ridge behind Wongaling Beach one
morning, watching two of them as they drove around and visited a
couple of houses. Nobody around here was crazy enough to be in a
house in clear weather during the day, so it was a fruitless exercise.
We were all there except Kieran who had headed off with Bruce to
do some hunting earlier; he knew well enough to stay out of sight.

The facemask they wore must have severely restricted their
vision and it all looked ridiculously cumbersome. They already

moved very slowly, so with this outfit on, watching them get around was almost painful.

As we watched, they drove up one of the smaller roads close to the rainforest and stopped at a house. They completed their inspection of the house and headed back to their car when all of a sudden, we saw Bruce come running out of the forest at full stretch and he latched onto one of the Lizards, dragging it to the ground. Kieran was right behind him with his machete held high, it was a short dash before he reached the other lizard, and he brought the knife down across the back of its neck. He then raced across to where Bruce had the other one pinned down and he hacked at its head several times.

Jared, who was beside me, swore loudly and said, "Come on, we'd better head down there."

We ran down there as fast as we could. Fortunately, there were many well-worn paths now, which were mainly free of *wait-a-while*.

When we arrived, Kieran was standing beside the jeep with one of the alien weapons in his hands.

"Kieran what were you *thinking*?" asked Jared, out of breath.

"They've killed enough of us; I had the chance to return the favour," said Kieran defiantly.

"Return the favour! They'll probably level this place because of it."

Kieran scoffed. "Come on, they won't know who did it, maybe I'll chuck the bodies in the river and let the crocs get rid of the evidence."

Jared shook his head. "Mate, they don't care who did it. They'll just bomb the crap out of this whole town... Help me get the bodies into the jeep."

"What're you going to do with them?" asked David.

"I'm going to drive them out of town. There's that old house a few kays up the road that nobody lives in. I'll park it there and hope they bomb *it* instead of us."

It seemed like a good plan to me. Kieran really was reckless to do this without any thought of the consequences. I could see Jared was annoyed and to be honest, so was I. Everyone in this town was doing their best to avoid detection by the aliens and we were doing well at it too. This will bring a spotlight on us we didn't need.

We bundled the bodies into the back of the jeep. It was our first chance to see them up close and I really wanted to study them. What I'd noticed already was their blood; it was blue/green in colour and smelled disgusting! It had also coagulated almost immediately on contact with the air.

Jared jumped in the driver's seat and said to Kieran, "You're coming too. Leave Bruce, he smells bad enough as it is without sitting in the back with those two."

I suspect Bruce wasn't too unhappy about being left behind. He was still rolling his tongue around his mouth, apparently trying to get rid of the taste of the alien. I really wanted to go too, just so I could study the aliens. "I want to come,"

"What for?" asked Jared. "This is too risky Jess; we can't afford for you to get hurt."

"Yeah well, I want the opportunity to take a look at those two closely. We might learn something from them," I said, climbing in to sit beside Jared. Kieran shrugged his shoulders and climbed in beside me.

The smell in the vehicle was overpowering and the guys rolled their windows down as soon as they closed the doors.

We took off in the direction of the road out of town. I thought Jared was driving really fast until I looked at the speedometer. It said we were doing sixty!

"It feels strange to be going this fast after so long walking, hey," Jared said when he saw me looking over at the gauges.

"I'll say! I can't believe this is only sixty kays."

We bumped and rattled our way out of town, and we came to the old house, but Jared kept going. "I'm going to go further, it's riskier but we need this thing as far from us as possible."

"Remember we have to walk back as well," said Kieran.

"I haven't forgotten... You'll owe me beers for this," laughed Jared.

Kieran just laughed.

I was keenly aware of the bodies in the back, not just the smell of them, but that there were two dead aliens within a few feet of us. I looked over my shoulder at them and Kieran must have seen me.

"They're very dead, Doc," he grinned. "They're not coming back to life."

I laughed; intellectually I knew that of course. But it was hard not to wonder if they could.

We finally came to another house another five minutes later. It was derelict but still standing.

"This'll do," said Jared, pulling into the driveway. We pulled up at the front of the house and got out.

The guys went straight to the back and began pulling the aliens out.

"Jesus, they stink," said Kieran screwing up his face.

"I really want to get a closer look, can you cut one of their suits open?" I asked.

"We'll leave one in the back and put one in the front seat," said Jared.

They picked up the first one and shoved it in the driver's seat before returning to me around the back. Kieran used his hunting knife and cut open the suit. The smell was even worse.

They are pretty much human shaped, but their skin is like dry leather. Not scaly but more leathery like a dried up green tree frog.

"I'll gut it, let's find out how to kill the bastards," said Kieran.

"We really don't have time for that, guys," said Jared.

"This could be important," I said.

"Righto." He sighed. "But make it quick."

Kieran took his knife and cut the alien from the base of its throat to its groin. He struggled to get through its version of a rib cage. Unlike ours, it is an extremely *hard* solid bone, which hooks back up under to protect the organs. I couldn't see where it hinged to allow expansion and contraction and only in hindsight did I think that perhaps muscles in the lower abdomen move in and out to allow the inflation/deflation of the lungs.

Without using complex medical terms, I'll explain what we found.

There was very little blood or fluids and what there was, gelled as soon as it touched the air. They have an oesophagus similar to ours but there is no stomach. The muscular oesophagus is extended down into the lower abdomen and is wrapped in large blood vessels with small muscular tubules radiating outwards, which taper off after about one hundred millimetres.

It's where the faeces are formed or stored. I don't know which, but oh my God, the smell!

We found packets of the food they eat, which appear, (and smell) partly digested, so the body is able to process it quickly, I guess it didn't need an elaborate digestive system.

The smell inside them is something I'll never forget. Like the worst dead rat smell, mixed with very dead fish, sulphur and ammonia. They have lungs and a heart, but neither is much like ours. I couldn't discern any other organs like liver or kidneys.

Kieran has gutted more animals than I care to think about, and he was unable to locate much that resembled the familiar organs in mammals, fish, or reptiles.

We did find various things that we couldn't identify at all, and with my limited knowledge, I wasn't able to ascertain what their functions could have been.

They possess no reproductive organs I could find, or any opening other than their mouth, nose and ears, so we have no idea how they reproduce.

Where Kieran had cut into the skull with his machete, we found the brain of similar consistency to Earth's creatures, but the cranial fluid was more a paste than liquid, just like all the liquids in the body. This may have been a post mortem reaction and while the body was less than thirty minutes dead, I can't know without studying a live specimen. That's not something I would look forward to doing.

"Right, let's get the hell out of here," said Jared. As he closed the rear door of the jeep with its dissected cargo inside.

Kieran reached in and grabbed his new weapon from inside the jeep. "Can't forget this!" he grinned.

"Careful you don't blow your foot off with that," Jared said with a wry smile.

We set off at a jog along the cleared ground under some power lines through the forest. I already missed having a car but at least our packs were light, and we were still pretty fit, in spite of our pretty relaxed lifestyle in Mission Beach.

When I thought back to those first few days hiking when I barely made it through each day, I had to smile. I was a machine now; I could hike all day and wake up feeling fine. Ok, I would never be as strong as these guys. But I was infinitely fitter than I have ever been and my short height and light weight, really came into their own in the forest. I was more agile than they were, which meant ducking and weaving through vines and branches came easy and I was way faster than any of the guys. I still couldn't swing the machete, but as I grew accustomed to walking in the forest, I found that I didn't need to hack my way through. You can read the forest if you try, you can know where to expect lots of vines or wait-awhile and avoid them. While Jared always led in the early days, a few of us took turns now and it was interesting to see the different styles. Jared wasn't bad at reading the forest most of the time, but Kieran had a completely different approach. He chose a direction and bulldozed his way through. Making more noise than a heard of cattle, bashing and crashing his way through the bush.

I'd noticed all the girls had tuned in a little more to the forest and were quieter; leaving little trace we'd been there. The other advantage to that approach was less cuts and scratches to deal with.

We'd been going for maybe fifteen minutes when we heard an aircraft, it wasn't close to us, but close enough. We were nearing a small earth bank, so we scrambled over the top and hid in some tall guinea grass to watch. It flew straight to Wongaling beach where it disappeared for a few minutes. We couldn't see it behind the mountains, and we strained to listen for explosions, but heard nothing.

When it came back into view it was heading straight for us.

We all hid deep amongst the grass as it passed overhead, and we watched as it banked around after passing at speed over the house, we left the jeep at.

When it returned, it flew down and hovered just above the ground behind the jeep, and two Lizards jumped down from a door in the rear. They walked straight to the jeep and looked inside. One went to the back and opened the rear door. It then closed the door and looked around with its weapon raised.

"Christ these things are amateurs," Jared said.

"What do you mean?" I asked.

"They weren't even looking around *before* they went to the jeep, they only got nervous after they found the dead bodies. They're not like disciplined soldiers at war, they're more like civilians."

The aliens then walked quickly back to the aircraft, and it took off fast in a low banking manoeuvre.

"They aren't taking the dead ones with them?" I asked incredulously.

"Doesn't look like it," said Kieran.

The aircraft circled around and flew directly over the house. BOOM!

This was the first time we'd ever actually *seen* them drop a bomb and we were dangerously close to it. As I saw in the split second before Jared dove on top of me and the shockwave hit us that it wasn't a bomb, as we know it, it was almost a disturbance in the air that was directed downwards to the ground. It created a shockwave radiating out from the ground and I saw it bounce back and strike the aircraft, just before the wave reached us and blew us flat.

The earth bank had protected us from the worst of it but my ears were ringing. When I opened my eyes, Jared was already climbing up to look over the bank again. He turned to me and said, "Ok, Jess?"

I nodded. I was ok this time, but when I looked across at Kieran, he sat up with blood coming from one ear. He'd ducked against a large round granite boulder pushed up by the bulldozer that had made this track many years ago.

In my slightly dazed state it dawned on me that it wasn't weak eardrums that caused the damage, it was the reflected shockwave!

When that blast that hit us on the mountain, many of the girls were leaning up against the rocks; the guys were on the flat ground. I had ducked between two rocks, which must have doubled the shock, but each kind of cancelled the other out. It went some way to explaining why I took longer to recover than the others; I'd had a very different experience to them.

The bomb dropped in front of us was a shaped implosion like we'd seen elsewhere. It covered a large area around where the house once stood, maybe a football field in size, totally levelling the forest and turning it into a five meter high bank of debris ridden dirt.

"Did you guys see that?" asked Jared.

I nodded. "It's not a bomb at all, it's a shockwave."

"Yep, and did you see what happened to the aircraft?" he asked, smiling.

"It got hit by it's own bomb," said Kieran with his hand over his now quite sore and deaf ear.

"Exactly!" said Jared. "These guys screw up... They aren't the boogeyman. They make mistakes, and by the looks of it they screw up all the time!"

"How do you figure that?" I asked.

"Well look at what just happened, Jess. Just one guy, with a machete and a dog, killed those two Lizards. They weren't guarding each other, neither of them were looking out for danger and that's either arrogant or incompetent. Then the aircraft went looking for them in town before they came out here so they must be able to track them, or their vehicle, and what that says to me is instead of just looking for them, they went looking for the last place they should have been. Again, incompetent because if you have tracking tech, then there's no point if checking where they should be, you check where they *are*. They landed and checked the vehicle, without checking out the area from the air first, they waltzed up to the jeep without even thinking about hostiles, until they saw the bodies. They got scared and went back to the ship and dropped a bomb on the place without checking altitude to make sure they were at a safe height. What we are up against is their technology; the aliens themselves don't seem too hard to beat." He was grinning.

He had a point, I was no soldier, but everything he said made sense, even to me.

Kieran laughed. "So what you're sayin' is, they don't know what they're doing and are as dumb as dog poo, but they have some great guns. Yeah?"

"Ha, yeah in a nutshell," said Jared.

"Well, that makes me feel better about losing a planet to them hey," said Kieran. But he wasn't smiling.

"Not much we can do about it mate," said Jared, just as seriously.

As much as this was an interesting conversation, we had a long walk home to look forward to, so I said, "Come on, we can talk about it on the way, I have to be back in time for any patients that might come tonight."

The guys agreed and we began walking. Kieran couldn't take his eyes off the weapon in his hand. To the point of him bumping into things because he wasn't watching where he was going. Jared quite rightly told him to concentrate, which he did, but I could see he was still keen to have a proper look at it.

His chance came when we stopped for a drink and a quick rest. The weapon looked very much like a stick with a swelling at either end. It looked more organic than made. I couldn't see any seams or screws in it at all. "I can't find a trigger on it," he said, puzzled. He tried pointing it and squeezing various parts, but it didn't fire.

"Come on, you can play with your stick at home, let's keep moving," said Jared.

Kieran was reluctant but agreed to head off, so we kept walking and were home just before dark. Once in the house and with an exchange of stories complete, which included a blow-by-blow of the flyover the aircraft did of the house. We all had a close look at the weapon. We were careful to keep it pointed at the forest outside in case it went off, but nobody managed to get it to fire.

Kieran in particular was frustrated with it and tried every which way he could, but never managed to make it do anything at all.

In disgust he decided he'd pull it apart. Kyle, being an auto sparky, was keen to assist. But as Kieran tried to dig the tip of his knife into what looked like a seam and prise it open, it must have short-circuited something and there was an almighty BANG!

When the thick black smoke cleared, Kieran was flat on his back, still holding the knife, which was now minus about thirty millimetres of blade tip. Kyle was also laying on the ground. Both were covered in some sort of greasy soot from the waist up.

I was heading for Kieran who was closest to me when he sat up with his face as black as shoe polish, eyes blinking red and white in the blackness. He gave a cough and said, "Bugger me... I wasn't expecting *that*!"

Kyle also sat up and laughed between coughs. "Well, that was interesting." He managed to get out. After that it was agreed that we wouldn't attempt to dismantle one of those things again.

New Hope

'Hope is a waking dream' -Aristotle

It took weeks after we dissected the alien for the bombing runs to reduce in numbers and frequency. Jared was right, there were repercussions from killing the two Lizards. Every bit of clear weather was marked by an increased number of aircraft flyovers, any number of jeeps around town and with that, an increase in patient numbers. People were spending less time in houses and more time in the forest so there was a marked increase in rashes, insect bites, injuries associated with falls and of course infections. The wet season brings with it hot humid conditions which is perfect for breeding bacteria.

I treated my first crocodile bite victim, which also involved my first amputation. It was barbaric and brutal to take the arm off a man without general anaesthesia. The crocodile had grabbed the man's hand while he was retrieving a crab pot from the river. When the animal rolled, as they do to tear off a part of their prey, it dislocated the elbow, shattering the joint and tearing every ligament from the bone. The puncture wounds from the teeth had caused necrosis in the skin; Kieran said he'd read once that it isn't bacteria on their teeth but the sheer bite force that causes the death of the skin around the puncture. That's what causes the horrible infections.

And as the blood supply to the lower arm was also compromised, there was no choice but to remove it or it would kill him. There was a chance he would die from shock or loss of blood during the surgery but as I told his wife, he will die if I don't do this. The poor woman was distraught, and I left her with Julia to try and calm her. I could understand why she felt like she did, to lose your husband would be bad enough, for it to happen now could mean life or death for her too given how much everyone relies on each other.

David once again borrowed from his marine work history and told me that you can use lime wash to sterilise the walls of a room before doing surgery. He told me that in the old days, that's what they used to disinfect the timber holds of sailing ships after there was sickness on board. I'd never heard of it but was happy to be able to make *some* attempt at making a sterile environment. A quick trip to what was left of the local hardware store provided the bags of lime and hacksaws needed. We converted the storeroom of the clinic into a makeshift operating theatre. Someone organised a camp stove and Jared took charge of boiling absolutely *everything* he could that would enter the room.

I can't tell you how nervous I was going in there. Sure the books had taught me how to do this, in theory anyway but actually cutting a man's arm off was a world away from the sort of things I'd been treating. I remembered Dr Jacobs saying he didn't think I was qualified for surgery, but I don't think he foresaw this situation. What I was doing could kill him, but I told myself he was dead anyway. It had been twelve hours since the injury and the bruising was horrific, the muscles that had torn away from their attachment points on the bone and had bunched up on his shoulder. The blood had pooled in the upper arm and the lower arm was cold to the touch, I assumed it meant the artery was damaged. Maybe a skilled surgeon could have saved the arm, but I knew I certainly didn't have the skills to even attempt it.

Amy assisted me and as had become the norm; she exceeded any and all expectations. Kieran was also there to act as nurse because he had the least amount of squeamishness over blood and gore. I had given the patient some of the precious few morphine tablets I had, and he was conscious, but only just. I just hoped he wouldn't remember it.

Kieran held him down and the man cried out when I first cut into him, I almost lost my nerve. I couldn't do it while he screamed, but fortunately for both the patient and I, it only lasted a few moments before he became unconscious from the pain. We had to work fast then to get it done before he woke up.

As it turned out the damage was way more extensive than I thought, so I was right to take the whole arm, all the way to the shoulder.

I took the arm at the socket leaving no sharp edges of bone to contend with. The blood vessels were either tied or cauterised with a hot iron, run in from the fire outside as needed. The smell of the cauterising was awful, it had a rich kind of coppery/metallic smell combined with burnt meat, which made feel queasy each time I touched the iron to the blood vessel. It was effective but gruesome. With a flap of skin stitched over to cover the wound and a drain hose fitted, I felt pretty good about the job. The hose would be removed when the wound stopped bleeding internally. Mercifully the patient didn't wake up during the ordeal and while he looked a bit pale, his vital signs were good. He slept for almost twelve hours, Amy and I took turns monitoring him and keeping notes. I had no way to give him painkillers intravenously so he had to wake before I could give him anything. I did insert a hose in his rectum to keep him hydrated but questioned whether I should put morphine in it. I really didn't know enough about it to risk giving it any other way than orally.

I expected a rude awakening for him and as it turned out it wasn't too bad. Of course, that's easy to say when it's not you in pain, but when he woke, he was in reasonable spirits. As soon as he was capable, I sat him up and gave him the painkillers and the start of an antibiotic course to stave off any infection before it began. I ordered two weeks of bed rest minimum, but I was told later by another patient that he was up and moving around within a few days.

On the whole we deemed the operation a success, and the "surgical team" celebrated with a nice dinner.

While the patient was recovering, a strange thing happened. Jared had been down to town and was told that the Lizards had been posting flyers all over town. Written in English, what they said was"

PEOPLE OF THIS TOWN.

The new rulers of this planet are offering you refuge.

We have set up a refugee facility where you will be given FREE:

Food

Accommodation

Medical care

Resettlement to permanent housing under construction.

Your town is scheduled for complete destruction so you will only have this opportunity once.

You are advised to accept this generous offer and meet at:

<u>TULLY AIRPORT.</u> On <u>THE DAY OF THE NEXT CLEAR FULL MOON. AM</u>

For relocation to the refugee resettlement facility.

Please note: If it is not clear weather, your relocation will be postponed until the next full moon.

Weapons must be surrendered before boarding the aircraft.

Travel light; you will be provided with everything you need.

There will be no aircraft or ground vehicles in the lead up to resettlement day to allow you to travel in peace to the pick up location.

This caused a buzz to go through the whole area. Groups were traveling all over town to discuss what it meant for us all and the next full moon being just a week away, it left no time to lose.

The discussion within our group went on into the night when we first heard about it. The medical clinic was closed for the night; the rain was so heavy that it was too difficult to travel around anyway. Besides, everyone knew where we lived if there was an emergency.

Jared was firmly in the '*don't trust them*' camp.

"Look I just think it seems odd that they go from killing everything that moves, to welcoming us in the space of a day. I don't trust them," he said.

Amy said, "Maybe they've had a change of heart. Maybe they have won everywhere now and don't need to keep killing us."

Jared scoffed. "They bombed the crap out of Jacko's place the day before yesterday, those flyers would have already been printed."

Jacko was the leader of another group close by, that Jared had become good friends with. He'd taken Jacko and his family's deaths pretty hard.

The group was fairly divided on it. We were all sick of being hunted, but on the whole, we were doing pretty well.

Kieran said, "I'm with Jared on this, I don't trust them, we're doing ok here so why go looking for trouble?"

"Because they are going to flatten the whole town," said Louise. "If we don't go, there will be nothing here for us anyway."

"We don't know that," James said. "It could be all crap, if they were going to, or able to, they would have done it already. They've stopped using the shaped bombs, maybe that's because they're running out. Maybe they're running out of fuel for their aircraft."

Kyle said, "Jared, you said they weren't a bomb but a shockwave."

"Yeah," said Jared. "But maybe it uses some kind of power charge that they can run out of. I have no idea how they work."

Louise shook her head. "No, that's the trouble, we have no idea about anything, but we do know they have the technology to do exactly what they said."

Peter said, "Look guys, I thank everyone for the lifestyle we enjoy. We really are doing well compared to others, but I didn't spend six years at uni to live like a rat. My family was fairly well off and I've never really had to go without. In this group I simply don't have the skills that most of you possess to earn a rank above labourer, so if the Lizards are offering resettlement, I'll be going. It may be a chance for me to return to a position... more suited to my skills."

The whole group sat in stunned silence until Jared spoke. "I had no idea you felt like that, Pete...and just for the record, nobody outranks anyone in this group, that includes me. We each do what we can for the good of the group and that's why we do so well, we were lucky enough to have the right people."

"Exactly," said Peter. "You all have practical skills in survival except me, please don't take offence, I'm just being realistic. Some people are just better suited to positions where they make decisions for practical people to carry out. I'm one of those but I'm in an environment where I don't have the practical knowledge to do so. Maybe in resettlement I will find a niche."

Everyone sat in silence while they mulled over what he'd said. Was it a left-handed insult? Did he just tell us he was *above* us? He did it so well, I really wasn't sure, and I think everyone else was in the same boat.

Jared finally said, "Well, again, I'm sorry you feel that way." He then addressed the whole group. "For now, I think everyone needs to have a think about what they want to do. I can't make that decision for us. I think it's too important. What I will suggest is that we at least get out of town, head for the hills behind Tully in case they do come good with the threat. At least from there we can escape to the mountains if we have to. Those that want to trust the Lizards will be able to do so from there."

We all agreed and went to bed.

I thought about what Peter had said and started to understand a little. He was always there but rarely had input. He worked as hard as anyone, but I guess I just never thought of him as someone with ideas because he rarely offered them. It didn't occur to me that he was so far out of his comfort zone doing practical things, that he was clueless in this environment. I hoped he found his niche in resettlement.

For me, I really didn't know what to think. On the one hand we were doing ok and to risk that was a bit crazy. On the other hand, to miss an opportunity for it to all be over, was madness.

I didn't sleep much that night and I doubt anyone else did either. In the morning we all looked a bit wrecked, and it was raining heavily so we stayed at the house for the day. I found it amusing that nobody really believed the promise of no aircraft or vehicles, but several were convinced the resettlement offer was genuine.

The discussions continued a little less formally, but unabated.

Amy came to me and said she wanted to go. I was heartbroken when she told me. "I'm hoping my family is there Jess, I know you guys are my family now, but what if they're there and worrying about me? And maybe I can go back to uni, maybe change to medicine instead of botany, I was never really *that* into plants anyway." She smiled.

I tried to reason with her, but how could I without being dishonest. The truth was we didn't know what was going to happen, all we knew for sure was the Lizards had done everything they could to kill us, and now they wanted to help us?

The general consensus from the other groups who dropped in during the day was that they were going to take up the offer. In a way I couldn't blame them, many weren't doing well and there was only so much the guys could do to provide meat and fish for the community. A lot of people, particularly outside of Mission Beach were starving and this offered a way out of their misery.

As each came past saying they were going, my decision swayed slightly towards joining them. But there was something in the back of my mind that said not to trust the Lizards. I couldn't shake it.

By the end of the day we were all getting bored with the subject and it was still pouring with rain so we let our hair down a little and risked some music. The house with the fridge allowed us to charge some phones, which were still useless of course, but most of us had downloaded music on them so we could play tunes. It was funny how quickly we all went from our phones being our whole world, to them being a bit of a pain to look after. I hadn't even seen mine in over a month and didn't miss it.

Kieran surprised us all with his music. Lots of old songs from the classics like Elton John, Fleetwood Mac, and Pink Floyd. We all laughed, but when he put *'Tiny dancer'* on, it suddenly became karaoke time.

There was a lot of laughter and plenty of dancing that night. It occurred to me during a quiet moment, that if we ended up being all that's left to represent humanity, you could do worse than these guys... And we'd have saved some great tunes.

The next morning Jared and Kieran discussed what would happen if they did bomb the town and it was decided that we should empty the supermarket, chemists, and hardware and stash it all outside of town. They took off early in the pouring rain to pass the word around of what they were planning but were back by lunchtime. "We weren't the first to think of it," said Jared. "A few groups had got together and already did it last night in the rain. They took the risk, used three vehicles, and stashed it all in a derelict house on the other side of the range, to the west of town. They're passing the location on to all the groups in town."

It appeared everyone was taking the threat seriously. I looked around at the house that had become our home since we arrived here. I would certainly miss it if they blew it up. I was reluctant to go back to camping in the bush again and I have to admit, that was one thing weighing on my mind quite a bit. Yes I was being soft, but living in a house is *so* nice compared to camping in the forest, with the bugs and the damp.

We all had good tents again, every time we had the opportunity, we searched the sheds of bombed houses, and managed to get enough tents to go around should we ever need them again.

We emptied the medical supplies we'd stashed the various houses and took them to an old shed outside of town. It was almost completely covered in forest and would be all but invisible from the air. David stashed a load of fishing gear there as well and we spread the word amongst the other groups of its location. I'd kept a load of supplies to take with me, just in case, but I left the bulk of the medical books with the supplies. I thought whoever might need the supplies, might need the books.

With a couple of days left till the full moon and in clear weather, we set off for Tully. Everyone was in good health and Amy was back to a healthy weight, which made me happy. We hadn't seen any aircraft or vehicles, which made us feel a little more confident that the Lizards might keep their word.

When we left we fell into a line of groups all heading to Tully along the main road. There must have been hundreds of us. Many I knew as patients, but many faces I didn't know. I spent much of the trip helping with people's injuries and doing what I could for them. Looking at the line of people walking along the road, reminded me of images of refugees fleeing war torn countries. I guess we weren't any different.

When we camped that night, it was at the base of Mount Mackay, a tall mountain to the east of Tully overlooking the town. The bigger mountain on its western side, Mount Tyson was part of the Great Dividing Range.

The groups separated to find campsites and Jared chose a nice spot under an escarpment with a good flowing creek. We dropped our packs and rested a moment before setting up camp for the night. We easily slid into our routine of pitching tents, getting a fire going, organising food, and checking for medical issues. The only difference from when we first arrived in Mission Beach was that it was now the wet season. It was stinking hot and very wet. Even though it wasn't raining, the moisture level in the ground and the foliage was sufficient to make our boots soggy by the end of the day. Leeches were plentiful and we all spent some time getting them off. Keeping up with water supplies was a challenge for us as well. Hiking in the summer meant we were sweating profusely and consuming far more water than we ever did. With my trusty saucepan, I set about boiling water for everyone to drink tomorrow. Some of us may be planning on being flown to shelter, but they would do so with plenty to drink.

We could hear other groups in the distance but we hadn't met any yet. I guess everyone was keeping a low profile. They can't have been far away if we could hear them, as sound doesn't travel well in the forest. We were all quite nervous about what was to come.

Jared chose the eastern side of the airport to camp on as it gave us cover almost all the way to the runway. The downside was that it would contain us into one section of forest about forty square kilometers in area, the forest on the western side of Tully went all the way to Cairns in the North, and Ingham in the south, nearly six thousand square kilometers. It wouldn't be practical for the Lizards to bomb all of that. After much discussion it was decided that we should move to the western side. It was further to walk in the open, but if we had to run, it was a far better direction.

The next day we set off again and found a good camp near the base of Mount Tyson. There were plenty of creeks running at this time of year so campsites were plentiful. From where we camped, we could climb a small ridge and overlook the town and the airstrip with relatively good cover from the air.

We'd run into two other groups as we walked through town. They were all heading to Mount Mackay, which proved Jared right, but the rest of us stuck to our guns. They'd come from the forests to the west and looked like they'd done it tough. They were thin, seriously thin, and covered in sores that had become ulcerated, most likely due to poor nutrition, and the inability to keep their wounds clean and dry. Their poor diet and lack of medical care was written all over them and it made me appreciate yet again, how fortunate I was to have ended up in this group.

That night we lit a decent fire and enjoyed each other's company as a whole group for perhaps the last time. There was a lot of joking about things we wouldn't miss if we were going, Leeches featured high on the list, ticks, March flies and being constantly wet and stinking pretty much rounded up the feeling across the group.

I was certain we'd all make efforts to keep in touch, but it all kind of felt final. It was making me feel sick to my stomach. These people had become my whole world, I couldn't imagine, didn't want to imagine life without *all* of them now.

I'd already decided there was no way I trusted the Lizards enough to go with them.

Jared, Kieran, Paula, James, Kyle, Julia and Louise and I were going to stay.

Only Amy and Peter were going.

Part of me was very nervous about my decision, Jared had always steered us right and to go against his advice would be perilous. But while I had accepted our life as it was, it wasn't the life I would have chosen. The idea that a better one awaits in the resettlement camp, maybe I could find a way to continue my studies, perhaps even going into medicine with real training, instead of reading a few books and hoping for the best. Well, it was attractive, but I knew it was a pipe dream.

After dinner I found Jared up on the ridge looking out over the town. I could see him clearly in the light of the full moon.

"Hey," I said.

"Hey, come join me, Jess," he said, motioning to the rock beside him.

I sat beside him, and we looked out together at the myriad of small orange dots spread across the landscape from the campfires of the groups who were converging on this town.

"Must be thousands of them out there," he said. He paused for a little while and then continued, "Wish you weren't going down there tomorrow."

"I know Jared," I said. "I've decided not to go"

He glanced at me. "I'm pleased to hear it. I wish the others were as smart."

"It's ok, I know what you mean. It's a risk, and one I've decided not to take but I can't talk Amy out of it. Being with us has been an amazing experience for her and she wants to learn medicine for real, but I don't think that's the way. I can understand it, I wish I could get some proper training, Jesus I'm floundering about half the time."

"I think you're doing a pretty bloody amazing job as you are, Jess. We absolutely couldn't have done it without you. Half of us wouldn't have made it this far, what's left would have looked like those poor bastards we met today."

"Their diet was mostly the problem for them, I can thank you guys for keeping us fed, as well as housed and safe. I can't thank you enough for that," I said, with a tear rolling down my cheek.

And I meant it. If it wasn't for Jared, I knew many of us wouldn't have made it.

Jared smiled then. "We all had our part to play...I think that's what made us so strong. Everyone is doing their bit. You know I've never said so, but you did the right thing with Craig, he *was* an arsehole and had to go. He was a leech, and I knew it. But I choked at having to go through the confrontation, so you stepped up and kicked arse. I was in *awe* of you Jess." He turned to me and grinned. "I still am!... No doubt you'll make a kick arse doctor... I think you already are and there has to be hundreds out there," He swept his hand towards the glowing lights. "Who think you are too. I saw that guy with one arm today; he's alive because of you. No question he was going to die, even I could see that... But he's alive because you stepped up. We'd have lost Amy if it weren't for you. Plus, all the others you treated *before* it became serious. A lot of them wouldn't be here either. I reckon that's pretty awesome

Jess." He chuckled. "You know when I first called you *Doc*, I hoped you'd be our first-aider... now look at ya!"

I laughed. "Jesus that would have been nice. Patch them up and send them to a real doctor."

"Yeah, and since we didn't have one to send 'em to... You *became* one... Amazing.

"Look, whatever happens when the others leave," he paused. "Know that we all love you and are grateful you did what you do."

I was being strong till he said that, and a little sob escaped before I could stop it, he put his arm around me and gave a squeeze.

"Are we making the right choice?" I asked.

"Yep, I think so, I don't think anyone is going anywhere, but it's not for me to try and stop them... When the other guys go, do me a favour and hang back. Don't be up front, let's see how it all pans out."

The thought of staying up here and watching them walk down through town suddenly frightened me. I hadn't realised just how much of my strength came from us as a group and how much I'd miss them.

"Ok," I said. "Will we be going down to see them off?"

"We'll go as far as we dare. There's that river down there along the highway, there's trees for cover, after that it's open ground to the airfield and I'd rather they didn't know we were there. Anyway," he said, getting up. "We'd best go see the others, they'll be wondering where we got to, and you *know* how they love to gossip." He grinned and held out a hand to help me up.

I laughed. "Oh yeah, especially the ones who've got together, not happy till everyone's got together with someone."

As we walked back to camp, I started thinking about that. From comments I'd heard it was generally accepted that Jared and I would get together, but it just didn't happen. I guess I just hadn't had the energy for it. Jared's an awesome guy; a girl could do way worse. Nice looking and well built, but I didn't get *that* feeling about him, if I was honest, I just didn't allow time for it either.

Maybe I've missed that boat, I'm in the 'friend zone', I thought... with just a little regret.

When we arrived back at camp the others were sitting around the fire sharing a laugh. I knew I'd miss this. We just gelled as a group and I couldn't imagine any of us not being a part of it, and having it work so well. I thought back to when Craig and his mob were with us. It was a totally different dynamic, we were together, but everyone was for themselves.

These guys were all about each other.

The weather was clear that night so it looked good for the Lizards' arrival in the morning.

Spirits were high but there was an undertow of the impending splitting of the group. None of us wanted to be parted but there was a clear divide between those who were going and those who were staying.

Now that their departure was close, I admit I was having second thoughts, but a week of dreaming of a better life and waking up to the reality of what the Lizards are about, had cemented my decision. I wasn't going.

We shared memories into the night, and we all went to bed late, having exhausted ourselves with laughter.

When I woke up, I could smell the coffee. Jared was up to his old trick with the coffee being waved past our tents. I smiled knowing what he was up to.

When I dragged myself out of my tent, I found that I was the last one up!

I was greeted by everyone and handed a pannikin of coffee by Jared. "Glad you could join us." He smiled.

"Can't believe I'm the last one up," I laughed.

"Yeah, there's a first for everyone. Anyway, I've been for a look and there are already people gathering on the airfield. No sign of the Lizards yet though."

I drank my coffee and took in the sounds and smell of the morning. The birdsong was amazing as always, but today I paid more attention. I paid more attention in general.

After breakfast we heard the aircraft arrive. It started as a low rumble but soon we could hear the high-pitched whine as it approached. We all scrambled to the ridge and saw a huge ship settling on the airfield at the northern end. It took up more than twice the runway in width, and it's stubby wings extended to the trees on the side of the grassy area paralleling the bitumen landing strip. I could see many people gathered, waiting for its arrival. I have no idea how many, from here they were just a mass of dark.

"Well, I guess we'd better get down there," Jared said.

We all packed our tents in silence. I'd made a policy of spreading medical supplies across everyone to make sure we never place all our eggs in one basket. Just when I was starting to spread the medical *knowledge* to Amy, she had chosen to go to the resettlement and none of the others had ever shown interest in learning. So unfortunately, all the medical care eggs were going to be in my basket again. I never felt comfortable being the only one with those skills, if anything happened to me, they'd be in real trouble.

By the time we got through town we were joining many hundreds more walking towards the airfield. I had no idea there were so many still living around here.

Instead of going straight there, we curved around to the north following the river and the cover of the trees. We finally came to a stand of trees maybe one hundred and fifty meters from the refuelling apron where the aircraft was hovering. It was clearly different from the other aircraft we'd seen. Aside from its massive size it was more angular and appeared to have scorch marks radiating out from under the belly. "This must be one of the spacecraft they used to get here. Look at the scorch marks from entry into the atmosphere," said James, a little excited.

Bruce gave a low growl and Kieran gruffly said, "Leave it." The dog immediately sat down and began panting.

There were Lizards with weapon sticks lined up either side of a doorway, with a set of stairs leading into the belly of the ship. Beside the door was a raised podium with a fat human in a suit, who was speaking over a PA system to the people gathered.

"People, please leave your weapons in the container on the left hand side of the door, only bring essentials, everything you will need will be supplied."

There was a steady stream of people entering the ship in single file with a huge number still waiting to enter.

"There's too many," said Jared

"What do you mean?" asked David.

"Too many to fit on that aircraft. I mean look at it, it's big, but there isn't enough room on it to take that many. They would have been loading well before we arrived and they're still loading them, how is it possible they can all fit in there? You'd have to lay them all down on top of each other to fit."

"People, please place all weapons in the bin on your left, you cannot take them with you," said the fat man over the PA.

"Maybe it's like the *Tardis,"* joked James.

"What's the *Tardis*?" asked Paula.

James rolled his eyes and mumbled, "Never mind."

The people kept filing in one by one and a man in the back yelled at the fat man. "LOOKS LIKE YOU HAVEN'T BEEN DOING IT TOO TOUGH, MATE."

"It hasn't been easy for any of us, I assure you," he replied.

"WELL, SOME OF US HAVE BEEN DOING IT TOUGHER THAN OTHERS, HEY," yelled the man.

"LOOKS LIKE YOU HAVEN'T BEEN MISSING TOO MANY MEALS!" yelled another.

"We've all had to make sacrifices," The fat man replied.

"*SACRIFICES*?" The man laughed and was joined by many in the assembled crowd. "WHAT EXACTLY HAVE YOU SACRIFICED?"

"We all do what we have to in these trying times. If I don't do this, I don't get paid."

Half the crowd roared with laughter and there were many angry shouts.

"PAID? JESUS MATE WE'VE BEEN TRYING NOT TO *DIE*!" said another man.

"I WATCHED MY LITTLE GIRL DIE, AND YOU'RE WORRIED ABOUT GETTING *PAID*? YOU BASTARD!

TELL US WHY...WHY DO WE DIE AND YOU GET PAID?" asked woman in the front.

"You don't understand the question you are asking."

Angry abuse and boos, erupted from the unhappy crowd.

The man was holding his hands out, trying to calm them. *"People, PLEASE! We all just must get through this together. Just place your weapons in the bin and file on-board."*

There were a few more words of abuse hurled at the man, but everyone went back to filing on-board. They knew they had little choice.

I guess the fact that there was a human involved made me feel a little more at ease about Amy and Peter getting on board the ship, even if he was a self-serving bastard.

I turned to the others, and we began our goodbyes. It wasn't easy. I tried to give some last minute medical advice to Amy but she just pulled me in for a hug. Kieran grabbed her and nearly crushed her ribs with his hug and then finally Peter said, "Well I'm off. Let's go Amy." And stoically, he headed off across the grass towards the tarmac. Amy was still doing the rounds of hugs with her usual sweet words to everyone when suddenly there was a commotion at the spaceship. We all turned as a young woman with long blonde hair, scrambled back past the others filing into the ship, she was covered in bright red blood, and she screamed hysterically. "THEY'RE KILLING THEM!" She gasped a breath and yelled again, "THEY'RE KILLING THEM!"

WHOOMPH. One of the aliens shot her in the back, cutting a hole right through her.

There was an immediate uproar, people shouting, gunshots rang out. I have a mental picture of a bullet striking the fat man in the arm before he crumpled against the ship and the Lizards opening fire on the humans waiting outside. It was complete carnage. I heard rifle shots ring out from alongside me; it was Kieran shooting at the Lizards.

The Lizards were firing small projectiles that exploded above people's heads with an ear splitting WHOOMPH, which sent them sprawling. It was the first time we'd seen those weapons and they were frightening.

There were shots ringing out from all over the place, people were screaming. I saw Peter go down, hit by a projectile bomb right in front of me! Jared grabbed me and threw me to the ground placing his body over me. A few moments later he grabbed me and lifted me to my feet. "Come on, we're getting out of here," he said, and dragged me behind him, heading off along the tree line. "But what about Peter?" I cried.

"You can't help him, Jess. We have to save ourselves now," he said breathlessly.

I heard the ship take off and turned to see large doors open underneath it and bodies, so *many* blood-covered bodies, spilling out onto the ground along the runway as it headed south. We ran as fast as we could. We crossed the river, which was only waist deep; Amy had hold of Bruce's collar as he bounded across the water, dragging her along. We scrambled up the bank on the other side and headed west to the mountains... We kept running.

I was almost out of steam when I felt Kieran grab me under the arm and almost lifted me as he drove me forward. Louise had Amy on her other side doing the same for her. By the time we'd reached the forest on the other side of town we were all exhausted. We crumpled into heaps on the ground trying to get our breath, when we heard the smaller aircraft coming. "Keep moving," said Jared. We all got to our feet and ran on; we climbed the hill through the trees until we topped the first ridge where we stopped again to get our breath back.

We could hear the BOOM, BOOM of the bombs but they seemed to be concentrated on the airfield. We were in the forest so couldn't see anything which made the situation worse. We kept running and climbing, the further we were away from it, the less likely we were to get bombed, so we *ran*. When we finally reached a point where we could see out, the aircraft were gone, and we looked in awe at the sight before us. The airport was pock marked with bodies and circular discolorations from the bombs; the lower western side of Mount Mackay was almost entirely without trees.

We all sat down without a word. What else could we do, we'd just seen Peter, and maybe two thousand people die before our eyes.

"Those bloody bastards," Kieran said with uncharacteristic anger in his voice. "They slaughtered them in cold blood."

"At least now we know for sure what their plan is," said David.

James said, "Yeah, total extermination."

"Well, I guess we'd better get back down there," said Jared.

"Why the hell would we want to do that?" asked James.

"Because there might be people hurt," I said.

There was silence for a moment before James stood, picked up his backpack and sighed. "Let's go then."

We began the trek back down the hill and it was mid afternoon before we got back to the airfield. Already there were a half dozen people checking for wounded amongst the dead.

It was a grim sight and I have to admit that. Looking for survivors sounded like the right thing to do on the hill, but down here it was a gruesome task I wasn't sure I was prepared for.

Jared spoke to one of the people already there and came back to us. "They have a system already, so we'll join in. Each of us space out along the runway and check people as you walk south. Any wounded let Doc know ok?"

We all agreed and dumped our packs under a tree at the edge of the runway. "If the Lizards come back, head back to where we were this morning."

We all walked across the refuelling apron, the bodies on it had already been checked if the system worked. Kieran found Peter, Bruce sniffed him and started emitting a quiet, high pitched whine and sat close to Kieran. Clearly this upset him as much as it upset us. Our friend was dead and there was nothing we could do about it but look for others that may have survived.

We'd walked most of the way across the tarmac when the true carnage of the weapon sticks at close range could be seen. I found no compassion in me for the dead lizards; the blonde woman who likely saved us all was there. I nearly threw up at the sight of her, the massive hole in her abdomen a ghastly reminder of what I'd witnessed. There were dozens more like her.

Bruce stopped in his tracks and pricked up his ears, and we all stopped to watch him. He left Kieran's side and sniffing emphatically, he zigzagged his way between the bodies, until he found one and licked its face. The body was on its side facing away from us and Bruce began whining and sat down. Kieran raced over to the body, rolled it onto it's back and quickly checked its pulse, before pausing with a look of shock on his face. I'd got to him by then and saw who it was. Carol, Kini's mum, was lying dead in front of us.

Kieran suddenly burst into action going from body to body with tears in his eyes, "Kini, look for Kini," he said. We scrambled into action looking for her but after a few minutes we'd checked everyone on the apron. There were more than a dozen kids but as best we could tell, she wasn't one of them.

"She would have been with her Mum, if she's not here maybe she would have gotten away," said Julia.

Kieran kept looking, searching bodies like he was possessed, muttering "Bloody bastards," over and over.

We all had our moment of grief over Carol's death, just as we did Peter's and began the more urgent task of checking bodies for the ones we might be able to save. We went on for the next hour and didn't find anyone still alive. If nothing else... The Lizards were thorough.

I was nearly ready to give up when I heard an engine. I looked at Jared who held up his hand. *What's that about, why aren't we running?* I wondered. The sound got louder, and it definitely wasn't a jeep, it was a *big* machine whatever it was. I could hear it approaching the southern end of the runway and at last I saw it; a huge yellow bulldozer came rattling onto the runway. I was confused for a moment as to why this was happening when it dawned on me that it was coming to dig a grave.

It came all the way up to where the furthest bodies were and put it's massive blade down, it began gouging into the red earth, all the way to the refuelling apron. It turned and dug its way back down the trench, repeating the same thing over and over, each time getting deeper into the ground.

More people had showed up by then and there were quite a few of the bigger guys carrying the bodies to line them up alongside the trench that was to become their grave. The Lizards were left lying on the ground.

I was soon called away from checking bodies to treat the walking wounded who'd come back to this place. I didn't mind, it was much easier to take the blood and gore when the person was living, it's when they were dead that it truly affected me.

With the trench completed, the driver of the bulldozer slewed his blade sideways and drove along the edge of the trench, scooping the bodies into it. His face was grim and his eyes fixed forward as he came past us. I couldn't watch the bodies being scooped by a big steel blade either, it seemed disrespectful, but there was simply no choice when you have so many to deal with.

When he finished his run, he turned the machine around and came back pushing dirt back into the trench to cover the bodies.

By the time he was mostly done there was a shout, and I turned to see two army jeeps come racing onto the runway from the south. The man on the dozer turned the machine and drove it directly at them with great plumes of black smoke coming from the exhaust. The jeeps stopped and Lizards got out, pointing their sticks at the machine. I saw the dozer blade rise to protect the driver, but he didn't stop. I could hear the Lizards begin firing with the loud WHOOMPH sound, but each was followed by an even louder CLANG as the sound struck the blade. Still, he kept going.

Kieran and some others with high-powered rifles and telescopic sights began firing. It was a long distance away, but I saw two Lizards fall to the ground. Someone was a good shot.

When the dozer reached the jeeps, it simply drove straight over the one on the right, then turned towards the one on the left and stopped. I saw two more Lizards fall from rifle shots and it all went quiet.

Jared, Kieran, of course Bruce and several others ran down the runway with their rifles. "HEAD FOR THE TREES EVERYONE!" yelled Jared over his shoulder as he took off.

I couldn't, I was in the middle of stitching up a gaping wound in a man's stomach from a fall onto a machete while running from the bombs. How he'd got here without his intestines falling out was a mystery but there was no way I could go yet.

His friend was giving us a running commentary on what was happening at the end of the runway, so I wasn't completely blind to what was happening. "The driver of the dozer is dead," he told me. "Looks like the guys are carrying him to the trench. Your mate with the dog has climbed onto the dozer, looks like he's gonna finish the job ... oh nah hang on, looks like he's turning those jeeps and the Lizards into pancakes first."

I couldn't blame Kieran for that, I felt like doing the same.

With his little revenge over, Kieran did fill in the rest of the trench and then parked the dozer.

I finished stitching up the man's belly and got his friends to carry him back to their camp.

"Keep him still for at least a few days or he'll pull those stitches," I told them.

When the job was done we all met back at our backpacks, but Kieran was there already with an arm full of rifles he'd taken from the bin the Lizards were using to collect the weapons.

He handed one to each of us but when I took mine it nearly hit the ground. It was so heavy! He grunted and pulled out two target pistols and handed one each to Amy and myself. "Close range only," he said. I looked briefly at it, before shoving it in my backpack. It was a nice looking gun if you like that sort of thing. But I was never really that into guns.

We headed west to camp for the night. We'd gone maybe halfway when we heard an aircraft approaching. We dove into some trees for cover and watched as it flew over the runway. Kieran lifted his rifle and took aim but Jared put his hand in front of the telescopic sight, "No mate, they'll just bomb the crap out of us."

"Bugger 'em, they can't get away with it," said Kieran angrily.

"I know, but us dying, won't hurt *them* a bit, hey."

Kieran lowered the rifle, and I could see his jaw muscles flexing and he ground his teeth.

The aircraft made several passes over the airfield; it dropped one bomb and then headed off to the south again.

When we made camp near the base of the mountains the mood was understandably cheerless.

The creek we camped near was deep enough to lay down in and we all took a proper bath to try and wash away the blood, and more importantly the *memories* of the day. It didn't work of course, but I did feel a little better for it.

There were a lot of tears that night as we sat around the fire as everyone vented and talked out their feelings, it was like a group therapy session. Surprisingly there were no tears from me, and I don't know why, maybe I hadn't processed it all yet, but it meant I could spend much of the night giving comfort to my friends. We would all miss Peter and to lose him like that, right in front of us, was something that would take a long time to fully get over. Amy was particularly upset. She was two goodbyes from being right beside him. Suffering from grief and I think a little survivor guilt, she was really upset, and it took a lot of hugs to calm her.

Kieran just sat and fumed. I could feel the white hot rage emanating from him, and we all tiptoed around him that night for fear of setting him off. I hoped a good sleep would help calm his rage but doubted it.

Fight or Flight

'If angry count to ten. If very angry count to one hundred.' -Thomas Jefferson

The next morning, we were greeted by another clear and stinking hot day. With yesterday's happenings, I'd failed to boil water for drinking and thankfully David had started the process already.

When we all had a coffee in hand we sat again around the fire, but this time in silence. We'd all nearly finished our cups when Kieran finally spoke.

"I'm gonna fight back."

Jared nodded and said, "Yep, figured as much."

Kieran went on. "They're just gonna keep hunting us down, killing us one by one until we're all bloody gone, I'm at least gonna take a few with me."

"Yep," said Jared

"How can we fight back?" asked Louise "We have nothing, a few guns and hardly any bullets. They have aircraft and jeeps."

"Yep," said Jared.

David spoke. "I'm all for it, but I'm not gonna go charging in on a suicide mission, bugger that."

Kieran said, "Got any ideas? I wanna hear 'em."

"No," began David. "But I think it's something we should plan, not go blasting in to get shot on day one."

Jared said, "Yep."

Louise cut in with her usual acidic tone. "For Christ's sake Jared, stop saying *YEP*! You're the army guy, you must have an opinion, let's hear it."

Jared took a sip of his coffee and began. "Look… I'm not saying anything because I already know what I want to do and it's not fair for me to influence this group either way. Not on something this important. I would rather you all come to your own decisions."

Louise scoffed. "That's a cop out, your opinion is what a lot of people will be looking for to help them make their decisions."

"Yep, that's why I am trying to keep my opinions to myself. But if you must hear them then here it is. I think Kieran's dead right. They will keep hunting us down till they've killed us all. I think they haven't already wiped us out of here because it's too wet for them on foot, and they can't bomb the entire bush, it'll take them a year. But that doesn't mean they won't eventually. We most likely can't win," he paused and shook his head. "Nah who am I kidding, we can't possibly win against them, but as Kieran said, we can take a few with us."

The group was silent for a moment while we all digested Jared's information.

"I don't want to see any more killings," said Julia. "It's just so awful." She put her face in her hands and sobbed. Kyle put his arm around her and pulled her to him.

Kieran said, "The killing will continue whether we like it or not."

"But we don't have to go *looking* for it!" Julia replied through her tears.

Kyle said, "And what about the bombings, if we piss 'em off, they just bomb the hell out of us."

"Yep, there is that," began Jared. "But I'm thinking we won't attack them here. I'm thinking we would take the fight to them. From what we know they are based in Townsville, we can stir all sorts of crap down there, and they won't associate it with this area."

"What sort of crap can we stir with a few rifles?" David asked.

Jared looked thoughtful for a moment before saying, "Look I don't want to discuss too much until everyone has made their decision, but I will say this. Ever tried to sleep with a mozzie in the room? Even small things can give you grief... I'm thinking of *guerrilla* style hit and run tactics. Sabotage, not all out war... We'd definitely lose if we took them on in a battle... But for now, I think we should all just have a think about where we stand. Let's not try to make a decision yet, just have a think about what you want to do, and tomorrow we can decide."

We all agreed to leave it till tomorrow. We set about making breakfast and getting our day underway.

I didn't know where I stood. I knew nothing about war, and I seriously doubted I could kill, but these weren't human, and they deserved what they got. Yes, that's how cold I'd become having sifted through thousands of innocent dead people, looking for survivors of an unprovoked and despicable attack, made under the guise of friendship. I was angry and wanted revenge on these creatures.

But to make war was something so foreign to me that I couldn't even imagine it. I didn't even like watching war films! I thought if I was torn, I could imagine many others would be feeling the same. I couldn't see Julia agreeing to it and where she went, Kyle would go.

Paula would most likely go with Kieran... And Louise, well I could see her getting into it.

Amy, oh my god, Amy! I seriously couldn't see her waging war with *anything* and I wouldn't want her to. I'd come to think of her as a little sister and the thought of her risking her life in a battle just horrified me.

The day dragged on and anytime the subject of war came up Jared shut it down. "Guys I think discussing it is not fair on those who are undecided. It means they could be swayed by a good argument and that's not fair. This is a conscience decision and it's up to the individual," he said.

It didn't help my decision at all, but I understood his standpoint. My usual way in this sort of situation is to listen to which way the tide is running when people start voting, and go with it, but I know that's cowardly and I had to make my own decision on this, as it was simply too important.

It made it easier to imagine it would be a secret vote and I wouldn't be able to see a show of hands. That meant I had to decide *beforehand.*

The night went without discussion and it was in general pretty quiet. We were far from recovered from the ordeal the day before, so we were a long way from our usual banter and laughs.

The morning came and once we all had a coffee Jared sat down and said. "Right folks we've all had a night to sleep on it. I guess we'd better make our decisions. Anyone have anything to say?"

"I do," said Kieran "I'll be fighting back."

"And me," said Paula.

"And me," said David.

"Yeah, and me, better that than waiting to die," said Louise.

"I'm not a soldier," said James. "I think I'll head back to the coast and try to make some sort of life for myself for as long as it lasts."

"Same for us," said Julia. "We," she motioned to Kyle and herself. "Have given this some thought and come to a decision. If we only have a short time left in this world, we would rather be happy together, than trying to kill things. We'd like to go find somewhere on the coast and live for as long as we can."

"Ok," Jared said. "At least you have a plan and I'm sure everyone would join me in wishing you well."

Everyone agreed.

"I really want to help fight back," said Amy. "But I don't know how much use I could be to you."

"You've been training with Jess. Of course, you would be a great help." He smiled.

"I'll be fighting back too," I said and Jared smiled broadly at me.

There, I'd said it and it felt good. No more sitting and waiting to be bombed, I was going to go out and make a difference. Well, I hoped so anyway.

Jared said, "Right, well now that's over with I guess we'd best get organised. I was thinking we should try to recruit as many of those people helping at the airfield as we can. You guys who are heading for the coast, stay for a while or head off. It's entirely up to you but let us know if you need anything. You all know where the supplies are stashed and I'm sure you've picked up a few tips on fishing from David, so you should do ok I reckon."

We all broke camp and headed back towards the airfield. The weather had turned overcast, and it threatened to rain so we were feeling pretty safe. As we approached the airfield, Kieran grabbed one of the flyers that had been stuck to a tree and asked, "Hey anyone got a pen?"

"I do," said Amy and she pulled a thick black permanent marker from a pocket in her backpack.

Kieran took the pen with a "Thanks" and started writing on the back of the flyer.

WE ARE FIGHTING BACK!

Join us or wait to get bombed.

Army trained leader.

Let's make those bastards pay for what they did.

Meet us at Tully airport.

"Jared, how's one week sound to meet back here?" Kieran said.

"Yep, day of the three quarter moon. Gives us almost a week to get the word out," said Jared.

Kieran continued his flyer.

... The day of the ¾ moon. Afternoon.

If it's raining... bring an umbrella!

Signed

Jared's Group.

Satisfied with his work, he handed the pen back to Amy and said, "Amy, is there any chance you could copy that onto any other flyers we see?"

"Yep, will do," she said, looking pleased to have a job to do.

Kieran spotted the bulldozer with its now very dented roof and decided to go check it out. The rest of us started slowly making our way towards some buildings, as the rain started falling, we stood under a verandah. Amy had set about changing a couple of flyers that were stuck to the wall. A few moments later I saw a large plume of black smoke come from the exhaust stack on the dozer and heard the roar of the diesel engine. Kieran did a few circles with the machine, then shut it down and jogged back to us.

"Bloody thing still goes," he said, shaking his head in disbelief. "Roofs dented to hell…and the bonnet…Machines been pushed six inches into the ground, but their bombs didn't hurt it."

"That's good to know," Said Jared. "But I bet you wouldn't want to be in it when it got bombed hey."

"Nah, even the foam in the seat was shredded," replied Kieran. "Nobody would survive it."

The sound of the bulldozer's big engine had brought a few faces out of hiding and we waved them over to us.

The first to arrive was a tall thin man in a farmer's hat and ragged clothes.

"You guys start that dozer?" he asked in a slow, farmer's drawl.

"Yeah, that was me," said Kieran. "Hoping a few people might hear it."

"What are yas up to?" the man asked.

Amy handed the man one of the flyers, which he quickly read and then let out a low chuckle. "You lot must be *Jared's group*? You don't *look* much like soldiers."

"Jared is ex-Army," said Kieran.

"You're gonna get yourselves killed," laughed the man, shaking his head.

"You saw what they did here and what they've been doing. We're going to die anyway, mate, might as well take a few of the bastards with us," said Jared.

The tall man pursed his lips and thought for a long moment before shrugging his shoulders. "Well... I can't argue with you there... What's your plan?"

"Hit and run guerrilla tactics, sabotage... No point going head to head with them, they'll win, but we can hurt 'em if we hit and run," said Jared.

The man nodded his head slowly looking at the ground. About a dozen more people had crowded in the verandah by now and they were watching the exchange between the men.

The tall man finally looked up at Jared and said, "Well...We've been wondering how to get back at 'em, count me and my lot in." He held out a hand for Jared to shake. Jared grinned and shook the man's hand. "Welcome aboard mate, great to have you with us."

There were introductions all round. Most of the dozen or so people were in this man's group. The other group's leader introduced himself and quickly joined the cause.

Our numbers had increased from six to eighteen people in a morning. In a time without the Internet, I figured that was almost going *viral*.

Discussions went on for an hour or so as they quizzed Jared on his plans. He deflected most of them, he really hadn't had time to formulate much of a plan, but nobody could have sensed that from the way he handled himself.

When the rain stopped, everyone dispersed with a goal to spread the word, but before they all left, one man came to me and said a little sheepishly, "Hey... look you guys have girls in your group, I was wondering..."

I was immediately on the defensive, which he picked up on.

"Nah, nah, nothing like that," he said quickly, holding his hands up. "It's just that I know of a group nearby that is all men, but they've picked up a few kids after...Well the other day." He motioned behind him to the runway, "They have no idea what they're doing but they're doing their best for the little ones."

"We'll take them," said Julia who was standing behind me.

Kyle who was standing beside her said, "Julia, I dunno-" Julia shot him a look that would *cut glass,* and he didn't finish the sentence.

"We'll take them," she repeated. "Where are they?"

"I'll take you there if you like. It's not far, just up the back of town," he said with a big smile. "Thanks... Those kids need... Well, someone a bit softer than a bunch of blokes," he said awkwardly.

I went to Jared and told him what was happening, and we all set out following this man. He took us to a small weatherboard house set back against the rainforest on the edge of town. He yelled out *Cooee,* and three men came out of the forest behind the house. Their faces lit up when they saw us.

"Got someone willing to take the little ones off your hands Bill," the man said.

"Thank Christ for that," grinned a short, shirtless man in his sixties. He followed with an apology. "Excuse the language girls."

He turned to the man beside him and said something we couldn't hear, before the other man returned to the rainforest.

There were introductions and the man called Bill spoke to us about the kids. "Girls, these kids have been through hell. They need a woman's touch...Well, what they need is their mums, but they're all gone. They're pretty messed up; one hasn't said a word since we picked her up. She's terrified of us; the poor little bugger and she won't eat or drink anything we give her."

Julia said, "I should go to them. It'll be less scary than coming out to another group of strangers."

"Yeah, fair enough luv," Bill said. "Come with me."

Julia asked Paula to go with her and they headed off into the forest. We waited for maybe fifteen minutes before they re-emerged with the kids. Julia was carrying one who was clinging to her neck. The child's skinny legs were swinging with each step. Paula emerged leading two small boys with terrified looks on their faces. I looked across and saw all the guys with stern, worried looks on their faces. "Smile you lot," I said.

They all plastered on silly grins, which probably looked more like The Joker from Batman than friendly, but it was an improvement.

When Julia reached us, she turned her back to us and said, "Look who I have here."

Looking over her shoulder was an extremely thin looking face with big eyes in sunken eye sockets. Her tears having cleaned little rivulets down her cheeks in the dirt on her face, it was hard to recognise this child, but there it was. She was a very grubby Kini!

When she looked at me, I could see a faint recognition in her eyes, but then she looked down and saw Bruce. Her face lit up and she wriggled and squirmed until Julia let her down. She raced over to Bruce and threw her arms around his neck. Bruce's tail wagged like it would fly off! Kieran knelt beside the dog and said. "Hey Kini, how are ya?"

Kini slowly looked up from the dog's neck and saw Kieran. Her eyes went wide, and she launched herself at him, trying to bury herself in his neck. There wasn't a dry eye in our group. We were all so glad to see her.

"You lot know this girl?" asked Bill.

"Yeah, we know her, mate," said Kieran, wiping away the tears. "Long story."

"And this is Shaun and Jake," said Julia by way of introduction for the two boys holding Paula's hands.

We all said hello to them and introduced them to Bruce who just sat and let them pat him without trying to lick them. He was so good with kids he was a marvel. I could see every bone in his body wanted to lick them half to death but his self-restraint was amazing.

Bill said, "If you guys are willing to take 'em, we'll help you keep 'em fed. Where are ya camped?"

"That's very kind of you... we were in Mission Beach, and plan to head back there," said Julia.

"Yeah, we were too, but came here for the resettlement. That all turned to hell, and we've been trying to work out what to do with the kids since then."

"Three of us are going to settle at the beach again while the rest will head off to fight back," said Jared.

Bill thought for a moment and said, "Yeah well. We're all a bit old for all that, but I'm glad you're gonna have a go. I reckon we'll head back to the beach now, so why don't we travel with your people. We'll know where they are then and can drop off fish 'n stuff when we can."

"Mate, that sounds like an awesome idea. Thanks," said Jared.

I saw Amy was having a careful look over the kids to check their health. I was going to do the same but thought I'd let her do it instead. She needed to gain confidence in her abilities and seeing her take on the role was gratifying to say the least.

We waited for the four men to grab their gear and I spoke quietly to Amy. "How are the kids?"

"They're ok in general," she said. "Need feeding up. Kini is seriously thin and dehydrated but at least she's drinking now. The old guys look in worse shape." She smiled.

"They'll all need a doctor, Amy."

She squirmed a little. She knew what I was implying. "I want to help fight back," she said,

"No point in fighting back, if there's nobody left to fight *for*," I reminded her. "Those kids are the future. Isn't having a future the best way to fight back against extermination?"

She was quiet then with her brow furrowed, and I let her digest it.

I really hoped she would go back to the beach. Not just because I wanted to keep her safe, it was so there was someone else to carry the torch of medical care if anything happened to me.

Jared turned to Julia and said, "Well we all might as well come to Mission Beach I guess; we can get you all set up and see if there is anyone else there who wants to join us."

"Thanks, Jared. It'll be a big help," she said,

The men returned with their gear, and we all set off with Jared in the lead. Kini had gone back to being carried by Julia and Kieran carried Julia's pack. Where Kini's little pack went we didn't know but it didn't matter, I was sure they'd find things for her at the beach. The two boys were still holding Paula's hands but had relaxed a bit. They were older than Kini, maybe about eight or nine and were talking in brief sentences with the others when asked questions whereas Kini, had yet to speak a word.

Jared said, "Look, we're never going to make the beach today. What do you reckon we make camp for the night somewhere along the way?"

We all agreed, and Kieran said, "Make it sooner rather than later mate. I'll see if I can get us a feed, put some meat in those kids' bellies."

"Great idea, mate," said Jared.

It was raining so we just walked along the road and I looked longingly at some houses we passed.

"This rain is pretty set in, Jared, do you think we could borrow a house?" I asked. "For the kids of course," I added.

Jared laughed, "Yeah I reckon we can do that."

We walked into a housing estate and naturally headed for the houses closest to the rainforest. We found one that looked older than the rest and possibly not part of the estate. It was more a roof with large shutters that swung out on sticks that propped them open. Inside we found it empty and in reasonable shape but full of leaf litter and spider webs. Better than a tent in the rain anyway so we checked it out. It was small, especially for our larger than usual group, not just the three kids but five extra guys to find room for. There were no insect screens fitted to any doors or windows, but it was at least out of the rain.

Kieran headed out the back door and came back soon after. "This place is on gravity fed water off the mountain, and there's a donkey for the hot water!"

"Woohoo!" I said.

"What does that mean?" asked Amy and Louise almost in unison.

"A donkey is a drum of water you heat with firewood. It means we might get a hot shower!" I said excitedly.

The excitement caught on as others learned of the possibility of our first hot shower since it all began.

Kieran had left the hot water to the others to sort out and went hunting with Bruce, but Julia had a hard time convincing Kini that he was coming back soon. She became quite upset when he left. The poor girl had every reason to be suffering separation anxiety and it would take her a long time to get over it. It was going to be hard when he left her in Mission Beach.

Everyone separated into rooms to find an area to roll out their sleeping bags. I chose the main living area with the kids.

There was a sharp yell from one of the other rooms just as I rolled out my sleeping bag. One of the men said, "Snake...! Bugger, its a bloody *Taipan!* Everyone out while I deal with it!"

Snakes are something I fully expected to have to deal with in the forest, but as it's turned out we've seen very few. There's been the occasional tree snake but nothing poisonous. Now our first real encounter is with one of Australia's most dangerous snakes. Without anti-venom, a bite from the coastal Taipan is almost always fatal.

We all bolted outside and stood in the rain while the guys from the other group dealt with the snake. We waited for maybe five minutes until we heard a shotgun blast and then silence. Shortly after one of the men came out with the dead snake held up. It looked to be two meters long and as thick as my arm.

"It's all good, you can go back in now, he said, flinging it into the bush. "Wasn't taking any chances with that one, cranky bastards."

With the drama over we all went back inside, but our cosy house didn't feel that great anymore. I chose to set up my tent instead and threw my sleeping bag in. Everyone followed suit. It took up more room, but I wasn't chancing having something like that curling up with me.

Not long after we had all our beds ready one of the men came in from the back door and said, "Donkey's lit. Give it a half hour and there'll be hot showers all round." He winked.

There was a loud cheer from all of us.

We elected to bathe the kids first and the men graciously offered to let the girls go before them. There was just one bathroom for twelve people plus the kids, so there wouldn't be any long lingering in the shower. But nobody was complaining, even though it was still stinking hot outside, it was sheer bliss to get properly clean.

Kieran returned with two wallabies already cleaned, and he began looking for a way to cook them. There was no gas in the kitchen cooker so a rustic steel BBQ outside was the answer.

Kini was reluctant to eat; well in fact she point blank refused, until Kieran acted hurt that she wouldn't eat the food he'd gone out in the rain to get for her.

That worked and she slowly took a bite. As she did so, I saw her eyes half closed in bliss, and we *all* heard her tummy grumble, which made everyone, laugh.

She took to the rest of her food with gusto, and we declared her fasting over. David suggested Julia to only give her a little to start with, as she'd not eaten in days. Too much would make her sick. He was dead right and I thanked him for the reminder.

In no time Kini seemed more animated and a bit of colour returned to her cheeks, which was a bit of a relief. Like Amy, Kini can ill afford to lose weight.

The kids all bunked with Julia in Kyle's tent, which meant Kyle was out in the cold for the night, but David volunteered to share, so all wasn't lost.

I told Kyle the bonding time with Julia was important for the little ones right now. He just smiled and said, "Yeah I know, Jess... These are the reasons I love her."

The night went without much fuss. I heard the kids grow restless a few times and some whimpering, but Julia's calm soothing soon put them back to sleep.

The next morning saw a rush for the one toilet, and thanks to the gravity fed water, it still worked! The men all went outside to pee; that made things a lot less congested, but unfortunately it was raining heavily. So they were quick trips, which made for a few laughs.

We were organising some breakfast for the kids, when an engine starting up outside made us all freeze. The men all grabbed their rifles and positioned themselves at each of the doors and windows.

Jared and Kieran began venturing outside with their rifles at the ready when the engine stopped and a moment later; Kyle came running in out of the rain. He reached the verandah and stopped with his hands up. "Relax guys, it's just me," he said grinning. "I got us some transport."

The transport he meant was in the shape of an old Toyota minibus he'd found in the shed.

"I was thinking," he began explaining his idea. "It's pissing rain so there's no chance of Lizards on the ground or air. They bomb what's been changed yeah? So don't change anything. There is a door on that shed, so the Lizards won't know the van is gone if we close it behind us. All we need is a place in mission beach, that has a garage or shed with a door that we can close behind it and we can travel in style."

"The perfect crime," grinned Kieran with eyes wide.

I have to say it was good to see some of the old Kieran back. I was starting to get worried we'd seen the last of the lovable joker. After what happened at the airfield, he'd become quite dark and I put much of his recovery down to Kini's miraculous survival.

"Well, I like the idea," said David.

"I do too," said Jared. "But how does everyone else feel about it?" He turned to Kyle. "And do you know of any places like that in Mission?"

"Several," said Kyle.

"Yeah, me too," said David. "We found plenty of empty sheds with closed doors when we were looking for fishing gear."

"Well," Jared said. "Unless anyone has an objection, I'd say it's a bloody good idea."

Bill's group all agreed that it was a good idea but I could tell they were nervous about traveling by car. Nobody had done it safely since this had all begun. The squashed cars littered the roads as testimony to what a bad idea it was, but as Jared explained to them.

"We know more about them now; we know when they travel and when they don't. They have bombed at night, but only in the beginning and nobody has seen an aircraft or a Lizard at night since then. Nobody has *ever* seen one of them in the rain."

There was a lot of head nodding as everyone considered what he'd said.

"I reckon unless anyone has an objection, we should load up and *drive* into Mission Beach." He gave an idiotic grin with eyebrows bouncing up and down. The kids laughed.

Nobody objected and everyone set about finishing breakfast and packing up their gear.

Kyle was first out the door, and he brought the minibus up to the front of the verandah for everyone to load their gear. Paula was first in the door, and she stepped back out saying. "There's no seat!"

Kyle laughed and said. "Yeah, it looks like they were in the middle of converting it into a camper. Seats are in the shed, but it'd take too long to put them back in. Hang on." He raced around the side of the house and came back with an old milk crate and plonked it on the floor of the bus beside a window. With a graceful sweep of his hand and a bow he said, "There ya go, madam, a seat just for you." He grinned.

Paula laughed and said, "That's very nice of you, thank you." And with her nose in the air, proceed to get on the bus and take her seat.

The others piled in and sat on the floor or one of the two-wheel arches in the back.

The engine was noisy and rattled a lot, but it was transport! Bruce was almost last in and was sent right to the back and given a window seat, which was opened wide, for him. As soon as he came in, *all* the other windows were opened. We all loved Bruce, but that smell of his really hadn't ever gone away.

Heading off and creating a breeze through the bus was welcome relief from Bruce's pong and the general smell of the rest of us who, while washed, were still in the same clothes we'd been in for days.

As we approached the intersection on the main road I heard Kyle revving the engine and changing down gears quite loudly. When we got to the corner, we went round it way too fast causing everyone to hang on.

"Sorry folks, I forgot there's no brakes," said Kyle over his shoulder.

Julia sounded horrified. "There's *kids* on board and you've got *no brakes*?"

Kieran laughed. "Relax Julia, there's nobody to hit! Besides, I reckon brakes in a vehicle show a distinct lack of commitment on the part of the driver."

Everyone laughed. I guess it didn't matter. The ground was flat all the way to Mission Beach and there were certainly no moving cars to hit.

The wind buffeted in the back and the rain poured in, but it still beat walking all this way in the rain. Having no brakes was a small price to pay in my book.

In the time it would have taken us to walk to the main road, we had passed the turn off to South Mission Beach and were heading into Wongaling beach. Kyle slowed down a bit and many of us got up and knelt on the floor to look out the windows. It hadn't changed since we left as far as we could tell. So much for the threat to destroy it. Kyle drove past the supermarket and turned up a small road into an estate. The houses were fairly spread out, so I guess it wasn't worth a shaped bomb. He turned into the driveway of a bombed house and slowed right down. A shed, right at the back of the block was unharmed and had its door closed. "This is your stop folks; I'll just pull up here and let you out. Just hang on first ok?"

He slowed right down and turned off the ignition while it was still in gear. The van lurched a few times and stopped hard, causing us all to lurch forward momentarily in response.

In all, it was a successful stop for a vehicle without brakes.

David slid the door open, and we all piled out taking our gear with us. James opened the shed door and the old guys helped push the van inside.

The roller door was closed, and we'd successfully made it to Mission Beach in one piece.

Spirits were high in general as we set off to our old house. In the short term it seemed like a likely place to stay. In my mind it seemed a good place for them in the long term too. It was out of the way, large enough to accommodate them, easy forest access and it was our *home*.

As we walked David and Kyle had begun talking about maybe rigging up a *donkey* and gravity feeding water to the house. I expected someone to warn them about making changes, but I guess a pipe through the forest wouldn't be obvious from the air.

Amy had yet to make any comment on my suggestion that she stay, I just hoped she was still thinking about it. Of course, we didn't know yet how many people were in Mission Beach anymore. But if all Amy did was look after the kids I'd be happy.

Entering our old house was just like coming home. It had only been a few days since we'd left, but so much had happened, it seemed like a lifetime.

I volunteered to go to the fridge house and get some frozen meat for dinner while everyone chose rooms. I didn't need to be there for that, as I'd take what was left.

The fridge was exactly as I'd left it and I felt a little sadness again that my fridge pen pal was gone. I shook it off and grabbed enough food for everyone as it was going to be a full house for dinner tonight. We'd invited the men's group to join us for the first night back.

When I got back, most were in the lounge room discussing getting some supplies from the stash and finding out how many people had returned to Mission Beach. Nobody had any idea how many would be left now. It was not even lunchtime, so it was decided that we'd do a bit of a walk around during the day while Julia got the kids settled. I was thinking we might find some kids toys and clothes somewhere to help them settle in.

A few of us went for a walk around town. It was still raining but knowing I had a nice dry dress to get into later meant I could live with being wet for now. The rain in the tropics is warm in summer anyway.

As we walked Amy made a point of grabbing flyers and writing on the back of them. It seemed too many for who might be left in town, but she felt it was her job and we waited patiently for her to do it.

Town was very quiet as it was before, but what was missing was any hint of wood smoke. Before the settlement disaster there was always the smell of peoples cooking fires. Often you had no idea where the smell came from, but it was always there. Now there was nothing but the damp smell of the rain and the forest, and a slight hint of rotting flesh. Nothing like Babinda, but it was still there.

We found a house with some kids' playground equipment in the backyard and knocked but there was nobody there. Inside we found two rooms of toys and clothes for kids roughly the right age for Julia's kids. We grabbed armfuls of clothes, books, and toys for them and shoved them in our backpacks. It felt a little like Christmas shopping for my nieces, but these weren't new things I was buying from a shop, they belonged to kids, and I had no idea what may have become of them. I was rifling through a drawer when I found a hand-made "Birthday card for Mum", half finished and hidden in the drawer to keep it a surprise. It made me suddenly quite sad and Amy must have picked up on it. She gave me a one armed hug and pulled me away from the drawer. She was right to do that. There was no point in dwelling on these things, it just tears you up inside and can never bring these people back. All you can hope is that they got away somewhere and are safe.

For now, though there are three kids who will think it really IS Christmas when we get back, so we closed our packs and headed off.

We went via the school to have a look at the notice boards. There wasn't much new on there except someone cursing the Lizards after the settlement disaster. Whoever was updating the boards before, wasn't doing it anymore. Amy grabbed a flyer and stuck it to the notice board.

"You never know." She shrugged.

I grabbed the whiteboard marker and wrote.

Medical care available again. You know where.

If enough people need it, I will open the clinic again. Dr Jess and Dr Amy.

"You never know," I said with a laugh. I then smiled at Amy and rubbed out my name. "All yours now Doc," I said.

"I haven't agreed yet," she said, laughing.

"Oh, *oh yeah!* I'm sorry Amy; I guess I just want it so bad I made it happen in my head. We can rub all that off again."

"No! Leave it, Jess, it's ok, and you were right about what you said. The kids really are everything now, and I'm so glad you think I'm ready to treat people."

"Amy, you are far beyond where I started and will be beyond my knowledge in a matter of months. I'll be coming to *you* with questions soon."

"I don't think that'll ever happen, but thanks," she said smiling and gave me a hug.

We headed off back to the house. When we arrived and opened our backpacks it was such a joy to see their little faces light up. Kini still hadn't spoken but she was becoming more normal all the time. I missed the little chatterbox with her one hundred questions an hour, but I felt that after what she'd been through, she didn't need anyone pressuring her and she'd speak when she was ready.

Julia was constantly chasing her around with food and water so I was confident she would regain the weight she'd lost.

The kids had one of the rooms with the twin single beds to themselves. The boys were going to be sharing one bed and Kini the other. It would be Kini and Julia in the other single bed together for a long time to come. Poor Kyle had inherited three kids and everything that entails, but he seemed to be taking it extremely well. Kyle took a double bed, as did James, while Amy took the other room with singles in it.

James' plan was to go find somewhere to live but he'd only said that once, and it seemed he was making himself comfortable here. I'm certain everyone preferred it this way.

I must admit it was fun to see the house so full of people; it kind of reminded me of when the relatives visit at home. Lots of people you barely knew invaded your house, but everyone was having fun, it was so filled with laughter and warmth, and it made it ok.

The men's group headed off to check on their place and were back in the late afternoon with bottles of their home brewed beer. It was bloody awful and as strong as rocket fuel, but I drank it anyway.

"First couple of days it'll go straight through ya, after that you're right," said Bill with a laugh.

Excellent, so a little colon cleanse with your hangover. Something to look forward to, I thought wryly.

They'd also brought with them an old one hundred-litre oil drum, which they assured us was going to be the donkey the kids would need for hot showers. They said they knew where they could find some black poly pipe to route the water from the creek to the house, so all the plumbing would work.

Jared was congratulating their ingenuity as they rolled the drum under the house and Bill said quietly to Jared, "One advantage of gettin' old mate is that you've picked up a few clues along the way. We'll look after this lot for ya don't you worry. You just go get some payback hey."

Kieran took Kyle and James out hunting the next day, so they could learn the ropes. They came back with a small pig, one wallaby, and smug looks on their faces, so I assume it was them that did the hunting. Kyle had been with David a few times fishing so had a few clues on that.

With the men's group to help, who were all keen fishermen, a good knowledge of where all the fruit trees and vegie gardens are locally. I was confident we were leaving them all in a very good position. I'd handed many of the medical books I had over to Amy, so she could continue her study. It was a shame the clinic was no longer needed as it was a great learning tool, but the books would have to do.

When we visited the supplies stash, I stocked up big time on things I thought we might need to go to war. It sounded funny to say it even in my own head as I packed a big bag of things. But yeah, we were essentially going to war, and I was likely going to need more than a few band-aids and some antibiotics.

Our departure day rolled around too fast. Bill's group had done the rounds and came back with bad news as far as how many had returned to Mission Beach. "Few hippies and lots of oldies is pretty much all we've found. We got three guys willing to go, the rest were all too old or too stoned to be of any use to you," he said.

"They'll do fine, thanks, mate," said Jared.

"They'll be waiting at the South Mission turn off for ya, told 'em if it wasn't rainin', you'd probably travel at night."

"Yeah we were thinking we'd use the van again," said Jared. "And by the looks of it, this rain is set in for a while yet, so we'll be safe to use it."

When we all gathered under the house for our farewells it was a teary affair. We'd all been through so much together and hadn't spent more than hours apart since August last year! We'd become a family and it was so hard to leave them. Kini was not happy about Kieran's departure at all and refused to let go of his neck for most of the morning. When it came time to go, she was hanging onto Julia and quite upset.

I hugged them both and told Kini it was all going to be ok as we'd be back soon, and that she had two other kids to play with. I doubt it helped.

Julia whispered in my ear and said, "Soon she'll have another one to play with."

My mouth must have hit the floor. "You're pregnant?" I asked stupidly.

She grinned like a Cheshire cat and nodded. I gave her another big hug and said, "Congratulations! I'm so happy for you!" What else could I say? She seemed so happy.

I couldn't believe anyone would be silly enough to get pregnant, with all that's going on. The potential medical problems associated with childbirth and the risks involved. It made my head spin just thinking about it.

When I hugged Amy, I whispered, "Study that obstetrics book *extra hard* for me, Amy."

She pulled back with a puzzled look.

"Ha, not me don't worry. I hope to be back by the time it's needed, but you'd best study up, I haven't a clue unless it's got four legs."

We hugged again and she still had a puzzled look on her face.

We all piled into the van and Kieran called Bruce to jump in. But he didn't respond. Kieran was more forceful this time and Bruce, who was standing beside Julia with Kini in her arms, just sat down.

"What are you playing at, Bruce? Come on, we've gotta go." said Kieran pointing at the door to the van, but the dog didn't move. Kieran walked over to him and said quietly, "Wanna stay here mate?"

The dog didn't move.

"Righto, mate. Look after these people for us an-"

"Hang on, what are you saying?" asked Julia.

"Well, he wants to stay here," said Kieran shrugging.

"He's not staying here! You tell him to move, you're his boss."

Kieran laughed. "Ha, you got Bruce all wrong, he does what he likes, I just hope he *likes* to do whatever I ask him... At the time I ask him... If he doesn't wanna go, there's nuthin I can do to make him."

"He's a dangerous dog, I can't have him around the kids!"

"Jesus, Julia, the kids are the reason he *wants* to stay! He loves'em and he wants to stay with his mate Kini. He's no different to any other dog, just supervise him round the kids, don't let 'em play too rough."

"He stinks!" she said.

"Yeah I won't argue there," Kieran nodded with a grin. "Take him for a swim in the ocean, it'll make him smell better."

"He's not staying," said Julia with a finality to her voice. She handed Kini to Kyle and grabbed Bruce around the collar and pulled him towards the van. "Come Bruce," she said,

He didn't move.

"Bruce...COME," she said and pulled as hard as she could with both hands. Bruce just sat there with his tongue out one side and his tail wagging. He had no intention of moving and a woman who weighed half his own weight at best, wasn't going to *drag* him.

"How the hell are we going to feed him?" asked an exasperated Julia.

"Well like I've said before, it's the other way around when it comes to Bruce," said Kieran

"We don't know how to hunt with a dog!"

"Ahh, I might be able to help there," said one of the men's group. "I've had pig dogs most of my life. I'd be glad to take him hunting. What's he like, mate?" he said to Kieran.

"Well, he's ignorant, arrogant and stubborn, but take him hunting and he's like a well trained Kelpie... Best dog I ever took into the bush," said Kieran with a touch of pride.

"Well, he sounds like fun," said the man.

Kieran walked back to Bruce and crouched down in front of him. "You be good to these guys, mate," he said cupping the big dog's face in his hands and scratching both ears. "They'll be relying on you." The dog licked his lips a couple of times and slid his tongue out the side again.

Kieran got up and went to the van.

"He'll look after you guys, Julia. I promise," he said, and climbed in.

Julia looked at the dog, frowned, and said sternly, "If you're staying, you'd better go inside so I can wash you."

Bruce did exactly as he was told.

Kieran grinned from ear to ear and slid the door closed. Julia stood there with a stifled laugh all over her face and waved us goodbye.

A New Beginning

'*A true soldier fights, not because he hates what is in front of him, but because he loves what is behind him.*" -GK Chesterton

We picked up the three guys at the turn off to South Mission. They were all ex banana workers so reasonably fit. They were excited about it all and were awed that we were using a vehicle. They asked a thousand questions which, given we'd just parted with some dear friends, none of us felt like answering. Our plan was to head for the Army's Tully Jungle Training Facility on the Tully Gorge road. Jared had been talking about it for the last few days and we had no idea what to expect to get from there, but figured it was worth a look.

The drive through Tully was uneventful and it wasn't long before we were headed out towards Tully gorge. By the time we were ten minutes along the road we had to stop because of mud and debris across the road. When the aliens had destroyed the Koombooloomba dam wall, it must have flooded most of this valley. From there we had a very muddy scramble over the sludge left by the floodwaters. A bit further up the road cleared again and we continued on our way. I just hoped the rain didn't stop before we got back, or our new wheels were toast.

When we arrived, we found the gate open and many of the buildings bombed. It was a bit disappointing, but we had a look around anyway. Jared made a beeline to a particular building tucked away at the back. It had been bombed but he still dug away at the remains. It was entirely made of concrete; even the roof was concrete with steel reinforcing, so it was hard to make any headway. We went to help and one of the new guys grabbed a long steel pole from one of the sheds. We levered a big chunk of concrete out of the way and Jared scrambled under the concrete slab covering the contents. He emerged a moment later with a handful of bullets! He wiggled under again and kept doing so for quite a while, we'd gathered buckets to put the things in, He'd also found little green canisters like insect repellent cans which I later learned were smoke flares and flash bangs.

David found a small tarp to put over Jared and the buckets to keep them dry while he kept going for more. David decided there were too many of us there so suggested everyone spread out and look for anything that may be of use.

So that left David and myself with Jared. I just kept taking the increasingly small handfuls of things passed back by Jared. When he finally emerged, he shook his head. "Pretty much nothing but blanks left in there now," he said. "The smoke and flash bangs are good. But I was hoping for more ammo for the F88's."

"What are they?" I asked.

"They're the rifles the soldiers all use. We don't have the rifles, but if we have the ammo, we can get the weapons in Townsville. You follow?"

"Yep. So there isn't somewhere like this in Townsville?" I asked, pointing at the pile of rubble.

"Yeah, there is, but we'd have no hope of getting in there." He shook his head. "That's like the big boy ammo dump, full of everything the Australian Army has to offer. It'd be an underground bunker with bomb-proof doors' n' stuff. Take a pretty serious bomb to open that one up and there'd be nothing left in there afterwards." He shook his head again. "We'd hear the *bang* from here." He laughed.

The others started coming back with things they'd found. Louise managed to find a room full of old uniforms and was sporting a new Army shirt which she proudly showed off to the delight of the three newcomers who, let's be honest, hadn't taken their eyes off her since they climbed in the van.

"Uniforms are a good idea," said Jared. "Let's go get kitted out."

We all headed for the barracks and got our 'battle dress' as Jared called it. Everyone went searching for his or her sizes and to help me out, wound up searching for the absolute smallest ones they could find to fit me.

"I guess I was never built to be in the Army," I joked when I put on the smallest we could find and still had to roll up the pants and sleeves to comical amounts. I looked like I was wearing Dad's work clothes when I was little. I opted to forego the Army look and chose to stick with my grubby cargo pants and shirt.

"Do me a favour, Jess, at least take the shirt. They're bloody comfortable and there's good pockets on them."

I relented and took the shirt but planned to cut the excess sleeves off.

Kieran found a holster in a filing cabinet and got me to pull out my pistol. To be honest I had completely forgotten it was there. The day he gave it to me I was completely distracted and just shoved it in the bottom of my pack. I pulled it out and handed it to him. He checked it for fit in the holster and nodded with satisfaction and handed it to me. I did the belt up to the smallest hole and could have fit two of me in it. He took it back, poked a few more holes in the webbing with his multi-tool, and handed it back to me to try again. He then showed me how to fasten the leg strap, so everything pivoted with my leg, stood back, and smiled. "Look the part now, Jess, even I'm scared of you." He winked. "I should probably have shown you this before but we've been distracted. Pull it out for me."

I pulled the pistol out of its holster. It felt kinda wild west to do it and I smiled at the thought.

"Texas lawman now, eh?" he laughed.

He took a couple of minutes to show me all the features on the gun. In particular where the safety was, how to load and shoot it. It had a ten shot magazine which was full, so even though it was only a .22 Cal pistol, I had plenty of shots should I ever need to use it.

"Wait till they're close, Jess." He made me hold the gun up and he grabbed it in my hand and pointed at various places on his body starting with the head. Then the chest and then and the base of the skull. "Shoot here, shoot here, and shoot here. There's no point in shooting them in the guts with that gun, it's too small so you want *kill* shots only and from close range. Even a decent target shooter is going to struggle to hit anything past twenty five meters with a pistol in a hurry, and it's only a .22 so it has no hitting power at that range, ok?"

"Yep, got it," I said and then added, "You know I grew up shooting rifles."

"Yeah, I figured as much, you grew up on a station, but I saw how heavy even a small Cal rifle was to you and couldn't ask you to carry one too far. This is better for you."

"Thanks for thinking of me, Kieran," I said and smiled.

One of the guys surprisingly found a couple of ration packs, which piqued David's interest. "Are the chocolates still there?" he asked eagerly.

"Nah mate, the goodies are gone." He shook his head ruefully.

David swore under his breath.

So with our load of equipment, we headed off back to the van. There were a couple of vehicles there, which Jared checked out for fuel and a charged battery. They were both full of fuel and were ready to go, but we had to return the van to cover anyway so we set off back down the road to the van and kept the Army vehicles in mind for the future.

As soon as I started walking, I was intensely aware of the pistol on my leg. It was one of those cool looking holsters the anti-terrorist type Army guys use that puts the gun on your upper leg, not on your hip. I tried ever so hard not to walk with a swagger.

As I looked around our group, we'd started to look like we meant business, in our Army clothes and with rifles slung over shoulders. I guess in a news report we'd be called 'Rebel fighters' or 'Rebel militia', maybe 'Liberation Army'? I don't know, they all sounded cool, but I would never in a million years admit I thought that to anyone!

We headed back to the airfield and David spotted a big industrial shed near the runway. He said he could hide the van in it so we all piled out and he drove it in. Not long after he went in, we heard a loud metallic crash. He came out of the shed smiling and said, "Found the brakes."

It was sometime after noon by the time we'd gotten to the verandah of the building overlooking the runway. There were a few people already there, in fact quite a few and pretty much all were armed with rifles or hunting bows and all had backpacks. The doors to the building had been kicked in, so we all filed in to wait for anyone else that might be coming.

We gave it another couple of hours until there were maybe fifty of us altogether. A number I wouldn't have thought possible, given how many were killed here. Finally, Jared stood on a chair and got everyone's attention.

When he stood and faced the crowd of people, he did so with a confidence that completely belied the nerves he must have been feeling. He looked the part, and his voice sounded the part, it was strong and commanding.

The room went quiet while everyone listened to what he had to say.

"We're all here for one purpose. We want to fight back against an enemy that has walked in and destroyed everything we had... They've taken our families, our friends, our homes, and our *dignity*, just so that they can live. They didn't ask to share; they didn't come in friendship... They came to *exterminate* us. To wipe our *species* from the planet! Yes, their technology is advanced, I won't deny that, but it's not *so* different from ours that we couldn't fight back... Now how our *government SCREWED THIS UP*... I have no idea, but we can't change that now.

We don't know what's happening in the rest of the world. All we can know is what has happened *here*." He pointed out the window at the runway to illustrate the point.

"What we saw here at this airfield on the full moon... is enough for any man or woman to know that the Lizards have no conscience, they have no heart, and they have no *humanity*. That's the point, they aren't human, they are reptiles and are just as cold blooded. They must think us weak because we don't fight back. We let them walk in and *own* us...! Well, I'm DONE WITH THAT... and I think you all are too."

There was a chorus of agreement. Jared was gaining steam, feeding off the energy from the crowd. "We can sit here and get picked off one by one by these *bastards* until we're all gone, or we can fight back. I know I'm gonna and I hope you'll all join me... I can tell you now that we won't win..." He paused to let that sink in.

"It's true, their numbers are far greater than ours... We have no aircraft and too few guns. But we can either live like rats and wait to die on *their terms*... or we can take some of these things with us on *ours*!"

There was a cheer from the crowd.

"My plan is for guerrilla tactics...I wanna hit and run on their base in Townsville, I wanna sabotage their aircraft, I wanna disrupt their operations...I wanna kill some Lizards!

There was another, even louder cheer from the crowd.

"They may take our lives..." he continued over the noise. "But by Christ it's gonna *cost 'em*!

There was another, almost deafening cheer from the crowd... He'd won them over without a doubt, and I couldn't be more proud of him.

A voice from the back of the group said.

"Why go all the way to Townsville when they come here anyway, we can just shoot them as they arrive."

Jared was in full stride and was straight back at the man asking questions. "There are two reasons why, first let me ask you what your life is worth. How many Lizards are *you* worth?"

"As many as I can get," the man replied.

There were a few voices saying, "Bloody oath" and "Me too".

Jared continued. "Yep. But how many would it take for you to die happy?... Two?... Four?... Six? That's likely the most you'd get before they dropped a bomb and killed you. What I'm suggesting might mean *hundreds* of Lizards die. We don't know how many there are, but we'll take as many as we can. Reason two, we don't shoot the ones that come here, because there are still people living in this area. Women and children... old people... We shoot Lizards here and they'll bomb the crap out of the place. That's one of the reasons I want to take the fight *out* of this area. Make it look like they've won here so they'll leave our people alone."

"Yeah, and who protects the ones we leave?" asked the man.

Jared replied. "There are still people here to protect them...But if they stay in the forest and don't antagonise them, the Lizards will leave them alone. They hate the wet; they never go in the forest and only bomb what's changed. If the people are smart and we draw attention *away* from them, they will be safer here without us shooting Lizards locally."

There were no more questions from the crowd so Jared finished by saying.

"I guess now is the time for YOU to decide how it all ends. Are we going quietly to our graves... or are we fighting back and taking some of the *bastards* with us?"

A cheer rose from the crowd with a lot of back slapping around the room. Jared was the man of the hour, and many came to shake his hand. These men and women were ready to fight... We had our Militia and were going to fight back. It felt good to be a part of it, to be able to make a difference. Our group at least had something to fight for and it wasn't just about us now. We had people we thought of as *family* in Mission Beach, and we were ready to fight to keep them safe.

It was going to be a tough road ahead, but I was ready for it...

Stay tuned for book 2 coming soon!

About the Author

K A Allen Lives in Mission Beach Far north Queensland with
his wife and daughter. He's a retired helicopter pilot and marine
skipper with
a passion for the far north and the rainforest.

You can find out more about the author and this book at:
kaallen.com.au

Sign up to my newsletter from my website or social media to
keep up to date with new releases.

If you enjoyed this book, make sure you leave a review and tell
your friends!

Acknowledgments

Many thanks must go to Caryn Inall for her help in getting this book ready to publish. She is a part time Librarian, part time editor, and a full time legend.

And to my friend and fellow author Brenda May, for all her help and moral support while I found my feet. This is a much better book due to your efforts. Thank you.